Anabel Donald was born in India and educated at a convent boarding school in Oxford. She has been writing fiction since 1982 when her first novel, *Hannah at Thirty-five* was published to great critical acclaim. She has worked as a lecturer and is now a headmistress. She lives in Doncaster and is currently working on a third crime novel to feature Alex Tanner. *An Uncommon Murder*, her first Alex Tanner novel will also be published by Virago.

D0264280

In at the
Deep End

Anabel
Donald

Published by VIRAGO PRESS Limited, July 1994
42– 43 Gloucester Crescent, Camden Town, London NW1 7PD

First published 1993 by Macmillan London Limited,
a division of Pan Macmillan Publishers Ltd,
Cavaye Place, London SW10 9PG

Copyright © 1993 Anabel Donald

The right of Anabel Donald to be identified
as Author of this work has been asserted
by her in accordance with the Copyright,
Designs and Patents Act 1988.

All rights reserved

*A CIP catalogue record for this title
is available from the British Library*

Printed and bound in Great Britain by
Cox & Wyman Ltd, Reading, Berkshire

For the pupils of
St Mary's School, Doncaster

Monday, June 1st

Chapter One

The rectangle of pasteboard lay on the desk between us. My card. *Alex Tanner, Private Investigator*, it said. With my address and telephone number.

The man opposite me was pretending to read it. I say pretending, because he knew all the information on it anyway. That was why his secretary had rung me the previous Friday. That's why I was here now, in one of the larger offices in the newish office building in one of the narrow side-streets between the Strand and the river that housed the firm of Whyteleafe, Whyteleafe, Trigg, and Plummer, Solicitors.

My man was Plummer. He was in his late thirties, sandy-haired, balding, short and stocky beyond even the skill of what his pinstripe suit identified as an expensive tailor. In a cheaper suit he would have been simply fat. As it was his descending chins met his ascending neck over the white collar of a pink shirt, and when he smiled his pale blue eyes were submerged in flesh.

So far he hadn't spoken, except to greet me and, as it was teatime, offer me tea. I'd accepted coffee. I was tingling with curiosity – Why would a top London solicitor hire me? How had he even heard of me? – but I sipped the coffee and looked around, pretending to be relaxed. It was a pleasant enough office: uncluttered, thick-carpeted, book-lined. His desk was a good reproduction of an early Victorian design, mahogany with brass fittings and a tooled red leather top, bare except for a computer terminal, a telephone, a silver-framed photograph of his well-fleshed family, and my card. One wall of the room was glass and if I leant backwards a little in my reproduction eighteenth-century dining chair I could see the Thames sliding heavily past, unruffled by the light June breeze.

As I sat, I speculated on the cost of Mr Plummer's time. What did he charge per hour? A hundred and fifty quid? Two hundred? If it was

3

two hundred, the client, whoever he was, had just paid £23.33 for his solicitor to watch me drink a cup of coffee. I'd been there seven minutes.

He picked up my card and tapped it against his teeth. White, regular, sharp teeth, like a baby shark's. Otherwise he was more like a dolphin, sleek, friendly, no fool. Did dolphins have teeth?

'Miss Tanner. You seem very young,' he said, sounding pleased.

'Twenty-nine this week,' I said. It was true, but twenty-nine always sounds to me bogus because it's usually misappropriated. Like giving your occupation as model or your name as Brown.

'You look younger.'

People often say that. It could be the way I dress. I usually wear 501s, a T-shirt, and plain brown Doc Martens. I was wearing them now. Today's T-shirt selection: colour, dark green; style, short-sleeved. No logo.

I smiled and said nothing.

'How long have you been a private investigator?'

'Six months. Part time.' Very part time. Last November, by chance, I'd investigated the disappearance of a cabinet minister's daughter. Since then I'd decided to set up as a private investigator as a sideline. Not because I'd managed the first investigation well: actually, because I'd made a hash of it. I hate screwing up. I knew I could do better than that. I'd fixed it with my accountant, had the stationery printed, put an ad in the Yellow Pages and in local newspapers, and waited. I'd had one missing persons case which I solved in an hour. It was hardly enough to consider giving up the day job (freelance television researcher), but enough to keep separate accounts.

'You work alone?'

'Yes. And I've none of the usual experience. I haven't been in the police, I didn't learn my trade in a big agency, and I haven't even been a store detective. Most of the time I'm a television researcher. I started out at the BBC. My research skills are good, I have some contacts in the police, and I enjoy finding things out. But that's it. And I'm very much a beginner at the game.' There was no point in trying to flannel him. If I wasn't what he was looking for, the sooner we both knew it, the less time would be wasted.

'Thank you for being so frank,' he said. 'Your detective work is – shall we say a hobby?'

'My accountant doesn't think so. And I take it seriously.'

'Very laudable,' he said drily. Oddly, he sounded disappointed. 'Would you be free immediately?'

'To start, yes, but I've commitments later this month. It depends how long the job'll take.' My diary was full of three weeks of nothing – a freelancer's nightmare. Another reason why I sat so alertly in Mr Plummer's chair, ready to be his dream detective, if I could identify what that would be. My only clues so far was that young was in, serious was out. I sparkled winningly, trying to look like an early Shirley Temple.

'I imagine a week at the most,' he said.

'How did you get my name?'

He gave a sharp, white, pointed smile. 'You were recommended to me.'

'By whom?' I'd buy them a drink and urge them to keep up the good work: Whyteleafe, Whyteleafe, etc. were an extremely prosperous set-up. I didn't for a minute expect to get much of their business because they'd certainly use a top-flight international detective agency in the ordinary way, one of the big boys, full of ex-senior officers of the Met; but anything was better than nothing, and Whyteleafe etc. would be a good credit.

'By someone who praised your discretion,' he said. I nodded discreetly, still sparkling. He wasn't going to answer my question. Perhaps if I offered him £1.66 cash on the nail for thirty seconds of his time, he'd tell me. Then again perhaps he wouldn't.

'If you would tell me your fees?'

I gave him my daily rate. He tapped away at his keyboard. Now the computer knew my rates, as it presumably knew my name, address, telephone number, and reputation for discretion.

Another pause. Twelve minutes past four. I was running out of sparkle. Mr Plummer didn't speak and I didn't speak and I was beginning to find it odd. He didn't strike me as indecisive. We weren't exactly having a thrilling time chewing the fat and exchanging views on politics, art, and life. I wasn't wearing a skirt he could squint up and he showed no signs of finding me his type. So why were we waiting? The football chant began in my head.

Perhaps, I thought, he expected a sign from me. A masonic handshake. A password.

I tried small talk. 'It's a lovely day.'

'Indeed,' he said, and we both looked out of the window at the Thames. He didn't have to tilt his chair from where he sat.

'Are we waiting for someone?' I said.

He sighed as if he'd come to a decision, opened the top drawer of his desk and took out a folder. 'The information my client requires—'

'Don't I get a name?'

'I'm afraid not. My client wishes to remain anonymous. And the information he is interested in is rather – nebulous. Not a question of facts.'

'OK,' I said, to encourage him. He didn't want to spit it out.

'In late March this year, a seventeen-year-old boy named Olivier de Sauvigny Desmoulins drowned in the swimming-pool of his boarding-school in Oxfordshire.'

'Was there an inquest?'

'Naturally.'

'Accidental death?'

'Quite so.'

'Is it the accident that your client wants me to investigate? In case it wasn't an accident?'

'Not exactly. My client is interested in Olivier's state of mind before he died.'

I let that statement sit in the air a while, hoping he would focus its vagueness for me. Eventually I accepted I'd have to do it myself. 'When?'

'Before he died,' he repeated, puzzled.

'When exactly before he died? The seconds before? The day before? The week before?' We could go back as far as Olivier's nursery days.

'Say – the day before.'

I still didn't understand it. 'In case it was suicide?'

'Possibly.'

'And what exactly do you want from me?'

'A report. A detailed report. Who you spoke to, what they said. That kind of thing.'

'Any signed statements?'

'Not necessarily.'

'Tape-recorded interviews?'

'Not necessarily. A detailed report.'

6

'You say your client isn't interested in details of the accident? Just in case it wasn't?'

'Absolutely not. Just his state of mind.'

'And am I looking for anything specific, like was he being bullied or had he just had bad news – about his parents, for instance?'

'Why do you say that?' he asked, his voice for once as sharp as his teeth.

'No particular reason,' I said. 'Is your client a man?'

He hesitated, examined the question, evidently decided the answer wasn't compromising. 'Yes.'

Now I *was* suspicious. None of it rang true. 'Mr Plummer, you're holding out on me.'

He tapped his fingers on the folder. 'What gives you that impression?'

'You're a partner in a high-powered firm. Your hourly charge is probably my daily rate. Any client of yours is probably equally high powered, or solidly rich. Either way, he's not likely to ask such a fuzzy question and pay someone like you to find someone like me to answer it.'

'Grief does strange things,' he said.

'Certainly true. But predictably strange. You tell me a man wants to know the state of mind of a seventeen-year-old boy before his accidental death? I say that isn't true. Not for himself. Not unless he was in love with the boy, and probably not even then. Men are usually pragmatic. Sensitive, within a narrow range, frequently. Passionate, certainly. But not speculative if speculation gets them nothing but further suffering. It sounds to me like a guilty woman's question. So I ask you again, who wants to know this?'

He looked at me steadily. 'My client does.'

'Your male client?'

'Yes.'

I looked steadily back, and shook my head. 'I have to be able to trust you,' I said. 'I nearly died in an investigation last November because I was badly briefed.'

'That can't be the case here,' he said. 'There is no question of murder. There was an inquest. You must trust me.'

'And there's a cheque in the post,' I said.

'What do you mean?'

'Things you don't believe,' I said. 'Things people say, that are more

7

often lies than truth. I'll love you in the morning. There's a cheque in the post.'

'You inhabit a harsh world, Miss Tanner.'

'Yes,' I said. 'We both do. The only difference is that at the moment it suits you to pretend you haven't noticed.'

He cleared his throat impatiently. 'What, precisely, is your difficulty with the assignment?'

'If your client is a man, as you claim, I want to know his name, his relationship to Olivier, and his specific intentions. I'll keep it confidential.'

'I cannot answer your questions, I'm afraid,' he said. 'One further point. No one is to know the purpose of your enquiries, or indeed that you are enquiring about Olivier at all.'

'That'll double my fees,' I said. I meant merely that it would take much longer. He misunderstood me and tapped my new higher rates into the computer without a blink. I should have charged more to start with, I realized. Evidently confidential private investigators cost more than television researchers. I still didn't like the job, but now I couldn't possibly afford not to take it. Properly padded, it would cover my three empty weeks.

He saw the money was hooking me, and he pressed home, taking a chequebook from his drawer. 'I'll pay you for a week in the first instance, and add two hundred pounds as a float for expenses. After a week, report to me, please.'

'In person?'

'That won't be necessary. A detailed written report will be quite enough. I suppose you have headed stationery?'

Odd question. 'Of course.'

'Specifically in your capacity as private investigator? Not merely as a freelance researcher?'

Labouring the point seemed odder still. 'Yes,' I said.

'Good. If you find you need more time, telephone for further instructions.'

'OK,' I said, and watched while he wrote the cheque, then pushed it across the desk to me with a piece of paper from his folder.

I stowed the cheque away in a front pocket of my jeans, and looked at the piece of paper. At the top, the name and address of the school, together with the headmaster's and housemaster's names. Then two more names, under the heading: Olivier's special friends.

He was making 'the interview is over' movements, but I needed as much information as I could get. 'Now tell me about Olivier.'

'Why?'

'Well briefed is efficient,' I said. 'Like any enterprise. The more you know at the outset, the less you have to take time finding out. The family, for instance. His name is French, I suppose?'

'Yes. His father is French. Michel de Sauvigny Desmoulins, more commonly known in France as Michel Mouche.'

He waited for me to identify Mouche. I'm not good on France and I had to grope around in my memory. Eventually it came. 'The singer-poet-actor who looks as if he never washes, shaves, or sobers up?'

'Quite. Olivier's mother is an Englishwoman, Mary Anne Pertwee, better known as Freedom Mouche. She also has a career in France, as a minor singer. The parents have been divorced some years. She now lives in a commune in the Gers region of France. He lives in Paris. Olivier is their only child.'

I'd been taking notes but as he seemed to be opening up I took a tape recorder out of my big squashy leather bag. He saw it, and shook his head. I put it away.

'Where did Olivier live?'

'He was at boarding-school, as you know. During the holidays he spent time with his parents and grandparents. His English grandparents, Raymond and Alice Pertwee, live in Sydenham.'

Could the English grandfather be Plummer's client? Not likely, living in Sydenham. 'Raymond Pertwee's retired, is he?'

'Yes.'

'What did he do before?'

'He was an electrician.'

Certainly not Plummer's client. 'And the French grandparents?'

'Charles and Marie-Thérèse de Sauvigny Desmoulins. They have a flat in Paris and a house between Toulouse and Bordeaux.'

Much more like it, I thought. OK, French, but posh French. 'What kind of house?'

'How do you mean?'

'Small? Big? A shack? A château?'

'More a château than a shack.'

The boy had died in late March. A fatal accident at school, a child of minor celebrities – I was surprised I hadn't seen any coverage in the national papers. I asked Plummer about it.

'There were small paragraphs in the *Telegraph* and the *Mail*, I believe. Fortunately the Mouche connection passed unnoticed.'

With some help from Plummer, I guessed. He'd have been all over it like a winter-weight duvet. 'Why was Olivier being educated in England?'

'Desmoulins sons always are.'

Very posh. 'At this school? Rissington Abbey? I've never heard of it.'

He shrugged again. 'It is a small private school for boys from thirteen to eighteen. Run on military lines, but understanding.'

'What did they have to understand?'

'Olivier was unusual.'

Not very helpful. 'Unusually badly behaved or educationally subnormal?'

'Not educationally subnormal. He was very bright. He started at Eton, but – the school didn't suit him.'

'Or he didn't suit the school.'

'As you say.'

'Did they ask him to leave?'

'Yes.'

'Why?'

'A question of drugs. Several other boys left at the same time . . .'

'How old was he, at this point?'

'Fourteen.'

Young, I thought. Very young, to be expelled for drugs. Much more likely that they'd assume a fourteen-year-old was being led astray by older boys.

'And then he went straight to Rissington?'

'Yes.'

How come you know so much about him? I thought. He had the facts in his head: he didn't even have to look at his notes. The chances were that Mr Plummer had dealt with Olivier for years. A guardian, perhaps, or a trustee for the French grandparents.

'You've met Olivier, I expect,' I said blandly.

'Yes.'

'How did he strike you?'

He shrugged. 'He was an adolescent. Self-absorbed. Rather – theatrical. Prone to make scenes. Attention-seeking.'

And perhaps, with his background, he had plenty to make scenes about, I thought. Plummer hadn't liked him, that was clear.

'And you want me to poke around Rissington Abbey without declaring my interest?'

'Yes.'

'Difficult.'

'I understood that that was what I was paying for.' He stood up. I didn't. 'Do you have a transcript of the inquest?'

'Yes, but—' He just wanted to get rid of me now, and he saw I was going to insist. 'Very well. Get Mrs Sweet to photocopy this for you on the way out . . .'

Chapter Two

Mrs Sweet photocopied the transcript of the inquest for me in Plummer's outer office. She was fiftyish, with blonde-grey hair in a bun, good ankles, expensive shoes, and a forbidding manner. I'd no chance of getting information out of her, I felt, so I didn't try. I wasn't too nice to her, either. It's easy to feel patronized, if you're a secretary. So many office visitors chatter condescendingly, thinking they're being good with the help.

I took the photocopied pages, stuffed them in my bag, and ran down the stairs to the street. I don't take lifts when it's less than five floors; exercise.

Outside, it was five o'clock and the Strand was packed with workers going home. I don't mind London crowds. They're basically harmless, and there's hardly a person among them who wouldn't stop to help if they were really needed. Most people like helping strangers, it's easier.

Usually I'm in a hurry to get home myself, but not tonight. I had no solitary flat to look forward to, because Polly had bullied me into giving a party. So I chose to take a bus, knowing the journey would take at least an hour. That was OK, though. I'd helped Polly with food, drink, and cleaning all morning. The flat was ready; I'd even padlocked the French windows in my living-room to stop anyone going out on to the mock balcony. It was lethal, actually: a gardening-mad previous owner had made a platform for window-boxes, but made it balcony-size and given it little railings. He'd apparently done his gardening one-handed, the other clinging to a spike firmly cemented to the wall of the house. Why he hadn't just made a decent balcony I couldn't imagine. But, give him his due, he had half-tiled the bathroom all the way round.

So when I got home all I'd have to do was moderate Polly's efforts

12

to smarten me up. I feel foolish with expensive clothes and make-up, like the only child at a fancy-dress party whose mother bought the costume ready-made.

Polly and I have the two flats in a converted house off Ladbroke Grove. She'd decided (unilaterally: I never give parties) that, workwise, it would be a good move to signal my return to full health.

Last November I'd had my leg broken in two places and spent nearly six weeks off my feet. After that, restricted mobility and months in physiotherapy. I'd only been able to do titbits of library research.

When at last I was fully mobile, I'd gone to Dublin with a German film company, working on a doco shoot on the history of Ireland. Next, back in London, I'd done the preliminary interviewing for a programme on the menopause. Now it was early June and it also happened to be my twenty-ninth birthday.

'It'd be a good thing for everyone to see you're perfectly healthy. You know what rumours are like . . .' She was right: practically everyone in the media had heard that I was badly injured, but no one knew the details.

So we'd asked everyone who'd employed me in the past plus a few we hoped might, who I knew vaguely, plus any of my mates who were in the country. My friends are often abroad. The upside is that you get plenty of postcards. The other upside is that few of them are free to come to your parties. I'm not a hostess by temperament or training. I don't like spending money on anything as transient as an evening's pleasure, especially when, since I don't enjoy parties myself, I'm not even sure that most people find it a pleasure.

But both our names were on the invitation, and people who wouldn't turn out for Alex Tanner would certainly turn out for Polly Coyne, whether they'd met her or not. Although she'd retired from modelling two years ago, she'd been a huge name, one of those names you see in the gossip columns every week.

So even though I'd insisted we choose a Monday (Polly: That's a terrible day for parties. Me: Yes. Good.) the acceptances rolled in and I was to be on parade, fit, like a come-back boxer before the big match, jogging up and down on the spot, blowing from puffed cheeks, and giving lightning jabs with my right to show that the reactions were still there.

The final tally of guests was about fifty. The house is well big enough for that; we were using both flats. Food and drink downstairs in Polly's basement kitchen/dining-room, music for dancing in Polly's ground-floor living-room, quieter sitting-out and talking-over music in my living-room.

As the bus butted its way along Victoria Street, I sat upstairs, leaning as far into the aisle as I could to escape the strong smell which I refused to analyse which was wafting its way from the young man (Schizophrenic? Should I, for the moment, provide Care in the Community?) muttering and shouting to himself in the window seat next to me. My mother was a schizophrenic, once. Now she's in the twilight of Alzheimer's disease in a hospital in the twilight of the North Circular, and I only feel guilty about her when I'm really reaching for something to feel guilty about. But I still find schizophrenics touching rather than repulsive so I didn't move to another seat and I smiled at the young man when he caught my eye.

Outside, London was almost full of tourists. If you didn't know what the city usually looked like you'd think it was bustling and prosperous, but native Londoners could see the recession everywhere. Fewer tourists. Empty taxis. Tables at any restaurant you chose, that day. Tickets for any theatre you chose, that day. Cut-rate deals at even the grand hotels. More and more 'Going out of business' sales in the shops, a ticker-tape parade's worth of FOR SALE signs on flats and houses, a metallic taste of imminent panic in the mouth showing as blank endurance on the faces. You could see what they were trying not to think. Is this what I re-elected the Conservatives for? Will I keep my job? How high can the mortgage interest rates go? How little is my flat worth this week?

I'd stopped even wanting to know the depths to which my flat's value had plummeted. It was certainly worth thousands less than my mortgage. And the media business, my business, was on the skids. Very little work. Less payment. Even the big companies were defaulting now. I'd re-presented one invoice every month since last August, and I knew it'd never be paid. That's why I worked for the German company, when I could. They were demanding, arrogant, and hysterical, but they paid.

The bus was now stuck in a traffic-jam beside the walls of Buckingham Palace gardens. I looked through the leafy trees, past the lawns to the blank windows. Even the Royal Family was embattled. Fergie's frolics. Diana's marriage. Enormous Civil List allowances paid out of a bankrupt country's taxes. Widespread resentment: the least the Royals could do is set a good example. OK, the divorce rate in England was the highest in Europe, but the Royals should be different. We paid them to be different. We paid them to be our fairy-tale. We needed a fairy-tale, not True Confessions.

On the one occasion I'd been to Buckingham Palace (an assignment, of course, not a garden party) I forgot not to turn my back on the Queen and was frogmarched from the room so fast my Docs didn't touch the Aubusson. I don't think the Queen noticed, but she might have been pretending out of courtesy, what with all her breeding. She can name not only her father but her grandfather and all the way back to the Conquest. I come from a proud tradition of single parents. As far as I know.

The royal standard was flying over Buckingham Palace, and I imagined her sitting up the far end of the long, bare room I'd met her in, asking herself, like all the rest of her subjects, 'What went wrong?' And, like most of her subjects, it wasn't her fault. She'd been a decent old stick to me.

Change of scenery. The bus was now stuck in a traffic jam in Park Lane, between the fresh green of the park and the towering, empty hotels. I was getting nearer home, and nearer the party, and my stomach was beginning to churn. Not just because I hate parties, and because this was the first big one I'd ever given. Because, most of all, that evening I'd have to face Barty O'Neill again. Polly'd insisted we invite him, even though he and I haven't spoken for months. But Polly's been on my case to get in touch with him. She's an incorrigible romantic. I wouldn't be surprised if, as far as she was concerned, the main reason for the party was to get Barty and me together again.

Barty is an independent producer in his early forties, intermittently my boss. He made a pass at me last November. November the ninth, actually, at 9.37 p.m. If I'm interested enough to remember the date and time, why hadn't I responded?

Two reasons. The first is practical. I'm in a very chancy profession. I chose it for the freedom, but with the freedom goes the entirely unfree experience of being out of work, having no money, falling behind on your mortgage. I have absolutely no resources. As far as I know my only living relative is my mother. If my money runs out, that's it.

It's made me mean about unnecessary expenditure, like food, if someone else isn't buying it. I take a multi-vitamin pill every day, expenses food or not, and when I'm not working I buy bruised vegetables and fruit from the Portobello Market. I curry the vegetables and eat them with bread. Luckily I like bread. I liquidize the fruit and drink it with milk. I saw someone do that in a movie. They were in a beach house in Santa Monica, wearing cut-off denims and a bikini top. When I drink it that's how it makes me feel. One of my foster-mothers used to say, simple things please simple minds. Fantasy is cheap. It's also undermining. You end up living in it. I have to be careful about that too.

Barty's my most regular employer. Over the past four years he's provided about sixty per cent of my income. Affairs can go very sour. My affairs usually do. Then he'd stop hiring me.

The second reason is personal. I only get involved with men I feel superior to, and protective about: men who are less likely to criticize me. Men who feel grateful for my attentions. I have a low body image. I can only make love in the dark, and even then I shut my eyes and hope the man has the courtesy to do the same.

I seldom feel superior to Barty. I'd hate to be a disappointment to him. I hate being a disappointment to people, and when I am I get aggressive. I'd known for years that he fancied me. But when he finally made his move I'd blown it so badly that, if he hadn't been smooth and sweet about it, we probably wouldn't have spoken again. But we had.

And then when I'd been injured and was in traction he'd had me to stay in his house – fixed up his library for a sick-room, arranged the nurses – and he'd been very careful not to intrude on me. I'd felt even more of a burden and I hate being grateful, so I'd made no demands at all, and sometimes in the long evenings when I began, in desperation, to teach myself Ancient Greek, I'd thought of Barty sitting in the drawing-room upstairs and wished I had the nerve to call him in for a chat. I liked talking to him. But he couldn't have refused and I didn't know if he really wanted to . . . it had been a mess.

When I was better enough to leave I'd thanked him, of course, and gone home and waited for him to call. But he hadn't, not even to offer me work. If it hadn't been Barty I'd have thought he was sulking, but he's not a sulker.

The work was the worst part. He was involved in a project abroad and he hadn't told me what: most unusual. I'm his first choice as researcher, or at least I had been for the last few years.

Polly kept nagging me to ring him. She wanted to get us together. So, actually, did I, but I didn't know how. I'm rotten with human relationships and I didn't want to spoil this one. So we'd sent the

16

invitation and he'd accepted it – Polly took his call – and I was only hours away from facing him.

By now the bus was in a traffic jam in Westbourne Grove and I tried to dismiss the party and to concentrate on my recent success instead. Plummer had hired me for an investigation . . . I should be pleased. According to Freud, I should be ecstatic: he defined happiness as the fulfilment of childhood dreams. In my childhood, I'd dreamt of being a private eye. I'd actually wanted to be a middle-aged male private eye in Los Angeles, but we all compromise.

I was a step nearer to earning my living as a private investigator. I'd actually been hired by a solicitor. OK, for a peanuts job. If it hadn't been a peanuts job he wouldn't have hired me. But if I did it well he'd hire me again. Maybe I'd get something juicier next time. Like a real live murder.

Chapter Three

The party turned out like nothing I expected. Mostly because Polly's lover Clive chose that evening to tell Polly, already the Other Woman, that he had Yet Another Woman. Lousy timing. But perhaps there is never a good time for that kind of information; perhaps you should wait till the other person finds out. Perhaps he should just have tapered off the visits, the phone calls, until Polly herself said the magic words, Is it over? Much easier, then, to say yes and leg it for the door.

One positive aspect was that when he rang to break the news, ten minutes before the party was due to start (eight o'clock), Polly was in her bedroom putting the final touches to a very professional make-up job. On me. (She doesn't think I pay enough attention to Presentation.) So when she slammed the phone down and started throwing things, I was close at hand to restrain her. God knows it would have been a mess if she'd been in the kitchen. Wall-to-wall chicken mayonnaise, I expect. As it was I missed a difficult catch and her giant bottle of Poison shattered on the bookcase.

I didn't think it was genuine pain; she'd been muttering about giving Clive the push for months. It was more that her pride was hurt. So it should have been. Not only is she a famous beauty, she's also brainy enough to pass accountancy exams. She's not a girl who has to say, Well, so he's married, so he's a back-bench Labour MP, so he's nearly bald, so he's a bit of a git, but he's the best I can do. The best Polly could do was stratospheric. But she'd chosen Clive. Fair enough.

I knew that nothing I said would be right but I had to say something while I wrestled with her. 'Think about it tomorrow,' I said. I was panicking. A party without Polly running it – I couldn't. I'm a terrible hostess. Insecure, aggressive. Partly, I suppose, because I spent my childhood shuttling between foster-homes under the weary and moulting

18

wing of the Social Services. 'Polly, please. Don't leave me to do this without you – I can't. Please.'

As I said it I heard the selfishness, but she didn't. She's very kind. She heard the fear, stopped struggling, and hugged me. 'Stupid sod,' she said bitterly. 'Stupid, stupid sod. Don't worry, Alex, I'll be fine. I'll deal with him tomorrow. I'll cry tomorrow.'

'Loved the movie,' I said facetiously. 'Susan Hayward.'

'Rita Hayworth.'

'Wasn't.'

'Was.'

'A quid says it was Rita Hayworth,' said Polly, gritting her teeth.

'OK, OK. It was Rita Hayworth.' In the present circumstances I'd agree it was Michelle Pfeiffer. Which it probably would be in the remake.

Polly began to sob. 'Tomorrow, tomorrow,' I said urgently, but she stepped up the sobs to a wail. The doorbell rang; I went down to open it; there stood Barty whose pass I'd fumbled last year as badly as Polly's bottle of Poison, and who for some reason now took my breath away, almost as much as Polly's ex-bottle of Poison. He's tall and rangy and much stronger than he looks, and he stood in the doorway looking even taller in cream chinos and a dark blue silk shirt, sniffing suspiciously.

'Poison,' I said. 'Perfume. Clive's got Yet Another Woman.'

'Ah,' said Barty. 'Drinks?'

'Definitely.'

'Gin and tonic?'

'Stronger.'

'Vodka martini?'

'Don't forget the surgical spirit.'

'Sorry I'm so early. Did Polly tell you she'd asked me to come on the dot to help out?'

She hadn't. She was matchmaking again, but now wasn't the time to worry about that, and there are worse people than Barty in a crisis. You don't have to explain things to him twice. Often you don't even have to explain them once, because he's observant.

'Is that Barty?' Polly called down the stairs. 'Barty? You'll know. Who was the actress in *I'll Cry Tomorrow*?'

'Didn't know there was one,' Barty called back. 'The film star was Susan Hayward.'

Renewed sobbing broke out upstairs. 'Drinks in Polly's kitchen,' I said.

'Coming right up. For you?'

'Vodka martini,' I said. I'm not a spirit drinker but all in all it seemed the simplest way.

Three hours and at least four drinks later the party was humming along. People were lying to each other at the top of their voices. In the early part of the evening Polly'd soldiered on with ominously sparkling eyes. Latterly, she'd disappeared and I was half-looking for her when I was spotted by Alan Protheroe, who I'd just been working for on the menopause research. I'd seen him already when he arrived with a striking dark-haired teenager, but he was too busy showing her off to bother with me. Now she'd vanished, he was alone, and I was his best friend.

Alan's an acquaintance from way back, from my early days at the BBC. He's a conscientious plodder who spotted me as an efficient workhorse early on and helped with my promotion. For two years I'd been his production assistant. He nearly always used my ideas and seldom credited me with them, but it was worth it for the experience. When he went freelance he'd wanted me to go with him but I'd managed to wriggle out of it without hard feelings on either side.

He draped his arm over my shoulder and said, 'What did you think of Cloudier?'

'What's cloudier?'

'My new PA. That's her name. C-l-a-u—'

'Yeah, yeah, I get it. Most people say Clawdier.'

'She says Cloudier. I need to talk to you about her. Have you met her? She's around somewhere. Charming girl. She wants to work in television: needs someone to show her the ropes.'

'Why don't you hire a PA who knows them?' I asked. Before the words left my mouth I'd realized I shouldn't have asked: the drinks were slowing me down. Since his second wife left him, he'd taken up with girls in their late teens and early twenties, way above his sexual touch. He's in his early fifties, thin and anxious-looking, with wispy pale hair that he compulsively combs over an even paler scalp. He peers through beautifully designed Armani spectacles that he refers to as his 'bird-pullers'. They don't work. To get a girl to endure his company, he has to bribe them with the prospect of a glittering future in television. Even with this lure, what with education for women, the equal opportunities legislation, and natural female common sense, he doesn't get many takers. When he does, they're preselected for IQs in the low eighties and self-deception ratings somewhere in the top .0001 percentile of the population.

'Right,' I said meaninglessly. Claudia would be lucky if I showed her to the lavatory. No way would I share any of my hard-earned acquaintanceship with television ropes. 'How's our doco going? When do you shoot?'

'Not till the end of August. Some trouble with the money men.'

'Tell me about trouble with money men,' I said. 'Hardly anyone's hiring, and no one's paying. Can I get you a drink?'

'I've got money up-front for my current project,' he said smugly. 'Japanese money.'

Now I was interested. 'What's it about?'

'Education. They want to find out what's wrong with their education system.'

'I thought the Japanese education system worked wonderfully well for the ninety-nine per cent who didn't kill themselves.'

'They're worried about the one per cent who do. They're doing a world-wide survey on successful headmasters and headmistresses. I'm handling the European end. Working title, *Headache*.'

Typical Alan working title: uninformative yet unfunny. But, like a blaze of light, I saw how I could do Plummer's job, get into Rissington Abbey, and find out about Olivier without letting anyone know what I was after. I could use Alan's doco as a cover.

He'd had a few drinks. I fetched him another and twisted his arm. After a while he agreed I could give his sacred name to Mr Head at Rissington Abbey, at a price. I'd have to work, free, for two days when he started shooting the menopause doco in August. 'I'm not sure Claudia can handle it alone.'

That was all I needed, two free days teaching an airhead too thick to pronounce her own name. I'd have to find a way to add it to Plummer's bill.

Then Barty appeared at my side. 'Hello, Alan.'

Barty and Alan are both independent producers, but there the resemblance ends. Alan is a parasite. Show him power and he'll flatter it, call its taxis, and clear up the mess on its carpet. Barty is instinctively subversive. Alan's afraid of Barty, but he always keeps in with people.

21

If he'd been an independent producer in Nazi Germany, he'd never have turned up at Eagle's Nest without a freshly baked Black Forest gâteau. 'Good evening, Barty,' he said. 'Long time no see. What've you been up to? Is it true what I've been hearing? Can we lunch?'

'Fine,' said Barty. 'Great. I'll have my secretary call you, but right now I want to talk to Alex.' He gripped my arm and edged me away.

'Why are you talking American?' I said.

'That's not American, that's media insincere. I thought you had a good ear . . . Where can we go?'

'My bedroom?'

We pushed our way through the party and up the stairs, through the miasma of Poison which still hung about the staircase. There was somebody in my bedroom, on the bed. Two somebodies. We backed out of the room and sat on the stairs.

'Party's going well,' said Barty.

'Mmm. Thank god. I hate parties.'

'You're looking very attractive.'

'Thank you. The outfit's a present from Polly.'

'It's your face and body.'

'Don't make a move on me now, Barty, please.'

'I wasn't going to . . . I have a present for you.' He handed me an home-made gold paper envelope bunchily folded and held together with what looked like half a roll of Sellotape, so I knew he'd done it himself. (He's selectively clumsy. He can repair camera equipment and edit film with the accuracy of a neurosurgeon, but he can't pack two shirts into an overnight case.) Inside the gold paper envelope, a membership card. For the London Library.

'Why bother?' I said. I should of course have said thank you and told him honestly how delighted I was, but I'm always graceless when I'm moved.

'Because you like books. Because it's a good library. Because I knew you'd never spend your own money on the subscription,' he said. 'Because I hoped it would please you.'

It was one of the few presents I'd ever had which showed some understanding of me. Polly, a persistent present-giver, always tries, but she gives me what she thinks I need (perfume: clothes: earrings). In my interminable childhood, passed from hand to hand like the parcel that no one wants to open, none of my foster-parents had ever known

22

me well enough to choose a successful present: my mother had often been hard put to remember who I was.

So I was moved almost to tears. He saw, and knowing I didn't want him to see, pretended not to and chattered on. 'I stopped recognizing my own birthdays when I turned forty . . .'

I knew he deserved more than a flippant thank you. Something genuine, exchanged for a genuine gift. I gave him my best effort and shared my thoughts. 'It's probably the second happiest moment of my life,' I said.

He took it seriously: he's good at tone. 'What was the first?'

'When I opened my first payslip and knew I'd escaped the Social Services. Finally. I was earning my living. I could rent my own room and pay for it. Eventually, I knew, I'd buy my own flat.'

Silence. I looked at Barty, he looked back. He has dark blue eyes with an even darker rim, and very thick black eyelashes. His eyes were smiling though his face wasn't. 'Look, Alex . . .' he began, rather awkwardly. Then the bedroom door opened and a red-haired youth of about seventeen stuck his head out. 'Anyone got some Amplex?' he said urgently.

'In the top drawer of the dressing-table,' I said. He disappeared.

'Who's that?' said Barty.

'I think he's Polly's model friend Marcia's younger brother.'

'Who's he with?'

'Alan's new aspiring media bunny, Claudia.'

The head appeared again. 'Got any condoms, mate?' he said to Barty.

'Bedside table drawer,' I said, and he ducked back in.

'Oh, yes?' said Barty, widening his eyes at me.

'Don't you use them?' I said, unexpectedly embarrassed. I don't embarrass easily.

'Not in your bedroom,' he said. 'So far. Unfortunately. What do you suppose his next request will be?'

'Peggy Lee singing "Is That All There Is"?'

'Did he look like a virgin to you?'

The face appeared again. 'Don't have any soft cords, by any chance?'

'No,' I said. 'And the bed's a divan.'

'Scarves?' he pursued hopefully.

'I don't wear them.'

'Camera tape any good to you?' said Barty, producing a roll from his shirt pocket.

'Mind the wallpaper,' I said.

'Sure. Great. Thanks.'

He left us staring at each other. '*Camera tape?*' I said. With Barty, I didn't have to laugh out loud. Then I remembered. 'You were going to say something, before he interrupted.'

'Was I?' said Barty disingenuously.

'Yes, you were.'

'Sorry, it's gone,' he said.

I didn't believe him.

It must have been a good party. The last guest went home after three. By then I was exhausted, not from the late night (I don't need much sleep), but from the strain. Polly had flaked out at midnight and Barty took her home to sleep at his place.

Then he came back. I hadn't thought he would, but he came straight back and kept going, like a host, until he threw the red-haired youth and Alan's Claudia out of my bedroom and closed the front door firmly behind them. Then he helped me clear up.

That was when I discovered something else about him: he was the only man I'd ever met who didn't automatically assume that cleaning lavatories was a woman's job. I did. I went up to my bathroom, ready equipped with J-cloth, bleach, and rubber gloves, to find him on his hands and knees. 'Keep out,' he said, 'I've n arly finished the floor.'

'What about the toilet bowl?'

'Done it. Of course. You do the floor last, everyone knows that.'

I inspected his work. It was excellent. 'I'll go down to Polly's bathroom,' I said.

'I've done it. Bathrooms are the worst things about parties. Always get the worst over first.'

It was half-past four before we'd finished and the place – both places, Polly's and mine – weren't perfect but they no longer looked like a battleground. The clearing-up was the bit of the party I most enjoyed. Being with Barty under those circumstances, with something to do, was like working on a project with him. I could relax into his company without feeling awkward, and I liked seeing my flat emerge into being my own again.

We talked about what we were doing, and about the people who'd been there, and argued mildly about whether Alan was third-rate or fourth-rate and how long his current bimbo, Claudia, would last. I fantasized about telling Alan that it seemed she already knew the ropes, or at least the camera tape, and he'd better find another metaphor to apply to her comparative media inexperience.

Eventually we collapsed on my sofa. My feet were murder because I'd been wearing high-heeled shoes all night (Polly'd insisted) and my legs aren't used to them. I lay down with my feet on Barty's lap and he massaged them. His fingers rubbed my feet precisely. He was in non-clumsy mode. He'd made me a mug of coffee.

The sensation was delicious. I shut my eyes and enjoyed the touch of his fingers. When I first met him he didn't appeal to me particularly. He's not bad looking, but it's not in the style I like. He's tall, lanky, with a bony Irish face and thick curly brown hair. I've never liked curly hair. I like athletic-looking men, with muscle, straight locky hair, smooth oval faces, and strong white teeth. A down-market taste because the men I like are too muscled to look good in suits. Barty's body could have been designed to hang a suit on. The only bits that protrude are the bones. Odd, really, because when you see more of his body it's sinewy, with the long rangy muscles of a thoroughbred horse.

To distract myself, I asked him whether he knew a solicitor called Plummer, because he was the most likely person to have recommended me, I thought. 'The name doesn't ring a bell,' he said. 'Why?'

'He's just hired me. My first real job as a PI.'

'That's good,' he said, but he didn't sound entirely happy. I told him all about it but he still didn't sound happy. I hoped he wasn't going to get protective. A protective man I didn't need, but a quick-witted no-bullshit foot-masseur I did.

My feet were recovering, and my tiredness had disappeared. I had the Olivier investigation to look forward to, and the prospect of Barty. So what if he hadn't been in touch with me for months? He probably had a reason. I'd gathered from odd remarks that he'd been working in California for some of the time. Perhaps he was affected by West Coast neuromeltdown and was respecting my personal space.

Anyway, I was happy with my feet in his lap. Very happy. I wondered, as I told him about Olivier (I was already beginning to find the name familiar – he was *my* Olivier) what he really felt about me.

And then he told me his wife had just moved back into his house.

God! What an evening. First Clive, now Barty. It was his ex-wife, actually. Divorced ten years ago. A very beautiful woman. I'd seen photographs but never met her. Now, apparently, her second husband had left her and she was staying with Barty. 'Just till she gets herself sorted out,' he said, and 'I tried to tell you earlier,' and 'It's the least I can do. Really. We go back a long way together.' I snatched my feet away and tucked them under me. I was shaking. I couldn't possibly compete with her. They'd been married eight years, for a start, and she must know – everything about him. And a *first* wife. They sink their teeth in deepest, and when they leave the jugular goes with them.

Suddenly I was very tired again and I threw him out, but then I couldn't sleep. I imagined his house like a doll's house, opened. In a guest bedroom, Polly, sobbing or snoring off the martinis. In another room, Barty. Alone, or with his wife? It didn't matter. Of course it didn't matter.

Tuesday, June 2nd

Chapter Four

By six I accepted I wasn't going to sleep. I put on a track suit and trainers and ran a good way. Three miles? Four? I don't take my fitness for granted any longer. Before my broken leg I'd never ever been ill or injured, and I'd always relied on my body to do what I wanted when I wanted. It may not be tall and elegant but it's strong and sound and tireless, and now I'm careful to keep it like that. I jogged to Wormwood Scrubs – I don't like running hard on pavement – and then lapped the playing fields as the sun came up and I could see the scrubby, uneven grass at my feet and the black walls of the prison beyond the athletics track.

Back home, I went to Polly's fridge and fetched some cold salmon and mayonnaise for breakfast, had a bath, washed my hair, cleaned my teeth, packed a bag for a few nights in the country, and settled down at the kitchen table to read the report of the inquest until it was after nine o'clock and I could get a train to Banbury after the commuter rush died down a bit at Paddington. At some point this morning I'd ring Alan at his office, check on the details of my cover, and make sure he'd told his bimbo assistant that I was now on the strength in case the Rissington school rang back to check. Then I'd ring the school and try to fix an appointment. There was plenty of prowling round the town to do if they wouldn't see me immediately.

By the end of the inquest transcript I knew more about the circumstances of Olivier's death. He'd been drunk (blood alcohol .12 – well above the limit for driving). He hadn't been missed from his room but when his housemaster, Alistair Brown, went down to the indoor pool for a keep-fit early morning swim, he'd found him floating in the pool. By then he'd been dead some time. The pathologist reported injuries to his head consistent with hitting his head on the diving-board, presumably when attempting to dive in, and a time of death between midnight and two o'clock. There were traces of skin and blood on the diving-board. Apparently Olivier was a good diver, the best in the school. The suggestion was that he'd been practising alone, drunk, and it was an accident. There was a diving match against another school coming up the following week.

I had a few questions of my own, some of which the coroner had anticipated. The alcohol? According to the headmaster, of course it was forbidden, but Olivier had been caught with a bottle of vodka and warned before. Yes, said the headmaster, he was a troubled boy. The staff at Rissington Abbey were doing their best to help him. No, boys were not allowed to swim alone. Never. Senior pupils, with their parents' permission, were allowed to swim unsupervised in threes, but only at certain times, and never after lights-out, of course. The swimming-pool was locked at night.

Why wasn't he missed from his room? He'd had a room to himself. He'd been there at room-check, ten o'clock, when Alistair Brown had said good night to him. Brown gave evidence. Olivier had seemed quite as usual the night before. He'd mentioned the diving match, and that he was working on a new dive for it.

None of the other pupils gave evidence. That was where I needed to be, talking to them. There'd be any amount of rumour but there might also be some fact, and they'd know far more about his actual state of mind than the teachers.

I wondered, riffling through the inquest transcript again, whether any of his family had been there. Whoever was hiring me (the French grandfather?) was very interested in Olivier. Interested enough, perhaps, to have gone to the inquest.

I might get that from the local newspaper coverage. That was my first stop in the country, the office of the local newspaper. I'd get a picture of Olivier that way, and the reporter who'd covered it might have details he didn't put in the paper and that I could pump him for. He'd certainly have more information about the school than I had.

Local reporters generally come in two types. Rising Young (often female) and Drunken Has-Been (almost always male). Drunken Has-Been is more useful, but either will do. Both of them usually know where the local bodies are buried, if only because the editor's warned them to keep off.

As I packed the inquest transcript and locked up the flat, I felt guilty about ditching Polly. She'd probably be sleeping in at Barty's. She had no work to get up for – she was on holiday from her huge firm of city accountants (getting less huge by the day as they weeded out in face of the recession) and in the normal way I'd have gone over to Barty's place before I left and checked that she was all right. But I didn't want to see his ex-wife, I didn't (did I?) want to see him, and I told myself that Polly would be OK. It was only Clive, for Heaven's sake. She was better off without him.

So I bottled out. I left an encouraging message for her, hesitating at first between 'Good riddance' and 'Poor you, you must be feeling awful'. I compromised on the multi-purpose Irishism 'I'm sorry for your trouble'. That, at least, was true.

Chapter Five

On the train to Banbury, a nearly empty Inter-City, I had four seats and a table to myself. I opened my expense account with Mr Plummer. I took a new personal finance sheet in my Filofax, headed and dated it, entered the tube fare to Paddington and the open return ticket from Paddington to Banbury, and tried to remember if there was a nice, big, anonymous, chain hotel I could stay at in Banbury. I like big hotels, where nobody cares who you are or where you eat or what you're doing. Hotels with an electric kettle and packets of instant coffee in the rooms and no guff about ancient traditions of service which usually mean (1) they ask you how you are all the time, (2) if something's wrong they do sod-all about it, and (3) they disapprove of your clothes.

It was only ten o'clock and already hot. The sun shone unequivocally in through the windows and picked out the murky patches of old chewing-gum on the floor and the grease marks on the seats. A good day to go to the country, I suppose, if you have to leave London, which I hate to do. I'm a street rat. But even I have to admit that London isn't at its best in the heat. I've never understood how it manages to be at once humid and dusty.

At the station I hired a car. I like hiring cars with someone else's money. I can't see myself affording my own just yet. If ever. I chose a middle-range Nissan and checked that the radio and cassette player was working before I drove away towards a chain hotel clearly marked on the free map.

The hotel suited me nicely. It was on the edges of an industrial estate on the edge of the town, a range of low, box-like buildings in a concrete car park, flat Oxfordshire fields one side, factories the other. It was only two years old, the teenage desk clerk told me, but the carpets in the foyer were already stained and I could tell from his stuffed-fish expression that he had no idea who or what I was and didn't care. I gave him my expense account credit card, took the key, and found the room. I hung up my spare jeans and T-shirts, put my underclothes in the drawer and my washing things in the bathroom. The lavatory, a strip of paper across the bowl told me, had been sanitized for my protection. Looking at it, I wouldn't have guessed. Perhaps sanitizing was cheaper than cleaning.

I rang Alan's office. He was there, and fussing. Same old cowardly Protheroe. When I first knew him I called him Ping-Pong, because he had celluloid balls. When he overheard the nickname one day I said it was a reference to his well-known quick-wittedness. When he'd worked it out (some minutes later), he'd been flattered.

He was bound to be in a bad temper anyway after his girl's behaviour the night before, and when sober he was excessively cautious. He wanted to back out of our deal but I wouldn't let him. It was in his own interest: he knew he'd almost certainly need me to pick up the pieces of his autumn shoot. He knew, and I knew, that if the girl couldn't manage the PA work the shoot would fall apart and then I'd have to step in and do the whole thing. I'd researched it; I knew the material and the interviewees; I could PA it in my sleep. He needed Alex Safety-net Tanner.

Eventually we settled that I could say I was working for him on a freelance basis: tell Geoffrey Ellis, the Rissington head, that he was being considered for the documentary, and ask him if he'd be prepared to take part. That might get me inside the door, anyway. Alan moithered on about all the things I mustn't commit him to and I agreed. I would protect him, of course. With any luck the school needn't know what I was really after.

I made some notes on the angle he was going to take for the real documentary: it would save me having to invent one of my own, and would cover our backs with Geoffrey Ellis if the doco was ever made and shown, and he watched it: at least my questions wouldn't look too incongruous, in retrospect.

Next, I rang the school. 'Rissington Abbey GHQ. Good morning!' said an adolescent male.

GHQ? Had I heard him right? 'The Headmaster, please.'

'Is the Major expecting your call?'

'No. Please tell him it's Alex Tanner from Protheroe Associates.'

'May I tell him what it's in reference to?'

'No,' I said.

'Oh,' said the voice, in a much younger squeak. 'Just a minute.'

Click, click, silence. He made me wait much longer than a minute. Eventually: 'Ellis here!' I held the receiver away from my ear. 'Alex Tanner? I'm a very busy man. May I ask why you wouldn't explain yourself?'

'I was talking to one of the kids at your school, wasn't I?'

'You were talking to the private on telephone duty.'

'Isn't he a kid in real life?'

'Well—'

'And I didn't think you'd necessarily want the whole school to know what I'm calling about.' I waited for him to bluster, but he didn't. So I gave him the Protheroe cover story. 'Oh!' he said, moderating his voice from a bellow to a bark. 'Well . . .' he sounded doubtfully eager, as if his natural optimism had often been bruised by experience. 'A television programme? On the BBC?'

'More likely a commercial channel.'

'Still . . .'

He was nearly hooked. 'Of course, we have plenty of alternative headmasters to consider, so if . . .' I didn't think he'd let me finish, and he cut straight in.

'Give me your telephone number, and I'll ring you back . . . oh, you're at a hotel? I'd better have your office number as well, in case you're an impostor . . .' He chuckled. A half-impostor, I chuckled too. 'So you're at a hotel in Banbury. Are you going to interview another local head?'

'Possibly,' I said.

'And if I'm prepared to see you, when are you free?'

'Any time tomorrow. After that, I'm not sure. When are you likely to ring back?'

'Later this afternoon. Goodbye, Miss Tanner.'

'Goodbye, Major Ellis.'

I called the desk, told the boy I was expecting a telephone call and could he take a message. 'Of course,' he said huffily. I wasn't convinced but I could always ring the school later. Then I packed my bag with the

34

tape-recorder and notebook, and all the cassettes I'd brought with me. I'm trying to educate myself musically. At present I'm working through Beethoven, so the Nissan and I set off with the windows rolled down and the 'Emperor' concerto blasting across the hot concrete of the car park and the hot macadam of the roads.

Chapter Six

Banbury used to be, I suppose, a pretty market town. Now it's a one-way, pedestrianized waste land: drably urban without urban compensations. I parked in a multi-storey car park that served a shopping centre, went to the nearest newspaper shop, and wrote down the office address of the two local papers on sale. According to the Pakistani cashier, the nearest was the office of the *Banbury Courier*, just out of the shopping centre and down a side-street.

The side-street had been beautiful once: narrow, with medieval wooden buildings that almost met over your head. Now it was pedestrianized with cobblestones and flash shopfronts advertising only FOR SALE signs, with no pedestrians passing to read them. It was the grave-yard of the boom years of the eighties: you could guess the products that were now, in the grimmer nineties, unaffordable and unwanted, from the names and the littered, vacant displays. Water filters; fitted Swedish kitchens; one shop calling itself Countree Thynges still featured a few forlorn baskets of dried flowers.

The only businesses now trading were a video shop (everyone still had a telly, a video, and their dreams) and the *Banbury Courier*. I followed the signs through a door and up narrow, uneven, damp-smelling stairs. The girl in reception, very young, podgy-faced, podgy-thighed in black Lycra cycling shorts (a mistake), willing, understood simple sentences the third time around. She was usually occupied, I could see by the displays round the walls, in selling copies of the newspaper's photographs to friends and family of people featured in them, and she found it hard to understand and respond to another request. But she giggled and tried. Eventually I was established in a cramped room off reception with the two relevant issues of the paper, the one after Olivier's death and the one after the inquest.

His death was the lead local story that week. There was indeed a photo of him, a studio portrait by a top photographer of a dark French boy with thick floppy hair, good bones, and shadowy eyes. It was a head-and-shoulders shot: his bones had outgrown his muscles and he looked coltish, un-filled out. TRAGEDY AT LOCAL SCHOOL was the headline. The piece was boxed and featured with the photograph of Olivier and a shot of the school, a Georgian house, with modern buildings in the background, set in grassland and trees. I glanced through it, noted the byline (Martin Kelly) and turned to the inquest issue. Same byline, plenty of photographs in this one too. The Coroner, Olivier and the school again, and Geoffrey Ellis. He looked late fifties/early sixties with a military moustache, a firm chin, and a sombre expression. I'd have looked sombre too, in his place.

Then I read the articles through. Rissington Abbey was an exclusive, expensive school. Ellis was sixty-one, his wife Anthea fifty-two, housemaster Alistair Brown thirty. Nothing new on Olivier, and Kelly hadn't picked up the Michel Mouche connection, although possibly Banbury wouldn't have been interested in it anyway. I doubted most people in Banbury would have heard of Mouche. Still, Kelly could have made something of the mother: English girl, now French pop star, might have been worth a para. Chances were he didn't know.

The inquest one was more use. Olivier's English grandparents had been there – a blurred shot of two shabby old people, no comment – and so had Plummer, who'd given Kelly an anodyne quote. But Kelly had included some extra background material in the inquest article, most of it details of the school but including one interview with the old woman whose house Olivier and another boy had been painting as part of the school's service to the community programme. 'He was ever such a nice boy,' she said. 'Kind, thoughtful, sensitive.'

Kind? I hadn't got that impression from Plummer, nor from the inquest comments by the headmaster. 'Attention-seeking', Plummer had called him, which was probably solicitorspeak for 'a pain in the bum'. 'Troubled', the headmaster had said, presumably teacherese for the same thing. I'd make a point of seeing the old woman.

I persuaded Cycling Shorts to let me photocopy the articles and asked about Martin Kelly. Apparently he'd be in the local pub by now (quarter to twelve). I got directions. It would work quite well: I could have lunch at the same time. I asked for a description of him. 'He's old,' said the girl. Good, I thought. Even if her idea of old was over thirty, it probably meant Drunken Has-been. 'He looks like a priest,' she went on.

Did she mean in a black dress and a clerical collar? 'What does a priest look like?'

'I mean,' she struggled to express herself, 'he *was* a priest. So he looks like a priest. Not like a journalist. Like. If you see what I mean.'

'That's interesting,' I said, trailing my coat.

'It is. Isn't it?'

'Really interesting. Unusual,' I plugged on.

'Yeah. Really interesting.'

I'd have to prod some more. 'How did it happen?'

'What?'

'How did he stop being a priest and get the job here?'

'I think he just stopped. Like. They can't *make* you keep on, I don't think, but I'm not a Catholic, if you just say you don't want to be a priest any more, if you see what I mean.'

'I see what you mean. But how did he get a job on the paper?'

'He applied,' she said, wide-eyed. 'You write in. And send your curriculum vitty.'

'Yes, I see what you mean,' I said grinding my teeth behind my smile. 'But lots of people apply to newspapers, don't they? And he hadn't trained as a journalist, had he?'

'Hadn't he?' she said, surprised.

'If he was a priest, I mean.'

'Yeah. Yeah. I see what you mean.'

'So maybe there was another reason why he got the job.'

'Yeah. There might have been, I suppose, like.'

'Who owns the paper?'

'The paper?'

'The *Banbury Courier*. Who owns it?'

'Mr Flynn.'

'Is he Irish, maybe? With a name like that?'

'Oh, no. He lives in Birmingham, he owns lots of papers, all round the Midlands.'

'Is Mr Flynn Catholic?'

'Oh, yes, of course. He must be.'

'Why?'

'Well, because Martin used to be his family priest. In Birmingham.

Well, Edgbaston, like. Before Martin came to Banbury. He was the priest here, for a while. Before he stopped being a priest.'

That was all I needed. An innocent amateur, fixed up by a sympathetic ex-parishioner. I wanted an old soak who'd worked on a national daily, preferably a tabloid, as full of dirt as a Hoover bag.

Never mind, I'd give Martin Kelly a try. I also wanted some lunch.

Chapter Seven

The pub was big, dark, shabby, smelling of beer and smoke and chips and too many people, even though, as it was early, it was almost empty, apart from some adolescent boys playing pool and a man, presumably my man, at the bar. He was smoking as if the process needed concentration and skill, and filling in *The Times* crossword with confident expedition. He had very short brown hair and a clean-cut, wide-eyed, unlined but hollowed face that was hard to put an age to. More than thirty, less than fifty, was as close as I could get. He was wearing grey flannel trousers, white shirt, dark tie, and a dark blue lightweight jacket. A neat black briefcase stood at the foot of his barstool. Cycling Shorts was right, he didn't look like a journalist. More like the key member of an American evangelist's entourage, sneaking a smoke.

'Martin Kelly?'

He nodded and smiled, a tired, automatic smile. 'That's me. How can I help you?'

I introduced myself and offered my hand. He eventually shook it, but not before sharply withdrawing his own in a defensive reflex which I'd last seen in a concert pianist. I gave him the Protheroe cover story, saying I was looking for background on the school, trying not to let him see me looking at his hands. He held them with the fingers curled into the palm, and when he picked up his drink, newspaper, cigarettes, and briefcase to follow me to a grubby booth by an open window, I saw why. His nails were painfully bitten, rusty with bloodstains.

He heard me out courteously enough. I sensed another withdrawal, this time psychic, not physical, but whether it was a general reticence or a particular reluctance to talk about the school, I couldn't tell. When I'd finished he said, 'Ah. So that's the way of it,' in a resigned tone. Perhaps he just didn't want me to disturb his solitary lunch.

I offered to buy him another drink but he refused. 'One diet Coke's enough for now,' he said. His voice still had traces of a soft Southern Irish accent.

'The girl at Reception told me you'd be here,' I said. 'She said I'd recognize you because you looked like a priest.' I was fishing. I wanted to hear about his strange mid-life career change.

'Did she indeed?' he said blandly, lighting a cigarette. 'I've ordered my lunch. If you want to order yours, I'd advise the shepherd's pie.'

I fetched myself a Coke and ordered the shepherd's pie so as not to offend him, though it was the wrong weather for hot food. I needed to get his measure and build up a working relationship. I wanted not only what he knew, but what he'd guessed, about the school and Olivier's death.

'How did you get into journalism?' I said.

'The *Courier* is hardly journalism,' he said.

'Jobs are hard to find, though, even on a local freesheet.'

'I was lucky. The owner is an ex-parishioner of mine. Does that satisfy your curiosity?'

'I hear you were a priest in Banbury, before you left.'

'Yes,' he said, after a noticeable hesitation.

'And Rissington Abbey was in your parish,' I guessed, but spoke as if I knew.

'It's a Church of England school.'

Still guessing: 'With some Catholic boys.' The French were often officially Catholic. Olivier might have been.

He nodded.

'And you were responsible for the Catholic boys at the school?'

'They attended our parish church, yes.'

I'd pressed him enough. 'And how do you like being a journalist?' I said, and we chit-chatted for a bit.

The barman brought our lunches. The shepherd's pie was excellent. Real meat, real potatoes, plenty of Lea & Perrins in the gravy. Not surprisingly, the pub was beginning to fill up, mostly with minor businessmen in tired suits, some of whom nodded to Kelly as they came in. A middle-aged woman put a pound in the juke-box and a few seconds later Tina Turner was churning out her raunchy scream. I couldn't hear the words but the subtext was that it's Fun to be Fifty. I screened out her implied reproach: it was only intermittently Fun to be Twenty-Nine.

Kelly was explaining that he'd wanted space to reflect about himself and life. The priesthood was demanding: responsible, and emotionally draining. Working as a journalist, more detached from people, would give him scope to find out the truth.

'What truth?' I said. 'Is there one?'

'It's a big word. Perhaps I mean something much smaller. The truth about myself.'

The one unachievable truth, I thought. Always fogged by the bias of the observer. I wondered if it was a serious intention, or merely what he had chosen to believe, to give himself a purpose or to cover up guilt at his failure as a priest.

'Are you sure you really want to find it?' I said.

'I'm seldom sure about anything. At least I've learnt that . . . How long have you been a researcher, Miss Tanner?' We chatted on for a bit until we'd finished the shepherd's pie. Then he pushed his plate away and said, 'Right. I can give you a half-hour, then I'm going home. It's my mid-week afternoon off because I work Saturdays. How can I help you?'

He'd warmed up to me a little, by now, so I went straight in. 'Tell me about the school. What kind of place is it?'

He considered, started to speak, checked himself, and tapped his fingers on the table. 'What kind of a person are you, Alex Tanner?'

'Do you mean I asked a stupid question? Too general?'

'No. I wondered how you would describe yourself. With one adjective.'

It was a party-game. I don't like them. But you should never alienate a source. 'Curious,' I said. 'I'd call myself curious. I like to find things out.'

'All right then. Rissington Abbey.' He spoke deliberately. 'I'd call it evil,' he said.

I was rocked by the word. Evil. What sort of evil? 'Explain,' I said.

He paused again, for so long that I was about to prompt him. Then he went on, 'I've no time for private schools at all,' and I relaxed. If his objection was only ideological . . . He went on, 'It's a training ground for fascists. The boys wear paramilitary uniforms. They drill twice a day. They move between classes at the double. They salute the masters. They call the Headmaster "Major".'

'Is he a major?'

'He was before he left the Army, but that's not the point. Who'd want to run a school like that?'

42

'An old buffer? Someone who needs a gimmick to keep problem boys in line? While they're running and saluting, they can't get into trouble.' It didn't seem like a school I'd pick for my own son but I could think of a gang of boys from the council estate where (most of the time) I'd spent my childhood, who would have been better occupied at Rissington Abbey. Several cats the gang had tortured to death would have agreed with me, not to mention my mate Michelle who never really got over her rape, and the OAPs who couldn't afford steel shutters for their windows.

My scepticism was frustrating him. 'I'm explaining it badly,' he said. 'It's more like – a smell. A smell of evil. The place is rotten.' He stubbed out one cigarette, lit another.

'You didn't give that impression in your coverage of Olivier's death.'

'I've got a living to earn. And I've no evidence. It's just the smell. You can't miss it.'

I listen to experts on their own subjects. I suppose a priest, even an ex-priest, is an expert on evil. 'When did you first notice it?' I said. 'The evil. Was it the Headmaster, the place, what?'

'I covered their sports day, a year ago. They had a celebrity guest, Ellis rang my editor, he sent me along to cover it. I spent the whole day there, hanging round watching the races and talking to the Ellises and the staff.'

He hadn't answered me directly. Perhaps he couldn't. Perhaps his diagnosis of evil came from the earlier time when he was involved as a priest. 'Sports day,' I said. 'Ummm. It wasn't the celebrity guest, by any chance?'

'Hardly. That was Peter Hayes, the fifteen-hundred metre runner. A very genuine, uncomplicated man.'

'So the papers say.'

'You don't believe me about the evil.'

'I don't believe or not believe, yet. What you've told me isn't precise enough; I can't visualize it. You could mean you feel the place is badly run. You could mean it's an unhappy school. You could mean one of the people there is evil, just one of them, not the whole place.'

I was a lot less sceptical than I'd have been a year ago, before my first investigation. Eventually, that had smelt to me of evil, but then it was a very tangible smell, of excrement and blood.

I pressed on, since he was silent. 'On that sports day. You don't remember Olivier, the boy who died, by any chance? He was quite a diver, wasn't he? Did the sports include diving?'

'As a matter of fact, yes. Everybody noticed him. A very – striking youth. Confident, and beautiful. And no, I'm not homosexual.'

His sexuality was nothing to me either way. I gave a sympathetically butch smile, and pressed on. 'Did he seem happy, to you?'

'I watched the boy diving. How could I tell if he was happy? He was pleased enough at winning. How else can I help you?' he said abruptly, curling his fingers away from me again, so I couldn't see his bloody nails.

Martin Kelly, a man with a problem. Probably any ex-priest had a problem. Had he lost his faith? Had he been chucked out? One day a faith, a purpose, a place to live, the next day a life to rebuild from the roots. And drinking diet Coke, and chain-smoking. I wondered if he was a dried-out alcoholic. Not that that need impair his testimony. It might explain his nails.

'I could really do with any names and addresses of people connected with the school, however loosely, that I could talk to before going in there and seeing Geoffrey Ellis himself. Cleaning women, for instance, and the old lady you quoted in your inquest article, the one whose house Olivier was painting.'

He was looking at me. Not quite suspiciously. More assessingly. 'And you want this as background for the programme you're researching which is a character study of various heads?'

'Yes.'

'If you say so. I'd say you were interested in the boy Olivier.'

'I'm interested in him too,' I said. 'Background. I want to get the whole picture.'

'Ah.' His eyes met mine again, then slid away, full of some knowledge I didn't share. He might think the school smelt of evil but I thought he smelt of loneliness and pain, and I'm an expert on that.

'I'll give you this,' he said, and snapped open his briefcase. It was full of notebooks. That took me aback, even more than his statement about the school being evil. Why on earth would a reporter carry his dead notes about with him?

He selected two notebooks and flipped back through one of them. It was a standard reporter's notebook which he used in the standard way, from front to back on one side of the page, then from back to front again on the other, crossing through the pages with a single pencil

44

stroke when they were done with. He tore out a handful of pages, replaced them in his briefcase and passed the two notebooks over to me. 'You can have them. They're in longhand. God be with you.'

He got up to go.

'Thanks a lot. Here, take my card.' I scribbled the name and telephone number of my Banbury hotel on it. 'Where can I get hold of you?'

'Through the paper.'

'Don't you have a home address and telephone?'

'Of course. Why do you want it?'

'In case I want to get hold of you out of working hours. I'll be around Banbury for a few days . . . Maybe I could buy you dinner, on expenses . . .'

He smiled. 'I'm not very good company,' he said.

'It's not your company I'm after, it's your information,' I said.

But he still didn't give me his number.

Chapter Eight

His information was good, but why had he given me so much? The first notebook was last year's: towards the beginning, I found his coverage of the Rissington Abbey sports day. Some of his jottings were obvious, some obscure. I put it aside and turned to the second, recent notebook, which included Olivier's inquest. I sifted through it, back in my hotel room, with the rickety metal windows opened as far as they would go and the stiffly synthetic net curtains looped back to get every breath of the rape-heavy air from the fields. Plenty of names. The Coroner, the pathologist, the school doctor, the school matron. None of which were relevant: I wasn't investigating his death, something I found hard to remember.

Then, more useful to me, the charwoman who cleaned his room, the woman whose house he'd painted, the shop where Kelly thought he'd bought the vodka which had, indirectly killed him. It was near the school. A good place to find out his habits, perhaps, except that Kelly had spoken to the manager who'd denied ever selling drink to underage boys from the school. He wouldn't be keen to chat about the boys' real habits, since they were illegal and he presumably didn't want to lose his licence.

The mention of vodka reminded me of Polly and another wave of guilt swept over me. She'd be back at home by now. I rang her. Her answering voice sounded attenuated and distant. 'Hello?'

'Hi, Polly. It's Alex. How's the hangover?'

'Awful . . . thanks for clearing up.' Then silence. Silence. From Polly, the original natural geyser of chat, a Mannequin Pis of non-stop burble.

'I'm down in Banbury, staying at the Wanderotel. Do you want my number?'

'Oh . . . OK . . . hang on.' More silence. 'OK, go ahead.'

I gave her the number. 'I'll be back in two or three days. What'll you be doing?'

'Nothing. I'm just going to stay here.'

Bad idea. Bad, bad idea. 'Why don't you go home for a day or two?' She has lots of brothers and sisters, mostly living near her parents' house in Sussex. She'd be fine down there, with her bossy, affectionate mother, absent-minded doting father, and a revolving doorful of siblings, siblings-in-law, nephews, and nieces.

'I couldn't face it.'

'Give them a ring anyway.'

'Not just yet . . . I suppose I should thank you, Alex.'

'What for?'

'For getting Barty to take me home for the night.'

'Nothing to do with me. That was his idea.'

'But he wouldn't have done it, if it wasn't for you.'

Silence again, edgy this time. She was getting at me, I realized, surprised. She never got at me. 'Did you know his ex-wife was staying there?' she went on.

I bit my tongue. 'Yes,' I said neutrally.

'She's very nice.'

'Oh, good.'

'I'm going to ring off now, Alex.'

Just as well, I thought, though I said, 'Why?'

'I'm watching a repeat of *Cooking with Cassie*.'

The worst television programme in the schedules. 'You hate *Cooking with Cassie*.'

'Cassie is Clive's Other Woman. Maybe if I watch her I'll understand . . . Thanks for ringing, Alex. Goodbye . . .'

I didn't feel better for ringing. I felt worse. I wasn't used to sniping from her direction, and, besides, she obviously needed me there, to sit the other end of the sofa and watch Cassie cooking and bitch about her and say how much more beautiful, more talented, more loving Polly was, and then fetch sentimental videos from the corner shop and pass her the chocolates and Kleenex.

My hand hovered over the phone. I could ring Barty, tell him where I was, ask him to keep an eye on Polly. No, I couldn't. He'd enough to do looking after his ex-wife, and would be much more interested in doing it. He might think it was a pretext to call him. Which it wasn't, because Polly's mood worried me, seriously.

47

I'd have to go back to London tonight. Plummer's client could afford the petrol, and my unused bed in the Wanderotel. It was half-past two now. Time for one more interview, at least, today. Still no return call from Major Ellis, but it was too soon to chase him up.

I went back to Kelly's notes. He'd given me the name of the old woman whose house was being painted by Olivier, the old woman who had described him as 'kind'. I'd be interested in her comments. Maybe the kind boy had sat and chatted to the lonely old lady. Maybe one conversation with her would be my whole job finished. Not that I'd tell Plummer that, and not that I really expected it. The boy in the photograph didn't look as if he'd be interested in old women. He looked as if he'd be interested in himself first and everyone else a long way behind.

Matilda Beckford, the old biddy's name was, and the address 53 Foxglove Avenue. The boy, still on duty at the front desk, had no idea where to find Foxglove Avenue. He was a Wanderotel Accelerated Management Trainee, he told me proudly, spending three months working in Banbury. He was only on his second month and he didn't get out much so he didn't know the area. He worked punishing shifts. But he thought one of the cleaners would know.

One of the cleaners did, when he led me to the broom cupboard. She was sitting on a pile of used towels smoking a fag, illicit judging by the way she jumped when he came in. I always find that odd, when a woman in her fifties has to jump at the arrival of a pimply boy. I don't want to be in that position when I'm in my fifties. That's why I've got such a punitive self-employed pension plan. My money, when it doesn't go into the mortgage or the upkeep on the flat, goes to the pension plan. It's worth working for, though. It's a sort of freedom. Money is freedom. Freedom of choice. In a small country like England, there are enough restrictions anyway, without adding poverty to the list.

The cleaner, fagless, gave me directions to Foxglove Avenue, which was as its name might have told me on a new development of sheltered housing. Sheltered housing. I'll shelter myself, thank you.

The Nissan, Beethoven's Eighth Symphony, and I finally tracked down Foxglove Avenue between Bluebell Way and Primrose Grove. The houses were all very small bungalows, carefully kept. Not the sort of places you'd expect to need decorating by schoolboys broadening their curriculum vitae.

53 Foxglove Avenue had the regulation tiny square of well-mowed

lawn between the gate and the neat front door. It didn't have net curtains. Some did. I walked up the wide-slabbed path and rang the doorbell, taking care not to meet the eye of the person hovering inside the front-room window. At least I knew she was in, but if she wanted to pretend to be out, I wanted to give her the chance. Not that I'd let her get away with it – I was certainly going to speak to her – but it would be a factor to reckon with if she had something to hide, and I wanted to know.

She came straight to the door. She was really quite old: mid- to late-eighties, I reckoned, with thinning yellow-grey hair, a slow walk, and a stoop. She'd been tallish, once, but now she was shorter than me, and all her physical reactions were slow and anxious, as if a final fall was only a step away. Her substantial chest had shaken downwards like a sugar-bag and was held at the waist by the belt of her rose-printed cotton dress.

'Mrs Beckford?' I said.

'Yes,' she said, making no attempt to let me in.

'My name is Alex Tanner,' I said. 'I work in television and I'm collecting material for a documentary on schools. I wanted to talk to you about the Community Service programme at Rissington Abbey, because I believe you've been a part of it.'

A look of alarm flew into her watery, colourless eyes. Television frightened her, perhaps? Or everything did? I kept on talking reassuringly. 'You won't be on television yourself, of course. It's just background information. To give me a picture of the school. We're not even sure that we'll use the school, so it may all come to nothing – these things often don't—' What I said didn't matter. It was the warm, friendly, soothing tone of voice, like talking to an animal or a baby. 'And we won't use your name. It's very hot, isn't it?'

She blinked at the sudden change of subject. She was holding on to the door handle for balance, and concentrating on staying upright made it even harder for her to think clearly. She thought she didn't understand the transition because she was old. In fact I'd thrown her a curved ball. 'It's hot and I'm very thirsty. I wonder if I could have a drink of water?'

She stepped back and headed off along the wide short hall to the kitchen area, to get me a drink. I stepped inside and closed the door behind me. I had her.

On the way to the kitchen I stuck my head in the front room, which smelt of locked windows and age. Tidy, bare, over-filled by a blue velour three-piece suite bought for a larger room and a television with a giant screen. No family photographs. Either she didn't have children, or she didn't want to be reminded of them.

Actually it wasn't water she gave me, it was real lemonade, which she had ready-made in a jug in the fridge. She did everything efficiently but very slowly. While she shuffled from fridge to cupboard I sat at the kitchen table and watched her orbiting-space-capsule movements, not offering to help, logging the contents of the fridge. She wasn't starving, anyway. The fridge was full of small packages, clumsily wrapped in kitchen foil, presumably left-overs: looked like frugality, not poverty.

The kitchen had been recently painted cream. It was a smallish room, almost square, with worktops and plugs adjusted for wheelchair height and a door which led to a tiny back garden, a square of lawn bordered by raised flowerbeds, suitable for wheelchair gardeners. I wondered if she'd be better off in a wheelchair, and what it felt like to walk a wobbling tightrope over such a ubiquitous safety-net.

The painting had evidently been done by an amateur. There were patches where the last coat showed through, there were drips, now dried, and the gloss coat on the woodwork was uneven. But it had been done with care. What was wrong with it was inexperience rather than carelessness or illwill. If Olivier had done this, then he wasn't, or only, the spoilt, selfish adolescent Plummer had described.

'Will you repeat what I say to the people up at the school?' she said when she finally sat down. She had a rich local accent but she spoke grammatically and I reckoned that she would usually have taken me through to her front room, but that now, with age lapping round her neck, she was grateful to collapse on the nearest chair. Her eyes sought mine waveringly.

'Not a word,' I said.

'I've been very troubled.'

'About?'

'Did you read what it said in the paper?'

'Yes. I was very interested in your comments about the poor boy who died – Olivier, wasn't it?'

She made a humming noise and rocked backwards and forwards. 'That's what's troubling me,' she said.

'Tell me about it,' I said, completely lost. 'Tell me about Olivier.'

'I can't,' she said.

'Why?'

'The bit in the paper – the bit you read – it was a pack of lies.'

'Olivier wasn't kind, generous, warm-hearted?'

'I've no idea. I never laid eyes on him, my dear, not once.'

Chapter Nine

The obvious question was what Olivier had been doing with all those missing Wednesday afternoons, and that last missing weekend. 'I'm afraid I've no idea. No idea at all,' said the old woman defensively. 'Why should I?'

The possibilities began to excite me. It might have been ordinary schoolboy naughtiness; he might just have bunked off and gone to the cinema, or smoked behind the bike sheds, or done mild drugs somewhere. On the other hand he might have been doing something which, directly or indirectly, led to his death. Which I reminded myself I wasn't investigating.

But at the moment the question to ask the sugar-bag of summer cotton was obvious. 'Why didn't you say he'd never visited you?'

'You won't repeat any of this up at the school? It won't get back to the Major?'

She saw the Major as a powerful figure, I could hear from the anxiety in her voice. I reassured her again and complimented her on the lemonade. It was very good.

'You seem to be a nice girl,' she said, squinting at me. Her sight was as bad as her hearing but she was managing both, and there didn't seem to be anything wrong with her brain. 'You'll understand. I don't tell lies, as a rule.'

'So why did you, this time?'

'I did it for Tim.' As she spoke, she looked at a bookshelf in a corner of the kitchen, then, when my glance followed hers, sharply away. As far as I could see the shelf held cookery books and some fat brown A4 envelopes. Perhaps she hid her money there?

'Who's Tim?'

'Tim Robertson. That French boy's partner. Tim's from the school as well. They're supposed to do the community service programme in twos. But the French boy wouldn't do it. He didn't like doing anything he didn't want to.'

'How do you know?'

'Tim said . . . He made Tim not tell anyone. Tim was frightened of him, I think. So Tim never told anyone up at the school that the other boy didn't come with him. If they'd found out he'd have been in terrible trouble, because he's supposed to be in charge of the community service. He's the Officer Commanding, they call it. That's the point. I did it for Tim. So he didn't get in trouble. So when they asked me about the French boy, I just talked about Tim. He's a really nice boy. Gets pushed around up at the school. The Major doesn't like Tim because he doesn't fit in up there, and he's afraid of getting into trouble. And I didn't want him to, because he's been ever so kind to me. He's a duck.'

She was quite militant in defence of her Tim, who I couldn't wait to get hold of. The only thing better than an adolescent's friend, for information, is an adolescent's enemy.

'How can I meet Tim?'

'I'm not sure. He's finished with me, for the moment. He's got a new partner and they're painting the house next to the Warden's. Over in Primrose Grove. They might be there this weekend.'

Tim Robertson: a name for my action list. I left Matilda Beckford standing at the door of her house, clinging to the handle for support. When I got into the car, I waved, and she waved back. I wondered how many people visited her in her bungalow, purpose-built for decline, with its neatly cut lawn and sweet-smelling roses. She was still managing by herself; she presumably had enough money. A better old age than many.

Still, as I drove away, I felt a little guilty that I could. Then I pushed the sentimentality aside. I wasn't going to do anything to help Matilda Beckford, so any 'aah' saying was just sentimentality. I hate cruelty in all its forms, and sentimentality is just cruelty with icing sugar.

There were two messages waiting for me at the hotel desk.

2.6.92 pm Please ring Major Elvis at Rizington Abey Please ring Alan Rotherom

I hadn't underestimated the Accelerated Trainee, but I liked his version of Ellis. Perhaps I should alert the *Sunday Sport* to another sighting.

I rang Alan first, in case he had something to say. He didn't. He was wittering, about Ellis checking up, about me having to be careful, not doing anything to land him in it. I soothed him. Then I rang Major Ellis.

This time the duty private put me straight through. 'Miss Tanner,' said the Major, 'I'm prepared to discuss your project. Join me for dinner in the Mess tonight.'

I ignored the military flim-flam and refused the invitation. My evening was already committed to Polly's mess. After some negotiation, in which the subtext was how important, busy, and tireless the Major was, we settled that I'd see him at 0700 hours the following day.

Then I grabbed my tape-recorder, notebook, Martin Kelly's notebooks, and my toothbrush, and drove back to London.

Chapter Ten

It must have been a first. No one else, ever, could have watched a sixteen-minute videoed segment of Cassie preparing *Les Patates à l'Ail* for three and a half hours. She trilled on about the gastronomic delights of South-west France; I lay on the floor; Polly lay on the sofa and provided the voice-over.

'She's knock-kneed. Look at that skirt – if she bent over you could see right up her bony bum. She's got a speech defect. She can't even cook – look how she's holding that knife. Stupid pretentious cow, if I had an accent like hers I'd stick to English. Why can't she just say potatoes? Who gives a sod if the dialect word for *pommes de terre* is *patates*? Chances are she only found it out when the script rolled up on the monitor, anyhow. I wouldn't touch those potatoes with a barge-pole, not after she's shaken her dandruff all over them. I thought cooking was supposed to be hygienic. Why don't they make her tie back that verminous clump of hideous red hair?'

Every third time through, I made myself a cup of coffee and Polly a weak gin. At midnight, as Cassie bade us a tooth-flashing *Bon appétit*! for the thirteenth time and Polly pointed out that Cassie's gums were receding, I punched the stop button on the VCR. Polly blinked at the silence. 'What do you think, Alex?' she said.

'I absolutely agree,' I said. 'She's completely vile. I'm making scrambled eggs, known in Pyrennean dialect as oeufs for a pissed-off, beautiful lady. Want some?'

'How can I eat, at a time like this? Stop nagging. Stop trying to look after me. It's not a role that suits you.'

I made her the eggs anyway, and she ate some of them. I didn't understand exactly why she was so upset. She and Clive had never been serious. She'd told me she didn't want to marry him, she didn't want him to leave his wife, it was just an affair. She'd been planning to end it herself. Yet now she seemed completely shattered. It had hardly been more than twenty-four hours since she'd heard, and yet she looked older, sadder, reduced. Less beautiful, less capable, less Polly.

It made me feel reduced, too. I'd always depended on her bubbling optimism, her insistence on seeing the best in everything, the challenge in the disaster, the potential in the ugly duckling.

I wasn't so selfish that I wouldn't let her feel what she felt, but I didn't have the key to it. The underlying misery must have been something else. Not just because I thought no sane woman would have accepted a cup of coffee from Clive. Sexual tastes are irrational. But I'd watched Polly's sexual involvement ebbing. Once or twice, in the last two months, she'd preferred to stay in with me and a Chinese takeaway rather than scuttle over to his Pimlico flat for stolen hours of lust.

So if it wasn't the sex, what was it?

'What am I going to do, Alex?' she said, when I took away her half-eaten scrambled eggs.

'Go home for your holiday. Rest. Then resume your conquest of the world, I should.'

'I can't face them.'

'You needn't face them. That's the point of decent families, I thought. You just crawl in there and recover. You don't have to defend or excuse yourself.'

I didn't know that from personal experience, but it's the manifesto of the Hearth and Home party.

'That's all balls,' she said. 'I couldn't tell them about Clive. I shouldn't have been having an affair with a married man anyway.'

'So? It's not up to them to judge you.'

'Don't you ever judge?'

'Not my friends. That's the point, isn't it?' I was lying, of course. I do judge. I just don't let on I have. Behaviour is the test.

'Alex the admirable,' she said sarkily.

I hung around for another hour, until Polly fell asleep on the sofa; I covered her with a duvet and went upstairs to prepare my questions for the interview with the Major.

It was stuffy, a heavy London night, and not much better even when I opened all the windows in my living-room. The warmish, damp air seeped in and hung: you could almost touch it. With the windows open,

I could hear the traffic on Ladbroke Grove, and beyond it the rumble of heavy traffic on the Westway on the way to the M40. I ground some coffee beans, then while the cafetière plopped I pottered around putting the finishing touches to the post-party clear-up.

Then I sugared a mug of coffee and listened to the messages on my answerphone. The first two began with thank yous for the party and went on to offer me work. Polly's hacking was obviously a good idea. I pencilled in the dates, both much later in the year, and made a note to ring back. The third was a breathy, elfin, oddly accented gush. It wasn't recognizably foreign: I couldn't place it as French or Polish or Italian, straight off, but it wasn't any English accent I knew. Come to think of it, it wasn't so much the accent as the intonation that was unusual.

I'd spent the duration of the message trying to place the voice. I had to run the tape back and play it again, for content. 'Oh – hello – this is Claudia, Alan's friend . . . Thanks tons for the party, it was terrific . . . such fun . . . Actually I really need to speak to you, Alex, could you ever ring me, if you get this . . . well of course you can't ring me if you don't . . .' I took down her number automatically and forgot her call as I wrote the last digit. I didn't even have time to wonder what she was calling about, because the fourth voice was Barty's. He could have been in the room, and I wished he was.

'Hello, Alex. Thanks for the party. How's Polly? I wish you were in. It's midnight. Give me a ring if you're back before one. Otherwise ring tomorrow. I want to talk to you . . . Bye.'

It was nearly two. Should I call now? For a moment my hand hovered over the phone. He wouldn't mind being woken. But his ex-wife might . . . I'd ring tomorrow.

I re-recorded the answerphone messages, adding the number of my Banbury hotel. Then I sat down at the kitchen table with the notes I'd taken from my conversation with Alan about his *Headache* series. I might have to demonstrate an easy mastery of it at Rissington Abbey in five hours' time.

Wednesday, June 3rd

Chapter Eleven

I left London at quarter to five, in case the Major was obsessive about punctuality. It was too early for Beethoven so I listened to the World Service and then the news on Radio 4. I have to keep up with what's happening in the world. My job mostly depends on knowing about as many things as possible, so when I'm thrown in to find out the details, I have a framework to hang from. I routinely read three newspapers a day, preferably someone else's, and I listen to Radio 4 as well. I could have done without *Farming Today* but I listened anyway. There's always someone, somewhere in Europe, making a programme about the Common Agricultural Policy.

I reached Banbury early and spent half an hour with a cup of coffee in a truckers' café, full of men and steam and cigarette smoke. When I came out the sun was just beginning to be warm on my back. No sign of a cloud. We were getting all our summer in early June, as usual.

The school, surrounded by its walled grounds, sat oddly in the scrubby north-east outskirts of Banbury, skirted by industrial estates and the new, still unconvincing landscaping of the M40. The drive was long, about a quarter of a mile, and the grass borders were mercilessly trimmed. All the grounds looked over-disciplined: the bushes pruned, the flowers planted in rows. Most of the work was probably done by the boys. At least twenty khaki-clad adolescent figures were hard at work in the grounds as I drove. Punishment or honour, I wondered. Whichever, they were all working hard: they hardly looked up as I passed.

On the right of the drive was a line of trees: on the left, lawns, sloping down to a distant wall. Parallel to the wall, a group of older boys, almost men, were running at an impressive speed. They, too, were dressed in khaki, and although they were too far away for me to be sure, I thought they were wearing heavy boots. If so, their speed was even more impressive. They were led by someone wearing a blue track suit. The PE instructor? Whoever he was, he was very fit, and he ran like an athlete.

It was like driving through an Army base. There were lots of little white signpost arrows with cryptic initials painted on them where the gravel roads crossed and where side roads went off. SH, they said, and MB, and DWA. I slowed down for six ramps and the Nissan bumped over them obligingly. The grounds were very large. I wondered what the property was worth, and how long it could remain here and resist the creeping industrialization all around it. The recession would help, of course. And the building regulations. Presumably the land was limited to educational use.

A little arrow with the initials GHQ pointed to the gravel sweep in front of the main house. The layout was half-familiar to me from the photograph in the paper, and the Georgian house was rather beautiful. Someone unmilitary had protected the red creeper that covered half the front.

I looked at my watch as I walked up the front steps. They were worn by generations of feet, first aristocratic, I presumed, now mostly army boots. I was two minutes early for my appointment. The front door, a large heavy one, was open, propped against a presently non-existent breeze by a foot-high black-painted iron bulldog. Winston Churchill?

Inside, more doors, this time glass. It reminded me of Ashtons Hall, the Mayfields' house, a main feature in my investigation last year, still an occasional feature in my dreams. But this was very different. If the Major had any sense, this would be the first and last time I ever came here. I'd have no time to get to know it.

The hall was empty apart from one person, the Major. His face was the well-proportioned, square-jawed face I remembered from the newspaper photograph, but he was much smaller then I'd expected, only about five foot six, a trim figure in khaki, savagely upright as if to get every particle of height he could, with stiff back and shoulders. He was standing in front of an empty fireplace, looking at his watch impatiently. He must have been going deaf because he didn't hear me come in, even though boots on a polished wooden floor can't be noiseless. 'Major Ellis?'

'Miss Tanner! Good morning! This is the hall.' Of course it was. I looked gratified, as if my idle speculation had been confirmed by his superior intellect and experience. He waved his arm at a large, mediocre portrait, painted in the fifties or early sixties, of a late middle-aged man in army uniform with plenty of medals, a white moustache, and a goggle-eyed pose which might have been intended to represent Leadership. 'The Colonel. The previous headmaster and our founder.'

'Ah.' We shook hands. He was strong but not strong enough to crush my fingers. He squeezed, I squeezed back. His palm was damp and his face was sweating lightly. Unhealthy? Or nervous? He had well-defined pepper and salt eyebrows, a clearly marked pepper and salt hairline, and round brown brainless teddy-bear eyes which widened when they met mine. It was an automatic trick, perhaps another attempt at Leadership. But his carefully clipped moustache was just too big: it looked as if he'd borrowed it from a bigger brother for family charades. To impress adults, he'd have to do more than widen his eyes. His act might go down OK with the Lower Fourth.

'Follow me. These are the front stairs . . .' He moved at a smart pace and I clumped behind him up the wide, shallow wooden staircase that looked as if it was designed for women, dressed for the evening, to make entrances down. 'I'm taking you to our private quarters. I can spare you thirty minutes, should be long enough, huh?' The noise was a curious one. Not the American huh but a very English, semi-strangled grunt.

'Should be,' I agreed as we sped along a corridor, through a fire door, round a corner to a door marked *Private*. There were no boys in sight but there were voices and running footsteps as a constant background murmur. Clearly the school had been up some time.

There was a tray waiting, with a teapot and cups. My heart sank. 'Tea,' he said. 'Earl Grey. Milk or lemon?' I accepted lemon. I dislike plain tea: I detest perfume-counter tea. But he drank it thirstily.

I sat back in the place on the sofa that he'd pointed out to me, mimed sipping at my cup, and looked around the room. It was L-shaped, probably once the master bedroom, predictably (*Country Life* would have said elegantly) proportioned with long sash windows and delicate plaster ceiling decorations of vine leaves and grapes. It had been furnished by someone equally uninterested in comfort or style, with an eclectic approach to floral prints. The sofa and armchairs (chintz-covered, cream background, giant blue roses) were ageing, middle-range John Lewis. The upholstery had gone and it was not easy to find buttock-sized spring-free regions. The curtains (chintz, yellow background, sub-William Morris tiger lilies) were almost tattered, the carpet (pink, yellow and green roses) was worn.

So far, so predictable. Then I looked at the walls. My first impression had been of a battalion of photographs, in orderly rows. I expected them to be school groups, but I now saw they weren't: they were arty shots, in black and white, slightly out of focus. It wasn't easy to make out, from where I was sitting, exactly what the settings were, although most of them seemed to be outdoors.

The pictures closest to me each featured a girl, probably the same girl, from early childhood (three?) to adulthood. She was never in the foreground: usually half-hidden by the branches of trees or dappled by light streaming in to an interior. She had long, thick, curly dark hair and she was always dressed in the same type of garment, a thin pale dress, ankle-length, with short puff sleeves and a broad ribbon sash tied, at mid-rib level, in a bow at the back. As she matured the sash outlined her breasts.

I couldn't date them: no earlier than the twenties, probably, but that was as close as I could get. The model might be drawing her pension now, or she could be reading Media Studies at Hatfield Poly and taking her floaty dresses home to Mum to wash at weekends. But the Major would tell me about them soon enough, probably prefacing his remarks with 'These are photographs.'

I looked out of the window. A terrific view for the first few hundred yards, of the grounds and the khaki figures tending it. Beyond that, the M40. A bit like my flat, give or take twenty acres of land.

I couldn't feel any evil – the evil Martin Kelly had described. Just a naïve little clockwork man, Officer Commanding a 1950s theme park, and a touch of the Lewis Carrolls in the photographs.

'I haven't been idle, since you rang,' said the Major. I didn't suppose he was ever idle, but I looked surprised, since he seemed to expect it. 'Time spent in intelligence is never wasted, huh?'

'Always make your plans three deep,' I replied obligingly.

'Quite,' he said. 'Absolutely agree. Monty?'

It could have been a maxim of General Montgomery's. Then again I could have lifted it from Robert B. Parker's Spenser, my second favourite fictional private eye. 'I can't remember,' I said. 'What did your intelligence work reveal?'

'I spoke to an old Rissingtonian well placed at the BBC. Asquith, 75–80.' He waited for a response. I could have asked what he meant by 75–80, but you'd expect the Major to talk like a school magazine, and I could guess. Instead I said I knew Asquith, which I did, very slightly. I'd worked for him once, years ago. I didn't add that I'd found him a lazy, arrogant wanker who delegated everything except credits and credit.

'He tells me Protheroe will do,' he said. 'Huh?'

For the Major's purposes, perhaps he was right. Alan Protheroe had never in his career willingly offended, or even opposed, anybody above the figurative rank of corporal.

'He's an excellent producer,' I said, lying.

'And you're working for him. So I can trust you. Huh?'

'Yes,' I said.

'And we'll give you all the help we can. Go anywhere, talk to anyone. I'm proud of Rissington Abbey. It's been my life's work.'

'You were in the Army for some time, surely.'

'Of course. Of course. And the Army's more than just a career. I'd thrown myself into it, heart and soul. No private life. Too much so, p'raps. When I left, I was at a loose end. I tried my hand at business – I'm not bad at man-management, but shuffling bumf was never my strong point. Then I saw an advertisement for a housemaster's job here, and met Anthea – my wife Anthea – and there I was, both at once, private life and a worthwhile job, d'you see?'

'Where's your wife now?' In bed, if she had any sense.

'She's away, visiting a friend. She's taken a few weeks off, this term. A well-earned rest.'

A rest? For a headmaster's wife, in termtime?

'She'll be back next week. You can talk to her then. You'll want to do that. She's a key figure here. Wonderful woman. But I mustn't dictate to you, must I, huh? Choose your junior officers wisely and then let them get on with it. That's my motto. Just let me know your plans.'

So I was to have *carte blanche* at Rissington Abbey.

Good, in one way. Plenty of access to the people I wanted.

Bad, in another. Such was the Major's ingenuous enthusiasm – he was chuckling, widening his eyes at me, rubbing his hands together – that I could see myself having to absorb cassettefuls of unwanted detail, with him breathing down my neck. How could a sixty-year-old headmaster be so naïve? If he really invited a cynical documentary production team to his teddy bears' picnic, he'd sure as hell get a big surprise.

'That's wonderful,' I said, 'but you realize that this is just preliminary research. Alan hasn't yet decided who we'll use for the programme.'

'I understand that,' he said buoyantly, 'but I can't believe he'll decide against us. Not once you really find out what makes us tick. You will be filming soon, won't you? This summer? The grounds look their best in summer.'

'No chance,' I said. 'Even if Rissington Abbey is chosen, the project is still only at the research stage. It'll be shooting next year, sometime.'

'As late as that?' He was obviously disappointed. Childlike, I thought. He wanted what he wanted, now. It wasn't as if the school was going anywhere. 'Never mind. Never mind,' he said wistfully. 'Let me put you in the picture,' and he was off.

I'd set the tape running so I watched him and only half-listened. He was rather charming, I realized, perhaps because he was so passionate and vulnerable. The more I was with him, the more I liked him. Not that I ever thought we'd be mates: he would never be my choice for an evening out. But I wanted to protect him.

He talked about the school with the irrepressible eagerness of a genuine enthusiast. As enthusiasts often do, he told me more than I could take in, or wanted to know. He described how they overcame problems I didn't understand, how they improved on arrangements he hadn't properly told me about in the first place, all with a springy optimism that began to make me feel almost guilty. I'd never use any of this, I thought, as he outlined his dream programme for me.

'One of our best views? Huh?' he said, pointing out of the window. 'We think so. You'll want to use that. I thought you could begin coming up the drive, p'raps, show how well the boys keep it. All the work in the garden's done by the boys. Isn't that a thing?'

'Are they supervised?'

'Well, yes, of course. They are always supervised. That's the duty of care we owe them. The garden's under the very competent command of Lieutenant Archibald. Courtesy rank, of course. Used to be a RSM in the Scots Guards. Runs the CCF.'

'CCF?'

He laughed explosively. 'Sorry, m'dear. Keep forgetting you're a civilian. A young and pretty civilian, if I may say so.'

I didn't let men get away with that garbage usually. But the Major was beyond redemption. As well ask a Martian not to be green as to introduce him to the arguments of Andrea Dworkin. Not that I'd ever managed to follow them. I blamed her for that, not me. She didn't so much argue as swing an octopus around her head.

'The CCF?' I said again.

'Combined Cadet Force.' He explained.

It sounded like an apprentice scheme for the Army. I was listening enough to ask, 'So you have guns here?'

'Rifles, yes. No handguns.'

'Are they kept locked up?'

'Of course . . .' He explained some more. I wasn't really interested in guns.

He described Lieutenant Archibald's domain, presumably to reassure me that the guns were kept under a complicated system of double locking, burglar alarms, etc.

'Major, what would you say was the aim of the school?'

He stopped. We'd been standing at the window: he was pointing out the rifle-range. He'd want me to see that, I was sure. Maybe I could get out of it . . . 'A clean slate,' he said. 'Whatever their difficulties before they come here, they start with a clean slate. And we hope they leave with one.'

Apart from the school, he loved his wife. He talked of her proudly, with an almost painful enthusiasm. That was her idea . . . This innovation was one of her most successful . . . We must include the Annigoni portrait of her in the documentary.

Annigoni. That must have cost a bit, I thought.

'I'd like to see that. Where is it?'

'In the Mess. Of course, of course you'll see it. But you already know how beautiful she is.' He indicated the photographs. 'Black and white, d'you see? Huh? Wonderful, aren't they? The work of our Founder. He was Artistic.' So the pop-eyed white-haired git in the front hall, presumably her father, took the photographs of Mrs Ellis as a child and young girl.

'Artistic, aren't they?' he repeated. Oddly, it wasn't a dirty word to him, or a dismissive one. It was a fact of nature. Did I know that Monty did excellent needlepoint? No, I hadn't, and I didn't imagine I'd ever need to, unless I got terribly drunk one night and played Trivial Pursuits. That would be the only condition that would induce me to play it.

But Our Founder had taken photographs, and printed them himself, in the dark-room he'd installed in one of the cellars of GHQ. I should see it. We should use it in the documentary. It had been fully equipped several times since the death of Our Founder, of course, because technology changed so fast, and the boys had to have every chance. Every chance, I supposed, to be 'artistic', so when they were on the General Staff in World War Three they could while away the time in the headquarters bunker by playing the violin or taking photographs or doing needlepoint, like Monty.

Perhaps Monty was his hero because he too only reached average height standing on a breeze-block.

'Time marches on,' he said finally, checking his watch. 'Five minutes to breakfast.' He unzipped an inside pocket of his khaki combat jacket, fished out a pair of gold-rimmed spectacles, and put them on in a precise series of actions culminating in a final, firm, settling push up his nose. 'This is a list,' he said, glancing at it and then handing it to me. 'I prepared it last night. The people you'll want to see and the highlights of our life here. An oasis of decency and order in the chaos of modern society. Huh? The only area that's off-limits to you is the Sports Hall, during exam times. External exams in progress. Most important. We have excellent results. I'll show you the statistics. You'll breakfast with us, of course, in the canteen, and I'll introduce you to the school. After that I usually deal with the bumf, so I'll leave you in the capable hands of Alistair Brown, my second-in-command. And after break, at 1015, I'll be at your disposal.'

Chapter Twelve

Now I'd got the Major's go-ahead, I was going to do things my way. I thanked him for the invitation to breakfast, refused it, said I'd be back at ten fifteen and would find my own way about the school. Much better alone. If he could make sure everyone knew who I was and what I was after?

He didn't manage to hide his disappointment. 'I thought I'd just give you a few pointers. Huh? And you must meet Alistair. But you will, you will . . . And I won't forget it's your show . . .'

Back at the hotel, I had a bath, washed my hair, and towelled it dry. That doesn't take long, it's so short. Polly keeps nagging me to grow it longer and stop dyeing it red. She mutters about decent cuts and letting it grow out light brown and highlights and how good my features are. I don't know who she thinks she's fooling. Besides, I like it cropped.

Then I called Barty.

He answered on the third ring.

'Bartholomew O'Neill.'

'Alex Tanner,' I said, mimicking.

'Hello, Alex.' His voice warmed when he heard mine. I warmed to his warming. 'Thank you for the party,' he went on, and I chilled again. Barty's got a different background to me. He *has* a background. He's an honourable and his elder brother's an earl. Most of the time I think of him as a human being, but now he was in an insincere upper-class mode, thanking me for a party at which he'd done all the work.

'Not at all,' I came back to him in the same tone. 'Thanks for your present. And for all the help.'

'Now what's the matter?' he said. Affectionately, I suppose, but I snapped anyway.

'Nothing's the matter. Did you have anything sensible to say to me, or are you just following section 159c of the Bullshit Manners Manual for old Etonians?'

'How's Polly?'

'Not great. It'll take her a while to get over it, of course. I've got a room at a hotel in Banbury – that's where I'm speaking from – but I was back with her last night, and probably tonight too.'

'Any chance of seeing you?'

'Not tonight. I'll be with Polly . . .' Even as I put him off, I was glad he'd asked. I hadn't risked admitting to myself, all those months of not seeing him, how much I'd missed him. What I wanted to do, now this minute, was to abandon Plummer's stupid little job and drive straight up to London and Barty . . .

I took a hold on myself. If work went, everything went. It wasn't only the money, although God knows I needed it as sandbags against the tide of recession that was sweeping England. It was also my independence, and my self-respect.

'I'm working,' I said.

'Good. What about the weekend?'

'What about it?'

'I thought we could go away.'

'You and me?'

'Yes.'

'I can't leave Polly. It's a bad time for her.'

'What if she went home?'

'I can't persuade her to. I've tried.'

'If I persuaded her to, would you come?'

I hesitated. I didn't need to work the weekend, not by any stretch of the imagination. I'd probably have to do Plummer's job in slow-mo anyway, now that I was in at Rissington Abbey, because I couldn't afford to be paid for less than a week. The only thing preventing me from accepting Barty's invitation was fear. If you let fear kick you around, you end up unsafe and sorry. Easier to know than to act on.

'Yes, please,' I said. There was silence the other end. A pleased silence? I couldn't tell.

'Excellent,' he said briskly, as if I'd brought in a difficult shoot under budget. 'Where'd you like to go?'

'Up to you. I'll be ready to leave early on Saturday.'

'Don't you want to know what clothes to bring?'

Now he was teasing. 'Not particularly,' I said. 'Whatever you tell me, I'll wear a sweatshirt and my 501s. If you want me to change for one dinner, I'll stretch a point and bring something posh. Since you're paying. I suppose you're paying?'

'Just expenses. No daily rate.'

I went to breakfast in a splendid mood. I even looked forward to spending the day at Rissington Abbey. My feet hardly touched the stairs as I ran down, and that's not a frequent feeling in my weight of boots.

It was a commercial hotel, mostly, even now the tourist season was starting. The other breakfasters were men. One group was Japanese. Four Japanese in suits with the particular not-quite-polyester shimmer of silk, discussing balance-sheets spread out on the table beside them. I wondered what they were doing here in Banbury. Bringing business, I hoped, even if it was in the form of buying up bankrupt British companies and then running them at a profit using our comparatively skilled low-paid workers. Taiwan on the Thames.

Because I was so happy about the weekend with Barty, I couldn't manage to eat as much as I usually do, when it's free. But I concentrated enough to read the Rissington Abbey prospectus from cover to cover. It didn't take long. It was mostly advertising, as you'd expect.

I got a few more facts about the Major and his wife. They'd only been married since 1972, when he'd have been forty one to her thirty two. I'd already gathered that the Colonel, the founder of the school, had been her father. So presumably she was now the owner. Unusual for a school to be in private hands. Most English non-State schools were now charitable trusts, run by governors. The Major and Mrs Ellis were the autonomous gods of the imitation Sandhurst on show in the glossy, self-conscious photographs.

Inside the back cover was a little pocket with extra sheets, presumably the ones that needed constant updating. I glanced down the staff list: mostly Oxford and Cambridge degrees, very few teacher's certificates. Alistair Brown had an Edinburgh degree: the Major, no degree at all. You didn't need qualifications, when you married the owner of the place.

Then I looked at the fees and choked on my coffee. High. Astronomically high. Much, much higher than Eton or Millfield.

Why would parents pay that kind of money? To get rid of the deeply unwanted, perhaps. An element of revenge: strict discipline. And, at the same time, every chance that a boy who had already been thrown out of cheaper and more traditional schools might remain securely in the grip of a regime which promised, again and again, to be 'understanding', 'sensitive to the needs of adolescents', 'flexible in approach'.

And then I noticed an enigmatic footnote. 'The figures shown above are standard. A higher fee structure may apply in special cases.' Special cases where a boy was especially 'troubled', perhaps? On his way to prison, or a special clinic?

As I abandoned my second piece of toast I wondered who had sent Olivier there: who had chosen the school and who was paying. His parents, Michel Mouche and Freedom Pertwee, didn't seem at all standard Rissington material. I would have thought that the mother particularly, still doing her own late-sixties thing in a commune, presumably tie-dyed and marijuana soaked, would have disapproved of militarism and discipline in all their forms.

Which went back to the question of who was hiring me. That was still niggling me like a fragment of nut between the teeth, and my mental tongue kept trying to lift it out. My back teeth were full up, actually, because Martin Kelly was there too. What was evil about the school? Why had he bothered to tell me? Why had he given me his notebooks? There was masses of material in there which I couldn't use, most of it apparently not even relevant to the school.

My tasks for the day were clear, however. I needed to speak to one at least of the two of Olivier's friends I had on the list, his housemaster Alistair Brown, and Matilda Beckford's Tim Robertson. For cover, I'd start a general workup of the school and the Major. And for curiosity, I'd play 'spot-the-evil'.

Chapter Thirteen

When I got back to Rissington Abbey at 1015, the grounds around the drive were deserted. I parked the Nissan near the front door; when I got out I could hear boys' voices echoing from somewhere behind the main building. It was break time. Presumably they were getting their break rations from a canteen. I was going to walk towards the noise when a man came down the front steps. 'Miss Tanner?' he said. 'Alistair Brown, Second-in-Command. How do you do.' He had the traces of a Scots accent and a light, well-modulated, baritone voice. He shook my hand firmly, more firmly than I would have expected from his appearance. His handclasp was dry, warm, and, surprisingly, pleasant. I didn't get the full-scale, electric jolt of a handshake with a really attractive man, but there was an unexpected echo of it. I looked at him more closely. He was in his mid-thirties, tallish, slightly stooped, with thick-lensed brown-rimmed glasses, mouse-brown hair combed straight back from his forehead, and a mild, enquiring expression.

'How do you do. The teachers don't have to wear paramilitary gear, then?'

He laughed politely. 'No. We dress normally.' He was wearing a light tweed jacket, brown corduroys, a blue shirt, and dark blue tie. 'I wanted to catch you this morning, but I'm rather pushed for time. I'm Exams Officer, you see, and I'm due to invigilate in the hall in' – he checked his watch – 'ten minutes. After that, I'm off. It's my free afternoon.'

'Perhaps we can meet tomorrow, then?'

He smiled. He had very good teeth. I wished I could see his eyes clearly, but all I could catch were glints of blue through the glasses. It was a pity he blinked so much. 'Of course. But I wanted to welcome you, and see if you needed any help.'

'Thanks. I'd just like to wander round, if I may. The Major warned me about the exams – I'll be careful not to disrupt them.'

'Where are you headed now?'

'I'd like to see some senior boys, I think. I'm interested in your Service to the Community programme.'

'Ah. You'll want Tim Robertson, then. He's probably in his room now, in the Duke of Wellington Annexe. Shall I point you in the right direction?'

'Fine.'

'Just a moment.' He darted up the steps and into the main building. I stood alone on the gravel, tilting my face to the sun and thinking about Barty in a vague, pleasant way. Something to look forward to. Where would we go, for our weekend?

'Miss Tanner?' Alistair Brown was beside me again. 'Let's go, shall we? The Duke of Wellington Annexe is behind the main house. If we walk up the path here, we'll pass most of the school buildings, and I can give you a few pointers to where things are . . . This path is out of bounds to privates.'

'Privates?'

'Ordinary boys are privates, the prefects are non-commissioned officers, the masters are officers. The Major is the Commanding Officer. I'm the Captain, the Deputy Head. The other teachers are Lieutenants. Watch your step, the path's a bit slippery − it doesn't get much sun, and the moss tends to creep back. I'll have to put the next fatigue party on to it.'

'When I got here, this morning, some boys were working in the grounds. Would that have been punishment?'

'Not necessarily. All privates have fatigues − chores. We keep them busy.' He was walking ahead of me, sure-footed on the slippery flags of the path, and he held out his hand to help me up when the path reached narrow, broken stone steps, dark with the shadow of the house one side, the thick foliage of rhododendron bushes on the other.

At the top of the steps, in the sun, the view opened out to a flat, concrete area dotted with wooden temporary-looking buildings, and the volume went up on the boys' voices. 'That is the canteen, over there . . . most of the school should be inside, having their break squash and buns. They'll be supervised by two NCO's and an officer. The canteen is on the first floor. The ground floor used to be garages. It has been recently converted to provide a fully-equipped CDT block.'

I looked up, towards the noise. Boyish faces were pressed to the window, all with shorn heads, some still chewing, watching me greedily.

Very different from the lack of interest from the gardeners when I'd first arrived. 'I gather the Major's told the whole school about my documentary project, then,' I said.

'He has indeed. The younger boys are extremely excited.'

'How do you feel?'

He stopped and blinked at me. His lenses blurred the expression of his eyes. 'Ah, well, perhaps I'm a little cautious . . . The Major is an enthusiast. A visionary. He wants the British public to see what we achieve here.'

I'd stopped too. 'And you don't?'

'Let's say I'm well aware how easy it is for the media to distort things. Many of our boys are very vulnerable. Adolescents are.'

He was right, of course. 'I wouldn't worry too much. The series is going to concentrate on the headmasters themselves. Tell me about these buildings.'

He smiled, a wide white-toothed charming smile. 'And you've got a job to do. I understand that . . . On your right, the squash courts. We are proud of our squash team. Seven victories in the last seven matches . . .'

'Do you coach the team?'

'We have very well-qualified PE staff . . . On your left, the indoor swimming-pool.' He pointed at an ageing, battered wooden building like an aircraft hangar.

'The swimming-pool,' I said. 'There was an accident, wasn't there? I read about it in the papers.'

'Yes,' he said. 'A dreadful thing. I don't feel we should discuss it . . .' He went on guiding, as if I hadn't interrupted. 'During the Second World War the Rissington Abbey site was used as a military hospital. The pool was built at that time. It was intended as a temporary structure, but it's still giving us useful service.'

'The boy who died' – I pretended to look up the name in my notebook – 'Olivier Desmoulins. You were his housemaster, I believe?'

'I really don't feel . . .'

'This is a matter of public record,' I said. 'I already have what the *Banbury Courier* said. I'd like to hear your side of the story.'

I chose the words deliberately and he didn't miss the implication. 'My *side* of the story? Hardly. If you've read the *Courier* you'll know it was a tragic accident. The school was completely exonerated. Beyond the canteen is the Sports Hall, where the examinations are in progress . . .'

'Was he happy here?'

'Olivier?'

'Yes. Was he happy here?'

'Very happy. Not always well behaved, but very happy. The school suited him.' He started walking again, and I followed.

'So there's no chance it was suicide?' I'd keep trawling as long as he'd let me.

'Absolutely not. The day before he died, he was in excellent form.'

'Did you teach him?'

'Yes. He was in my history group, as lively and argumentative as usual.'

'What was he arguing about?'

'This time I think it was the causes of the Second World War. He blamed the British.'

'The British? How exactly?'

'Something about British hypocrisy. He often made much of the differences between his own country – he was French, you know – and ours.'

Mr Brown was quite ready to talk about Olivier's state of mind, I could see. Suicide didn't seem a bare nerve. 'Was he bright?'

'Very. Very bright. Especially since he was working in a second language . . .'

Time to leave Olivier. 'So you're a historian,' I said. 'How long have you been at Rissington?'

He went on as if I hadn't spoken. 'That's the Duke of Wellington Annexe, ahead, where the sixth-form boys have their study-bedrooms. The lower sixth share a two-bedded room, the upper sixth have a room of their own. My flat is at the end, on the left.'

The concrete area gave way to a gentle slope up to a ridge, backed by trees. The long, flat-roofed, two-storey modern building stretched along the crest of the ridge. The long outer wall facing us was mostly glass: I could see that many of the rooms were occupied. 'The senior boys aren't at break, then?'

'Only if they're on supervisory duty. We have our own kitchen up here. We go to the canteen for lunch and dinner. Each evening, some of us take it in turns to have dinner in the Mess, with the officers and Mrs Ellis.'

'What about the Major?'

'And the Major, of course.'

'Where is the Mess?'

'The dining-room in GHQ. The main house.'

We'd stopped at the foot of a flight of concrete steps leading up the grassed slope to a doorway in the middle of the building. 'Olivier was in the lower sixth, wasn't he? So he'd share a room. Who did he share with?'

'Tim Robertson. The boy you're going to see.'

'Why wasn't he called to give evidence at the inquest?'

'Miss Tanner—'

'Do call me Alex.'

He blinked shyly. 'I don't think . . . Miss Tanner, I don't see that this has anything to do with your brief here. As I understand it . . .'

'My job is to get a picture of the Major and the school. I'm a researcher. I ask questions. I don't always know where they'll lead, but the better the background, the better the research. So why wasn't Tim called at the inquest?'

Brown sighed impatiently. 'Because he was in sick-bay at the time.'

'And you've been at Rissington how long?' I pressed. I didn't know if he'd dodged my earlier question. Apparently not, because he answered readily.

'Six years, now. I heard about the vacancy through my mother.'

'Your mother?'

'She was the matron here. Before her illness. She still helps in the San occasionally, when she's well enough.'

'She lives here too?'

'We share the flat in the Duke of Wellington Annexe.'

'Is that difficult?' I said, knowing I was pushing it, but curious about a man in his thirties still living with his mother.

'Difficult? In what way?' He was blinking at me again, hunching his shoulders.

'If she's ill,' I improvised. 'Do you look after her? Isn't that difficult, with your other duties?'

'We manage,' he said, rather curtly. 'Now I'm afraid I must leave you: I'm late already. If you go in that door, you'll find Sergeant-Major Rees waiting for you. Perhaps I'll see you tomorrow.'

I thanked his retreating back and watched him. He moved well, springy, balanced. Pity about his posture and eyesight. And why wouldn't he call me Alex?

The foyer of the Duke of Wellington Annexe was empty. Dark red vinyl floor, cream walls: the left-hand wall taken up by a huge noticeboard covered with lists, time-tables, rotas, commands, and exhortations; the right-hand wall dominated by a reproduction of the Goya portrait of the Duke; the far wall, mostly glass, had a doorway to the woods behind. In a corner, a large leafy plant and a discarded khaki sock.

The building was almost silent. It wasn't well soundproofed so noises travelled, but they were the noises – cleared throats, scraped chairs – of a group of people being quiet. Possibly even a group of people listening. For me?

I looked at the room chart on the board. Robertson's room was on the ground floor, far end, left. I headed for it. As I passed a door it opened and a boy stepped out in front of me. He was perhaps eighteen, tall and heavy set, wearing camouflage trousers, Army boots, a khaki T-shirt tight across his well-developed chest and muscular arms. An apprentice Chippendale. His shorn hair was very pale blond and his eyebrows light, 'Can I help you, Miss Tanner?' he said, unsmiling. I felt his hostility like a wall as solid as his chest, and a corresponding wave of hostility surged in me.

'Sergeant-Major Rees?'

'Yes.'

'What does that mean in plain English?'

'I'm the Head Boy.'

'Hello. I'm fine on my own, thank you. On my way to see Tim Robertson.'

He stood blocking my way. I moved to go round him and he moved to block me again.

I'd had enough. I dropped my bag and, as he bent to pick it up, I stumbled against him. He lost his balance and fell sideways. I scooped up my bag and walked past him. 'So sorry,' I said over my shoulder. His pale face flushed crimson, with embarrassment or rage, as he scrambled up, but at least he had enough sense not to follow me.

When I reached the end of the corridor and turned to look, he'd gone.

I knocked on Robertson's door.

'Come in.'

I went in smiling. The room was almost dark, the curtains drawn. I blinked, my eyes adjusting to the sombre shadows, wondering if I had arrived at an awkward adolescent moment. The boy had said 'Come in,' though, he must be prepared for visitors.

When I could see, I looked around. I expected an ordinary, cluttered teenager's room, with a music centre, books, and the walls covered with posters declaring various temporary allegiances or hormonal impulses.

But this room was absolutely bare. Just built-in cupboards, two beds, two chairs, two empty desks. No photographs: not even a time-table. Perhaps the military discipline of Rissington Abbey dictated this more than tidiness, this Spartan absence of personality and work in progress.

Then I noticed that the cream walls were covered by cork boards, battered by generations of drawing-pin displays. So it must be personal choice, the choice of this boy who stood defensively with his back to a desk, his podgy thighs spread wide by the pressure. He was shortish and fattish and he held his hands in front of his chest, as if ready to be clenched into fists.

'Tim Robertson? I'm Alex Tanner . . . I think the Major told the school what I'm doing here . . . I'd like to talk to you about the community service programme. You're in charge of it, I think?'

'Yes . . .' he said. 'I'm Officer Commanding.' His words agreed but his manner and his body language screamed 'go away'.

'Is this a bad time to talk?'

'I'm a bit busy, at the moment,' he said. 'I've a history essay to finish before lunch.' If he was writing an essay, where had he put it? And why was he so tense, as if he was listening? Was he afraid to be overheard? I put my notebook on the desk and scribbled while I talked. 'We'll have to make an appointment, then, because I do think community service is an important aspect of school life.'

He scribbled in reply, closed the notebook, and handed it to me. 'Will you be here on Friday? I don't have any free time tomorrow but I could see you after break on Friday. 1045. If we meet then, I can have the community service records organized for you to see.'

When I was safely out of the Duke of Wellington Annexe I opened the notebook. Just two lines of writing.

Mine: *I know about Olivier. Must see you. When? Where?*
His: *2.30 today, McDonald's Banbury.*

Chapter Fourteen

McDonald's in Banbury was easier to find than I expected and I was there fifteen minutes early. I bought a cup of coffee, sat at a table by the window, kept an eye out for Tim, and brought my notes up to date.

After I'd left Tim that morning the Major had pounced on me and given me an excruciatingly thorough tour of the craft block, followed by school lunch (fish fingers, chips, beans: treacle pudding) in the canteen. I had enough carbohydrate loading to run a marathon and I'd be well versed if I ever worked on a doco on the National Curriculum requirements for Craft, Design, and Technology.

I'd kept the tape-recorder running because I found it hard to listen to his monologue. I could always listen to the tapes later, if I needed to check on details or identify the different members of the teaching staff I was introduced to. All men, most in their forties or fifties, anonymous and amiable enough.

It seemed that my meeting with Alistair Brown hadn't after all been arranged by the Major. He'd been surprised when I mentioned it during lunch. 'Really? Said he was busy, when I told him about you. Must have thought about it after we spoke, seen how important it was, p'raps. Huh? What did you make of him?'

'He was very helpful.'

'Remarkable chap. Remarkable. Thought you'd find him interesting.'

Interesting? I hadn't found him that. Puzzling, perhaps. I'd got no impression of him at all. 'He teaches history, I believe.'

'Some history. But he's mainly concerned with the sixth-form house. The housemaster makes the house; the houses makes the school. Huh? Fine athlete, too. Interested in the physical activities side. My wife thinks the world of him. Good judge of men, my wife.'

We were in the canteen. The noise level was astonishing. The huge first-floor room had low ceilings. There was harsh light in there, the kind of neon light that hurts the eyes. The boys' boots clattered on the floor, their cutlery clashed against their plates, and their several pitched voices squeaked or rasped or growled. There wasn't a separate staff table: the Major and I were sitting in the least crowded table of all, because boys went to sit anywhere except near us. It was a strange sensation. It wasn't because they were avoiding staff: I could see staff dotted here and there throughout the huge room, on crowded tables. I didn't know the reason. They weren't looking at me, either. None of the gaping and peering I'd seen at break. Not among the older ones. Some of the younger ones couldn't resist giving me sidelong glances as they passed.

'I'm looking forward to meeting Mrs Ellis. She comes back next week, you said?'

'Absolutely,' he said, looking guilty.

I should have pursued it. But I couldn't hear properly, I couldn't eat properly, and I suddenly wanted to be out of the school. I couldn't wait to get away. It was a relief to be in McDonald's.

I put yet more sugar into the coffee, hoping to swamp the taste, wondering why Alistair Brown had met me, why the head boy had been so hostile, and what was going on with Tim Robertson. Was it the evil Martin Kelly had warned me about, or just some adolescents, buggering about?

Talking of which, here was Tim in the doorway, looking round for me. I waved and he came over. He wanted two cheeseburgers and a strawberry milk shake, although I'd noticed him only an hour and a half earlier, at the far end of the canteen, at a table with much younger boys, eating a substantial lunch. I gave him a tenner and while he went to get the food, I logged the expenses for Plummer, and wondered why whoever bought Tim's clothes was too mean – Or perhaps too poor? Surely not, if they were paying Rissington's fees – to get him a new pair of trousers. He was wearing grey school trousers, too tight, too worn. They made him look fatter, and nature was doing a great deal in that direction already. His regulation blazer was too small, and shiny with wear. But his tie was neat and his shirt clean.

He sat down opposite me, gave me the Coke I'd ordered to keep him company, and started on his first cheeseburger. He didn't offer me any change and I didn't ask for it, but I was surprised. Was he dishonest, hard-up, or both?

Now I saw him in daylight I realized he had salt-shaker dandruff and a set of spots like a Braille version of the Bible; however he also had a pleasant voice and an engaging manner. If I didn't look at him, particularly at his face, all was well.

I began gently, with a pitch about the documentary and my need for background material on the school. No questions about the odd incident in his room. When I stopped talking, he nodded. He didn't look convinced, nor did he look sceptical. He looked as if he was thinking about something else. 'You said you knew about Olivier?' he said. 'In the note you wrote in my room. What did you mean?'

'I've spoken to Matilda Beckford. I know Olivier never did his community service, and you covered up for him.' He nodded again, and waited for a question to answer.

I banged on for a bit asking about the community service programme and the school in general. He answered through mouthfuls of food. His comments were fair enough answers but unexpanded and basically non-committal. Rissington was 'OK, I suppose'. The community service programme 'didn't do any harm' and was 'better than doing monkey-crawls across the Brecon Beacons'. He added to this, fair-mindedly, that lots of the other boys preferred doing monkey crawls, because they were better at it than he was. I was taping the conversation because I thought it might make him feel more important. The tape didn't seem to inhibit him.

'Did Olivier prefer doing monkey-crawls?'

'We called him Desmoulins at school, of course,' he pointed out sharply. 'Why do you want to know about him?'

'Background, I suppose.'

'Desmoulins didn't like painting houses and talking to old women, that's for sure. He didn't mind monkey-crawls.'

'When he didn't come with you on the community service programme, what did he do instead?'

The boy stopped chewing. 'Why do you want to know?' he said.

'Mrs Beckford says you didn't like him.'

'That's true enough.'

'And I was just interested. In the running of the school. How could Olivier get away with not doing the community service without the school finding out?'

'Easily, if I covered for him. It's not the school's fault. It's always

82

like that, in schools. They can't know everything, although some house-masters like to pretend they do.'

'What's Brown like as a housemaster?'

'He's OK. He doesn't count.'

'What do you mean?'

'He's not interested. If there's a foul-up, Mrs Brown deals with it.'

'And why did you cover for Olivier?'

There was a terrible sucking, glugging noise as his straw chased the last of the milk shake.

'I like McDonald's,' he said, apparently inconsequentially. 'You know where you are, at McDonald's.' He looked me directly in the eye, not something he'd done before. 'I'm not sure if I know where I am with you.'

'How do you mean?'

'OK, you tell me you're researching a television documentary. So how do I know that when you make it, you don't use something I say, and even if you don't name me, they'll know that only I could have said it, and then I'll be in even more trouble than I usually am?'

'Are you usually in trouble?'

'Answer my question first.'

'I can give you my word that nothing you tell me will be used on television in such a way that "they" know it's you who told me, if that's what you mean. Who's "they?" '

'How do I know if I can trust your word?'

This was an unusually suspicious sixteen-year-old. I sympathized. When I'd been his age, or long before come to that, I'd learnt not to trust anyone's word. Not necessarily because they meant to lie, but because they mostly couldn't deliver.

He was right, though. I'd waste a lot of time if I didn't tell him at least some of the truth. 'What I actually want to know is about Olivier. I am researching for a documentary, partly, and you can ring the producer to check if you like, but I'm also a private detective.'

I don't know what reaction I expected. I was showing off, a little. Never show off to an adolescent: they're connoisseurs. He looked at me with mild interest tempered by disbelief.

'I'm investigating the circumstances surrounding Olivier's death,' I said. 'But I must ask you to keep it to yourself.' I was stung. I suppose I expected him to find it as exciting as I still did.

'I'll keep it to myself, all right,' he said. 'Who are you investigating for?'

I wasn't tempted to tell him, since I didn't know. 'An unnamed client,' I said sniffily.

'Not the police?'

'No, of course, not the police. I told you I was a private detective.'

'Do you have any proof of that?'

I passed him one of my cards. He held it in his grubby-nailed, stubby plump hands. 'Is there much money in it? In being a private investigator?'

'Not steady money. I only do it part time.'

'I'm going to earn tons of money,' he said. 'One day,' and looked at me with the slight pity of one who would not be fat and spotty for ever, and saw his future in a merchant bank.

'Good. Meanwhile will you answer my questions about Olivier? And not tell anyone at school I've been asking?'

'OK,' he said. 'My fee is fifty pounds.'

'Right,' I said. Plummer's client could afford it. If he couldn't, he shouldn't have hired Plummer.

'Should I have asked more?'

Probably he should. I'd have paid it. What he had to tell me might very well be all I needed to know. 'Maybe. But you didn't, and it's too late now.'

'But we'd better leave here. It's out of bounds during the week, and there's no point in tempting fate.'

We ended up sitting on a rotting bench by the canal. It was too hot in the car. His skin looked even worse in full June sunlight. 'I've only got half an hour, so you'd better make it quick,' he said. 'What d'you want to know?'

'Tell me about Olivier.'

'He was a shit,' he said.

'In what way?'

'The usual way.'

'You'll have to give me more than that. I'm paying you, remember.'

'Not as much as you might have done.'

'And you're wasting my time. Fifty pounds for thirty minutes is a good rate. Now get on with it. Tell me about Olivier.'

'He wanted everything his own way. He thought he was terrific and everyone else was less than the dust.'

'Everyone else, or just you?'

'Everyone else, but especially me, because I'm pretty low in the pecking order at Rissington. Do you know much about it?'

'I know it's quasi-military.'

'It is, and I can't do military things. I'm slow and I'm clumsy and I'm not very strong, and I'm not at all interested. I think the Army is a crock of shit, frankly, and I wouldn't have anything to do with it if it was up to me.'

'So why are you there?'

'My stepfather wants me to be licked into shape.'

Neither of us thought that was likely or even possible, in military terms. 'Was Olivier good at military things?'

'He was OK. He was naturally athletic and a fascist by temperament. He liked running for miles and shouting out orders.'

'Did he like taking them?'

'That depended who gave them. He didn't take orders from me, for instance, and he should have done because I'm in charge of the community service programme so I'm the senior officer. But he wouldn't do anything I told him and he knew I couldn't make him.'

'Why didn't you report him to the Major?'

'What kind of berk would that have made me look? I've got to get a decent reference out of this school somehow.'

'For university?'

'Yes. I want to go to Cambridge. I'll get my four As at A-level, all right, but the headmaster's report can make a difference and I'm not going to risk it.'

'So that's why you covered for him?'

'Yes.'

'Not because you were afraid he might beat you up if you didn't?' I wasn't going to let his over-confidence run on too long. He might spin me a yarn because he liked the sound of his own boasting.

'He beat me up for fun anyway,' he said, unfazed. 'They all do.'

'If he was so unpleasant to you, did it make it difficult sharing a room with him?'

His eyes met mine and slid away. 'Not particularly. I managed.'

'You were in the san the night he died?'

'That's right.' He wasn't going to ask me how I knew. I guessed that information was a matter of pride to Tim, and he wasn't going to grant me the advantage of knowing more than he did.

'What was the matter with you?'

'Flu, I think.'

'Why can't you remember? Are you often in the san?'

'As often as I can manage, if it helps me get out of things. The food's better there, anyway.'

'When did you hear of Olivier's death?'

'Break time. Matron said I was well enough to move back to my room, and when I got there I saw that his things had gone. So I asked, and somebody told me.'

'Who packed his stuff up?'

'Dunno. Could have been Mrs Brown, or Mrs Ellis.'

'You weren't sorry when he died?'

'No, but I didn't kill him. Do you think it was murder?'

I wondered if I'd made a huge mistake. The last thing Plummer would want would be Tim spreading the rumour that Olivier had been murdered. Was it likely that he would keep quiet about such a juicy piece of information? He'd use it, surely, to impress the others. He was low down the pecking order. This might raise him a bit. Knowledge was power. I had to divert him from that idea.

'There's no suggestion of that,' I said. 'What I'm supposed to be finding out is Olivier's state of mind.'

'When?' he said.

'Just before he died.'

'It's a stupid bloody question,' he said. 'Who'd want to know that?'

I could hear and see myself in this unappealing, acute outsider, and I felt as impatient with him as Plummer had with me. 'I think my client's worried in case he committed suicide,' I said.

He shook his head emphatically, and I leaned away from the shower of dandruff. 'No way. Not Desmoulins. He'd never have topped himself. Much more likely to be an accident – he drank a lot. I can imagine someone murdering him, as well. But not suicide. Never.'

'Why?'

'He was too pleased with himself. He thought he was great. God's gift to everything.'

'Can you remember the day before his death?'

'Quite well. Because when he died, I wondered who'd killed him, and I tried to work it out.'

86

'Why?'

He sighed impatiently. 'Don't you know anything about power? I've got none, as I stand up. None. Not in that school. Nobody reads and nobody listens to music, and they're only interested in maths and physics if they're calculating the trajectory of a bullet. If someone had killed him I wanted to know, so I could shut up about it and keep out of their way. So's I wouldn't be next.'

'Are you serious?'

'Of course.'

'And what did you think?'

He looked at me unblinkingly. Even his eyelashes had dandruff. You could get an ointment for that, I fleetingly considered telling him. But he probably knew. Just as he knew he should use an anti-dandruff shampoo, get pills for his acne, and control his diet. Tim's problem wasn't what he knew but what he could make himself do.

'I had no idea,' he said finally.

I'd come back to it later. 'Tim, someone told me Rissington Abbey was evil. What do you think they meant?'

'Who told you?'

'An unnamed source. Is it evil?'

'Evil? It's bloody awful for me, I know that.'

'In the prospectus it says that there's a special fee structure for boys with problems. What kind of problems?'

'The usual. Getting chucked out of other places. Drugs, bunking off. Everatt broke his housemaster's arm, but he's a special case.'

'Why?'

'He's mad. The last Brecon trip, he tried to organize a party to torture sheep.'

Was he putting me on? 'Did they go?'

'No. They'd marched fifteen miles already. They were shattered.'

He was putting me on.

Two men jogged past us on the tow-path. Middle-aged, fit. Saturday football players, perhaps. A pet white poodle, picking its supercilious way along in front of its gay owner, almost visibly shuddered at their robustness. A canal boat chugged past: its waves broke on the walls of the canal. 'It's going too fast,' he said. 'They're not supposed to go more than four miles an hour, you know. It damages the banks.'

'I didn't know,' I said. 'Let's get back to Olivier's last day, shall we?'

'You've only got another five minutes, and I've plenty to tell you.

More than five minutes' worth. We can meet again on Friday and I'll give you the lot for two hundred quid.'

I thought he meant it. I gave him my telephone numbers at the hotel and in London and fixed another meet for two o'clock on Friday: he haggled me up to £200 per hour, and cadged a lift back to school. He made me stop down a lane three hundred yards from the school gates.

Chapter Fifteen

Tim had been very insistent that I wait a while before following him into the school. He didn't want 'them' to make any connection between him and me. I made a mental note to make him identify 'them' properly for me on Friday. Meanwhile, I was in no hurry. I didn't look forward to going back, myself. I found Rissington Abbey fifty per cent boring, fifty per cent spooky.

Probably I only found it spooky because of what Martin Kelly had said. And even if there was something crawling round under the surface there, something sliming and heaving in the depths, it was nothing to do with me.

I went back to the hotel. The Accelerated Trainee was off duty, but his spirit lingered on in the messages the girl at the desk gave me. I was to ring three people. The first two were easy: *Bratty* and *Poly*. The third hung me up for a minute or two. Who was *Klowdier*?

I tried the name out loud as I walked up the stairs. A Japanese passed me as I spoke and smiled in a paroxysm of embarrassment. I bowed: he bowed: we both bowed together and I nearly nutted him.

Safely at the top of the stairs, I clicked. Claudia. Alan's Claudia, still pursuing me. I wondered what she wanted, but not enough to ring her back. I made myself a cup of coffee from one of the Wanderotel's Complimentary Sachets, and I didn't spill a grain of the gritty powder. I cut off the corner with the scissors on my Swiss army knife. It's one of the small victories that makes me feel in control.

I was putting off ringing Barty because I immediately suspected he was ringing me to put the weekend off. I never trust looking forward, when it involves other people. I'd been let down too often.

My neuroses annoy me. My social worker used to congratulate me, distrustfully, on how 'well adjusted' I was. Whenever she did that I knew I was overdoing it and I'd break down and cry a little, to reassure her. But of course she was right: I was 'well adjusted' like a radio tracking a shifting FM signal, usually on beam after a fractional delay. It'd cost me a great deal to make the compromises I'd made. And I still tried to avoid disappointment.

When I'd been very young I'd believed my mother, and she had no grip on reality. One day, I remember, when I was about seven and I was back with her again, she seemed much better, and one day she told me to pack because we were going on a trip to see my grandmother. She described how we were going to a cottage in the country and how I'd have a little room to myself and how there'd be a pony and a dog.

It sounded like one of the books I borrowed from the library, one of the old-fashioned ones with small dense print and few pictures which I chose from the children's library because they took the longest time to read. Most children's books only took me half an hour. They had biggish print and contemporary themes, and if I wanted contemporary themes I only had to open my eyes and look.

I'd already known enough not to believe what my mother said most of the time, but I wanted to believe the grandmother story. I liked the idea of more family. I suppose I hoped that I'd find someone who could help me with my mother, because I couldn't look after her by myself. It was too much for me. So I'd believed this, and packed too, and begun to dream.

Then she did nothing else about it. The packed suitcases sat by the door all day while my mother went shopping for bruised vegetables. She made a good bruised vegetable stew. One of my few legacies from her: so do I. We ate the stew and the next day I unpacked and I didn't ask her about my grandmother because I hated seeing the bewildered look in her eyes. I supposed she'd forgotten all about it and I just didn't mention it and the disappointment was bearable, of course it was.

But here we were again with another disappointment, I was sure. Barty couldn't make the weekend.

So I rang Polly first. She sounded no better: much the same. Several hours dead is what she sounded. Then she said she'd decided to go to her parents' house for the weekend. She didn't say why, but I supposed Barty'd persuaded her. So chances were, my weekend was still on, and I needn't be disappointed. I tried to chat but she wasn't having any.

Then I tried Barty, but it was the answering machine, so I left it; but my spirits were restored.

It was lucky, I thought, that this investigation was so straightforward.

I wasn't concentrating properly. It was lucky I had such a lot of slack time, because I hate it when my concentration goes. You have to keep going over things again and again. You're not sharp. You can't be when you're mooning in a fantasy about what's going to be happening. And I'd trained myself to ignore bad feelings. That was easy enough: I'd had plenty of practice. It was ignoring good feelings I couldn't manage.

Four o'clock. I'd pop in to Rissington for a courtesy farewell to the Major, and then back to London.

London was hot. The temperature was building up, the nights weren't cooling, the air still hung like soup. I parked the car in Cambridge Gardens where there was unrestricted parking and locked it for the insurance company's benefit. Chances were it would be vandalized, but that wasn't my problem.

The three-hundred-yard walk down Ladbroke Grove was hard going. I'd brought my notes, Kelly's notebooks, and the huge wodges of material in brown manila envelopes, including the Rissington Abbey promotional video, which the Major had thrust upon me. He certainly seemed to do his paperwork three deep.

When I got to Ladbroke Crescent I went upstairs to my flat to dump my packages before looking in on Polly. Her flat was silent as I passed. At least she wasn't watching the Cassie video again: perhaps she was asleep. Best thing.

Her flat was silent, but mine wasn't. As I groped for the flat key I heard unfamiliar music: something French. It sounded like a sound library atmosphere track, the kind of predictable accordion onion-seller music a plodding director like Alan would lay over shots of Paris.

It rattled me. Polly had the key, of course, but why should she be upstairs in my place instead of in her own mourning bed? I dropped the packages on the floor to leave my hands free, pushed open the door, and said: 'What the hell?'

The accordion wheezed Gallicall on, and the girl lying on the sofa with bare feet looked up and said: 'Hi, Alex.'

It was Alan's Claudia.

'What the hell are you doing here?'

'I hope you don't mind.'

She wasn't pretty, but she was almost beautiful. She had a long, narrow face, with a high-bridged nose, a wide mouth, and an astonishing head of curly, shimmering black hair, caught behind her ears with silver-trimmed combs and tumbling down her back. Her eyes, too, were almost black, and very bright under strongly-marked eyebrows.

She sat up and began to put on a pair of top-of-the-range Nike trainers. Even bending over, her face was pale against her hair. She looked cool. Her white shirt was full and crisp, tucked into a wide leather belt and Naf-Naf jeans. It looked a designer shirt. She looked a designer girl. Not a fashion victim, just as if each one of the garments she wore would have an origin, probably Italy by way of Bond Street.

'I do mind.'

'Polly let me in.'

I took a deep breath. Polly, walking-wounded, was still safe from recriminations, however justified. 'Could we kill the French atmos?'

'Atmos?'

'Atmosphere. The bloody music. It's yours, I suppose.'

She turned it off. 'It's not mine, it's the radio. I tuned it to a French station. I'm sorry to barge in like this, I really am, but I must talk to you. You didn't ring me back.'

'No.' I picked up the paperwork, stacked it on my file shelf, and went through to the kitchen. 'I'm making coffee. Do you want?'

'Real coffee?'

'Yes.'

'Do you grind the beans?'

'Yes.'

'Thank you, I'd love some.'

She annoyed me, badly. 'In your position I'd accept a cup of coffee if it was made with instant acorn powder.'

'I can only drink real fresh coffee. Otherwise, I'd rather not.'

'And I'd rather you weren't here.'

'I've already apologized.' She spoke mildly but firmly, in her alien, stateless voice. She had the blithe self-absorbed self-confidence of an American girl, the kind who answers 'May I open the window?' with 'I'd much prefer you didn't', thus shaking the English right down to their socks.

It was a mode I didn't object to, usually. I prefer it to Uriah Heep. I took another deep breath. 'Come into the kitchen, watch me make the coffee, and tell me what you want. Quickly. Then I want you out of here.'

'It's very simple. I want to make a deal with you.'

'Tell me.'

'I want to be a researcher. I don't know anything about it. I want you to teach me.'

'No way.'

'Hear me out. I'll pay. You're a freelance, aren't you? OK, I'll pay. I'll hire you as a teacher. My money for your expertise.'

'Why me?'

'Alan says you're the best.'

'And you trust Alan's judgement?'

'Not Alan's. But what Alan says is always what everyone else says, that's why he says it.'

I turned on the grinder and pointed to a kitchen stool. She sat down, necessarily silent. When the grinder stopped, she started again. 'I wouldn't get in your way, I really wouldn't . . .' She kept talking and I thought. Of course she would get in my way. Bound to. My working life was postulated on the fact that you can almost always get more done by yourself working on your own. I'd have to explain what I was doing, I'd have to slow down to her pace.

Besides, I like being on my own. It suits me very well.

And the practical side of it. If she wanted to be trained as a television researcher, she'd have to come with me while I did some television research, and I wasn't booked to do any until the end of June, nearly three weeks away.

But I'd already promised myself this year not to turn down any work because I couldn't afford it. Times were very very hard.

So I'd probably have to take her on. Oh, God.

I passed her a mug of coffee, some milk. I guessed she wouldn't take sugar.

She looked accusingly at the milk carton. 'This is full cream. Got any semi-skimmed?'

'No.'

'I'll drink it black.'

'Oh, good,' I said waspishly.

'I'm eighteen,' she said. 'I've got my International Baccalaureat. I went to school in Switzerland. I speak French and German and I get by in Italian. I live mostly in Paris, sometimes Rome, because my second stepfather lives there and I stay with my stepsisters . . .' That explained the voice, I thought. She's a gilded Eurochild. 'My stepfather expects me to go to college here or in America, but I've had it with books, and I want to work in television.'

'Do you realize how much it'll cost, to pay me?'

'That doesn't matter. My trust fund'll pay. The trustees were expecting to shell out for my college expenses. The fees at Harvard or Oxford aren't exactly cheap.'

'And I'm not exactly Harvard or Oxford.'

'In your own line, you are. It isn't just what Alan said. The other people at your party, too, they all said you were the best.'

I'm as human as anyone. My first reaction to flattery is to enjoy it, to believe it. Then I look for the small print, which in this case was that I couldn't take her on if it would annoy Alan. I still needed him.

'No problem,' she said airily. 'I've sorted it with Alan. I made him think it was his idea. He's still a little pissed off with me about your party, anyhow. I said I'd go back to him when I'd learnt something.'

The money was tempting. I could just take her on and have her trotting behind me, but she was going about it the wrong way. I started to explain that she needed to be in a big organization, preferably the BBC, with decent current affairs resources.

She interrupted. 'I don't care about that. Basic techniques is what I need, and I couldn't get taken on by the BBC at my age anyhow.'

So then I told her that I wasn't doing any of the right kind of work for some weeks, that at the moment I was working as a private detective.

'Yeah. Alan told me. Look, this is how I see it. I'm learning nothing at Alan's except how to answer the telephone, and I knew that already. Give it a week's trial. I pay you your daily rate and my own expenses and I come along as your "gofer" – is that the right word? Alan said it. What does it mean?'

'A "gofer" is the person who fetches things. "Go for the coffee, go for the camera." That'll be five bucks, please.'

'I don't understand. Would you prefer to be paid in dollars?'

'Forget it.'

She shrugged. 'Fine. You answer my questions when you're not actually working. OK?'

'And you do what I tell you?'

'Of course,' she said blithely. I believed she meant it but not that she understood it.

'Everything I tell you to do, you do it, right then?'

'Sure,' she said.

'I have another problem,' I said. 'The private investigation I'm on is confidential. If you work with me, you'll know things you mustn't repeat. To anyone. Do you understand?'

'I'm very good at keeping secrets. I never tell anyone about my mother's lovers.'

'You've just told me,' I pointed out.

'In general. Not in particular. And I hardly think you'll tell Dieter.'

'Who's Dieter?'

'My current stepfather. He's . . .'

'OK,' I interrupted. 'Do you remember Alan's guide-notes about research for *Headache*?'

'Sure. I wordprocessed them. I've a copy at home.'

'Read through them tonight. And read this.' I tossed her my copy of the Rissington Abbey prospectus. 'Think of questions to ask when we go there tomorrow. Now finish your coffee and bugger off. Be here tomorrow morning at seven o'clock. Wear something you can move about in. Bring an overnight bag in case we stay over in Banbury.'

Give her credit, she went, without much blether. As soon as she'd gone, I rang Barty.

'Hi. This is Alex.'

'Six-thirty Saturday morning OK for you?'

'Fine.'

'I'll pick you up.'

'Fine.'

'Take care.'

'And you,' I said, and put down the receiver, grinning idiotically.

I sorted out my flat a bit and then nipped down to Polly's, taking the Rissington Abbey promotional video with me. If Polly showed any sign of trying to make me watch Cassie again, I'd fight back. But she didn't. I agony-aunted for a few hours. While she was still sober enough to listen I made her promise to watch the Major's video for me and report. She looked blankly at me from her duvet-nest on the sofa as I put the video on the floor beside the television. 'A school's promotional video? Are you serious? What am I looking for?'

'Evil,' I said flippantly. I'd told her the details of the Olivier case – anything to keep her off the subject of Cassie – but I didn't think she'd taken most of it in. 'The ex-priest I spoke to said the school was evil.'

'Well, they'll hardly put that in the video, will they?'

'Watch it anyway. See what you can see.'

'You're just trying to distract me. I think you should give up the mother hen bit. You're lousy at it.'

I didn't think about Claudia again until Polly'd sunk into a gin-soaked sleep and I was back upstairs. I undressed and lay in the bath, savouring my freedom. Tonight, I'd work for an hour or two; glance through the Major's material so I could pretend to be interested in Rissington Abbey's response to the challenge of the National Curriculum; check through my notes and organize questions for my interview with Tim Robertson; and, if I could be bothered, keep trawling through Martin Kelly's stuff.

Tomorrow I'd be joined at the hip with Claudia. On Saturday, I'd be away (where?) with Barty. But I wouldn't think about that now.

Thursday, June 4th

Chapter Sixteen

Next morning, Claudia's first test was in punctuality. I'd told her seven o'clock. I waited ten minutes, then left without her and enjoyed my own company and Beethoven's ninth symphony on the drive down.

Her second test, a very easy one since she had the telephone number of the hotel in Banbury, was to find me. That one, she passed. I was in the Wanderotel dining-room, only just starting on bacon and eggs, when she came in carrying a very big designer leather overnight bag. She was wearing different jeans, a different white shirt, a wide belt, a bum-bag, and a sulky expression.

'You left without me,' she said accusingly, 'I—'

'Lesson one,' I said. 'Be on time. Lesson two, if you're not, apologize.'

'But I—'

'Lesson three. Don't argue. D'you want some breakfast?'

'I don't eat bacon and eggs. Have you any idea of the cholesterol in that stuff? It's bad for you. And you drink full-cream milk—'

'We're staying in the dining-room another ten minutes. Here's the menu, there's the cereal and juice table. And don't tell me what to eat. If I wanted a dietary adviser I'd hire one.' I wasn't sharp, just firm, and I didn't smile.

She looked at me, taken aback. 'Don't you think it was clever of me to get here so fast?'

'No. Barely competent. Get your food organized and I'll tell you what we're doing.'

She settled for muesli and skimmed milk, and munched while I talked. The Olivier business sounded even sillier when I explained it to someone else. She was very excited when she heard who his parents were. 'Michel Mouche and Freedom Pertwee? Great! Have you met them? Is he as sexy in real life as he is on television?'

99

'I've no idea,' I said repressively, 'and that's not the point.' After that she had enough grip to listen in silence. When I stopped, she said: 'So really we'll have enough when we see Tim Robertson again?'

'Possibly. We can't go on one person's word, so we'll have to cross-check it with one of the other boys, or the housemaster. But effectively, maybe.'

'And we're going back to Rissington Abbey this morning?'

'Yes, and that'll be useful for you, because it's cover. I'll be handling it as if I was doing research for Alan, so you can pick up something from that. Maybe.'

Too many maybes. I took her upstairs to my room so she could dump her overnight bag and we could get started as I meant to go on. I wasn't going to let her disturb my routine.

'This is a really grotty room,' she said looking round. 'It's a grotty hotel. And my muesli wasn't even home-made. It was full of gritty bits. It might even have contained additives.'

'My heart bleeds,' I said. 'Get used to it.'

She fished a chequebook out of her bum-bag. She was rattled: her instinct was to pay. Perhaps she thought it would give her leverage. 'How shall we do this?' she said. 'Do you want a week in advance, or what?'

'Let's get this straight. You're not going to pay my daily rate, because you're not buying all my attention. You pay half, and I'll keep going just as if you weren't there. I'll tell you what I think you need to know and I'll answer sensible questions. You get this weekend off because I'm going away.'

'With your man?'

'My man?'

'The tall attractive one who threw me out of your flat after the party. Alan says you're an item.'

'None of your business,' I said, covering up pleased with brisk. 'You're with me today, tomorrow, and next week, Monday to Thursday. That's six days. Pay me for that, and next Friday we'll think again. And start an expenses sheet. Log your breakfast bill.' I passed her my organizer, opened at my Plummer expenses page. 'That's how you do it. Date, place, etc. In an organizer if you have one.' She showed me, proudly, a leather organizer with gold trimmings. Expensive, stylish, much too small. 'Get a bigger one,' I said, 'but that'll do for the moment. Now I'm going to have a bath. While I'm in there, go through this.' I tossed her Martin Kelly's notebooks. 'This is the stuff I told you about, from the ex-priest.'

'Defrocked,' she said. 'You should say "defrocked", not "ex-priest".'

'Are you a Catholic?'

'Cradle Catholic, educated by the Jesuits till I was twelve.'

'Good. That might be helpful if we have to get back to him. You can break the ice by chatting to him in Latin.'

'I can't *speak* Latin,' she began to explain. 'It's a dead language . . .'

Young, rich, nearly beautiful, and literal-minded. What had I done to deserve this? I took a deep breath. 'I know, I know. I was being facetious. I'm quite often facetious. It's an English trait, you may not be used to it.'

'My mother is English. I'm English—'

'Not exactly,' I said. 'You come from the crossroads where the Champs-Elysées meets the Via Veneto.' She opened her mouth, probably to correct my geography, then shut it again when she saw my expression. I waited, then went on. 'These are the ex-defrocked priest's notebooks. Go through them. Word by word, number by number.'

'What am I looking for?'

'Anything to do with Rissington Abbey, and anything that you're not sure about. Most of it's self-explanatory and nothing to do with us – flower shows, car crashes, court reporting of minor crimes. If it's obviously useless, tick the page. If you think it's useful, copy it out on another sheet of paper, date the entry, and star the page. I won't be long. Make yourself some coffee, if you want.'

She looked at the Wanderotel's instant coffee packets: she looked at me: she took a deep breath. 'Do you want some?'

'Yeah. Milk, one sugar. Not too much milk.'

She brought it in to me. In the bath.

I was lying there, naked (of course), and when she came in I scrambled to cover myself.

'Don't you knock?' I said sharply.

She was completely taken aback, shoved the coffee cup on the floor, and retreated, to burble at me from the other side of the door: 'Sorry . . . Gosh, sorry . . . I didn't think you'd mind. I mean, why would you? You've got a terrific body. I'd kill for your breasts.'

I looked at my breasts. They seemed to me, as they always did, too big. 'Just get on with the notebooks,' I called, 'and remember I'm your boss and I didn't go to boarding-school so I'm not used to girlish intimacy.'

'I'm really sorry,' she called back. 'Really.'

'Forget it. Get to work.'

Half an hour later I was ready to leave. She was still beavering through Kelly's notebooks, and I noticed that she'd copied out two A4 sides' worth of information. 'Thanks,' I said when she offered it to me. 'We'll look at that later. Now we're off to Rissington, on a general trawl. Have you got a recorder with you? No? You need one. Small, but make sure it uses standard cassettes.' I showed her mine. 'Always have spare batteries and tapes, and label the tapes as you use them. Date, place, person. Also read that into the tape. Any interview that might be challenged later should be taped. Safest to tape everything. You can use it for notes, too, if it's easier when you're walking about. Take mine today: you can practise using it.'

She nodded. 'Let's go, then.' She nodded again. Her silence was deliberate, but it wasn't sulky. She followed me downstairs. In the reception area, I gave her the room key. 'Take this back to the desk, and ask if there's any messages. Ask for messages every time you pass the desk, even if you've been in the hotel. Most hotels are inefficient. Most people are inefficient. Check everything, yourself, always. OK?'

'OK,' she said, and trotted off. The Accelerated Trainee was taken with her, I could see from his body language.

'No messages,' she said coming back, 'and a real creep on the desk.'

'Were you nice to him?'

'Are you serious?'

'Perfectly serious. If he fancies you he'll put himself out for you. He could be a source. We need the messages he takes. If they fancy you, cash in.'

'What possible use could that creep be?'

'You don't know.'

'But I—'

'No buts. When we leave, wave to him.'

'Wave?'

'Yeah. A little intimate waggle of your fingers, to show you've clocked him.'

'But he makes me feel sick.'

'You know that. I know that. We *never* let a possible source know that. Got it?'

She didn't answer, but when we reached the revolving door, she turned and waved. The Accelerated Trainee blushed and waved back.

'Well done,' I said. 'We'll go in my car. Which is yours?' She pointed to a green Mini Open. I tried not to remember how much they cost. If I was going to teach the child, I couldn't afford to be jealous of her. And after a bad misjudgement last year I'd promised myself never to be jealous of rich kids, ever again. 'Nice car,' I said, rather too heartily. 'Don't forget to log your mileage on that. Keep a record of *all* expenses, *always*. If you don't you'll cut down your profit . . .'

'Weird-looking place,' she said as I parked outside GHQ. 'Shaved lawns. Could have been a nice house, once.'

It was 1045, end of break-time. For me, it was a replay of yesterday. Warm sun, deserted grounds, boys' voices in the distance, and a one-man reception committee waiting on the front steps. But today, instead of Alistair Brown, there was a boy standing on the front steps. As we parked, he ducked into GHQ, and some moments later the Major appeared.

He was in good spirits. 'Another fine day! Sunny! Warm!' He shook hands with Claudia expansively, when I introduced them as best I could since I discovered I didn't know her surname. 'Welcome to Rissington Abbey! Always glad to show a new person round! We've nothing to hide here, as Miss Tanner will tell you!' He twinkled at me. The remark seemed intended to be taken at face value, but as the boy had clearly been watching for our arrival, presumably to see that we didn't move about alone, I wondered.

'I've some coffee up in my private quarters. Come and join me. We'll go by way of the Mess, then you can see the Annigoni.'

We followed him into the hall, past the stairs, and through the house. Claudia hung back to ask me: 'The Annigoni?'

'Fashionable portrait painter, fifties and sixties. Did Mrs Major,' I said. 'Admire it.'

She looked at me with astonishment. 'Of course,' she said. 'Do you think I'm stupid?'

Inside the Mess, I exclaimed at the painting. Mrs Major looked smooth, regal, and beautiful, but then all Annigoni's subjects did. Then

Claudia took over. 'Her hair – it's breathtaking – and he's picked up the wonderful flowing line in the figure—'

I left her to her high-quality creeping while I had a good look round the room. It was very large, oblong, and wood-panelled. The door was in the corner of one long wall, the painting dominated the other, and there were french windows to the garden in the short wall furthest away from the door. A long polished table ran the length of the room and there were small desks and easy chairs all round the walls. A set of pigeon-holes, labelled with names, a huge notice-board, and a trolley stacked with coffee pots and dirty cups, presumably from break, suggested that as well as the Mess it was also the staff-room. It smelt of tobacco and furniture polish. A comfortable place to work, Rissington Abbey. But I couldn't see any clues, even supposing there was anything to find clues to.

Up in the Major's quarters, we had our coffee and Claudia looked at the photographs, catching my eye behind the Major's back and pulling a face. She thought they were even more extraordinary than I did, it seemed, though she blethered on about their artistic excellence. One advantage of having an assistant was having someone else to do your smarming for you. The Major'd taken to her and was asking her about her background and schooling. He recognized the school in Switzerland she named. 'Les Trois Églises! Excellent!' They swapped a few names while I wondered why the Major had never asked me where I went to school. Perhaps he was astute enough to know that the answer would be a conversation-stopper.

Then she asked to go to the lavatory and the Major and I were alone.

He had been standing by the window, with the sun streaming through the slightly dirty glass on to his braced, upright figure. He moved to sit on the sofa beside me and looked directly into my eyes. 'Can I trust you, Miss Tanner?'

Now what was he up to? Half-exasperated, I acknowledged his charm. He was old: he wasn't my type: but when he looked into my eyes and asked if he could trust me, I wanted to tell him the truth, that he should chuck me out, and never let me back.

Only for thirty seconds, though. I gave him my best open-faced, innocent smile. 'Yes,' I lied. 'What is it?'

'This documentary is very important to me,' he said. 'The school. My life's work. Immortalize it. Huh? You'll have influence with this boss of yours, a smart girl like you. Could you arrange it with him, to use us?'

What was so important to him? I knew he was keen, but there was an extra urgency about this. He was determined. 'I can't promise anything,' I said, feeling a complete shit. 'You mustn't count on it.'

'Perhaps if you understood – I rose through the ranks, myself. Started out as a private. Went to Sandhurst late. Loved the Army, best possible way of life, but not always easy. Lose your old friends when you move up to the officers' mess. Forgive me saying so, but Asquith told me you were a ranker too, so to speak.'

'Television isn't a rigid hierarchy,' I said. 'It's not the same.'

'Not quite, p'raps. But there are lots of university types in the BBC, huh? Damn fools, most of them, I expect, get on your nerves. Plenty of officers got on mine, but that might have been my fault. Probably was. Chip on my shoulder. But then I found my place at Rissington, and Anthea. Everything I've always wanted.'

'You asked if you could trust me,' I said. 'What did you mean?' As far as I could see he was trying to manipulate me with a sob-story, but he hadn't told me anything confidential.

'I've a dicky heart,' he said, with an effort. 'I may have to retire soon. If I live that long.'

'I'm sorry to hear that,' I said, unmoved by the blatant attempt at tear-jerking, but surprised that he'd admit the heart condition. 'How can I help?'

'I know you'll do a good job. See the place as it really is. An outsider's eye. I want you to keep working here until you've got the measure of us.'

'I can't promise anything. It's not up to me. Ah, here's Claudia.'

The Major showed us the assault course, the firing range, the dark-room, and the fully equipped sanatorium. Up to then, Claudia had been keeping our conversational end up: all I'd asked about was the names of boys who passed us. I was still hoping for 'Olivier's friends', Jake Boswell and Peter Newman, to turn up without me having to ask for them. They didn't.

I perked up at the sanatorium. I wanted to know more about Alistair Brown's mother. I hissed at Claudia and she carried the Major away into the furthest room, leaving me with the nurse on duty, a stocky Welshwoman in her forties with a lively manner, false teeth, and one of the wheeziest set of lungs I'd ever heard. 'You're not Mrs Brown, then?' I said. She'd just been introduced to me as Mrs Owen, but I didn't expect anyone inured to the rigours of the Major's conversational style to find the remark unusual.

She didn't. 'Oh, no, I'm not. I'm the Matron now, Mrs Brown's not well.'

'So she's not working at the moment?'

'Oh, no.'

'What exactly is the matter with her?'

'She has multiple sclerosis. Poor soul.' She gave a sympathetic wheeze and started to cough alarmingly. 'But at least she can still make a contribution.'

'What contribution exactly?'

'The rotas. She can still do the rotas, and the ordering. She's the Domestic Bursar really except we don't call her that. But she's such a marvellous planner, never forgets a detail, always thinks a problem through. She's been an inspiration to me, I can tell you. It's so much easier to work when you can rely on the backup. I've never gone to the cupboard for a bandage and come back empty-handed and I've never had to do overtime because my relief hasn't turned up. At my last school it was always, "Sorry Mrs Owen, there's a bit of a crisis," and I'd have to work my free weekends. It's just not on, that kind of thing. But never with Mrs Brown. She thinks of everything.'

'Is she well enough for me to visit her?'

'Oh, yes. She's not bedridden. She's up and about in her wheelchair. I saw her about ten minutes ago, going for an airing up the drive with the Captain. He's so sensitive and caring. But then he would be.' She wheezed again, this time with admiring sympathy, and clacked her dentures.

'Why?' I said.

'What with his Call.'

'Call?'

'He misunderstood the Saviour's meaning, that's all. I'm a Baptist myself. I don't hold with Romans, in the usual way, and they're bound to make mistakes, aren't they?'

I struggled to make sense of the conversation: I didn't want to alienate her. 'His original Call was . . .'

'To the priesthood, of course. That's where he was before he came here, training to be a priest. Now he knows he has to do Christ's work in the world.'

Martin Kelly, an ex-priest. Alistair Brown, nearly a priest. It was a link, but I couldn't see the ends of the chain.

We had lunch in the canteen. Claudia's face was a picture as she gazed at the food, but I hissed 'eat' and she forked in tiny mouthfuls of steak and kidney pudding, baked beans, and chips. She wasn't doing badly. She'd been recording, and listening, and talking, and taking some of the weight off me, and I'd be interested to hear her impressions.

Once more, we sat isolated with the Major, though some of the other tables were overcrowded. This time I pointed it out, but he brushed it aside. 'Respect. Huh? Good thing, let us get on in peace. Now then – your movements this pip emma. I'm not going to be able to be with you, but I'm leaving you in Alistair's capable hands. We're meeting him in the Mess for coffee after this. I'd suggest you split up. Miss Tanner, you'll be with Alistair, of course, but what do you think if Claudia here goes to lessons with the Lower Sixth? Huh? Get a real feel of the education we offer. If you'll forgive me saying so, you're not long out of school yourself, you'll see how it compares.'

Claudia, smiling politely, caught my eye and I nodded. 'That'd be lovely,' she said.

On the way back to the Mess, under the stairs in GHQ, the Major stopped and pointed. 'The ladies' cloakroom,' he said delicately, and walked away from us.

I hustled Claudia in. It was a large, dark room, with bare wooden tables with vases on, two huge old basins, a cracked and peeling mirror and two lavatory compartments. There were more of the Colonel's art studies round the walls. 'I think the old man was batty,' said Claudia, looking at a particularly winsome version of ten-year-old Mrs Ellis clinging to the trunk of a large tree while her semi-transparent dress clung to her. I put my fingers on Claudia's lips to silence her and pushed open the lavatory cubicles. No one there.

'OK,' I said. 'You take the tape-recorder and try to get your paws on either of Olivier's friends.'

I was flicking through my notebook to give her the names, but she forestalled me. 'Peter Newman or Jake Boswell, it's OK, I remember. What do we want?'

'Anything about Olivier. Particularly his state of mind that last day. Plus anything on Alistair Brown and his mother, if you get the chance. Be careful.'

'The Major's got a heart condition.'

'How do you know?'

'When I went to the loo I checked through their medicine cabinet, and I made a list, see.' She produced a sheet of paper and waved it in front of me. 'Glyceryl trinitrate – it's for angina. My grandfather has it – and then there's Prempak-C, that's hormone replacement—'

'Does your grandfather take that too?'

'No, Kate O'Mara, I think – or maybe Mrs Thatcher – I read about it in *Cosmo*. Anyway, that'll be Mrs Ellis, and so will the Valium, I expect, and the Mogadon, and the Amytal. She must have tons of the stuff to leave so much behind.'

'Why did you look in the medicine cabinet?'

'Oh, I always do. It tells you so much about people . . . yours did.'

'There's nothing in mine.'

'That's what I mean. Not even paracetamol. Just low-protection sun-tan oil, which you shouldn't use, and multi-vitamins. You wouldn't need vitamin supplements if you ate properly. No proper facial care, either—'

'What?'

'I recommend the Clinique range, but perhaps you should consider Elizabeth Arden. My mother swears by it, for the older skin, and Mrs Ellis has the whole range.'

Why was she getting at me? 'Shove it, you little cow,' I said in a neutral tone.

'Well,' she went on reasonably, 'you talk down to me like – like a great-aunt. I admit you don't *look* old, but . . .'

'I must just check that all is well in the examination hall,' said Alistair Brown as we went down the front steps. 'Do you mind coming with me?'

'Not at all,' I said. I was with him for a reason, I supposed, either his reason or the Major's, and if I volunteered nothing then his purposes might become clear.

'Lovely day,' he said, and smiled at me. He was loping along beside me with his stooped, athletic walk. 'Do you know the Banbury area at all?'

108

'I'm afraid not. It seems very pretty.'

'It is . . .' He chatted on about the local beauty spots as we walked towards the canteen and past it to the Sports Hall, a large eighties building which I knew doubled as the study hall for examinations, and stopped by the outside doors. 'Just hang on here a minute, will you?'

As he went in, I looked through the doors. About fifty boys sat, head down, at desks dotted about the hall. Above their heads, in the high steel beams that supported the glass roof, ropes and rings were looped back: there were wallbars and basketball posts. Brown was headed for a teacher sitting at a raised desk, who looked up as he approached. Near him, at a smaller desk, sat Tim Robertson, reading. He didn't look up. The door swung closed before I could catch his eye.

I looked around the school, slumbering in the bright sunlight. It was quiet, peaceful: no boys anywhere. No movement anywhere. Afternoon lessons were going on, I knew. Somewhere in the sixth-form classroom block Claudia was being taught French, I hoped sitting between Olivier's friends.

'Now,' said Alistair Brown rejoining me, 'what would you like to see?'

By four o'clock I'd seen all of the school that I hadn't already seen and we were headed back to the Mess, where Claudia was to meet us. I'd waited for Brown's purposes to emerge: perhaps he'd waited for mine. I didn't think either of us was much wiser. I'd got used to his rather self-conscious baritone voice, with its faint intermittent Scottish burr, and to the supportive touch of his hand on my arm, around the rose garden ('Watch the moss on these flagstones—') helping me up steps ('Treacherous, these'), and through perfectly normal doors ('Rather a quick automatic close on this one').

I didn't like him touching me. Not because it was an unwanted sexual advance: because it wasn't anything. I felt like a car on an automatic assembly line being manipulated by a robot. I didn't protest because I was determined not to provide any input. Whatever happened, he must dictate. But as far as information was concerned, I got nowhere. I couldn't try him on Olivier again, and I didn't want to come out into the open about Martin Kelly until I was surer of my ground, so I just listened to his information about the school and thought how much better he'd look without his glasses, and if he'd stop blinking.

We were in the hall. He stopped, I stopped, and he blinked at me.
'Miss Tanner—'

'Do call me Alex,' I said for the umpteenth time.

'Alex – I don't – I wonder—'

'Yes?'

'Would you have dinner with me this evening?'

Chapter Seventeen

We were in my room by five o'clock. Claudia was full of herself: on the way back in the car, she'd wanted to babble, but I'd stopped her. I wanted quiet, to think. I had to decide whether to send her back to London for the night, and I weighed up the advantages of having solitary thinking time against the advantage of a thorough debriefing, extra productivity on Martin Kelly's notes and two heads, however inexperienced one of them was, working on the case.

Unasked, silent, she made me a cup of coffee, and that swung it. 'Claudia, go down to the desk and book yourself a room here. Unless you'd much prefer to drive up to London tonight and back in the morning.'

'I'll stay with you. But do I need another room? You've got two beds in here.'

'You need a room. I need peace and quiet.'

'I don't like sleeping alone in hotels,' she said.

'And I don't give a tinker's teacloth what you like. I want another room for you to work in and another telephone line for you to use,' I said. 'Go and book one.'

She didn't argue. She didn't pout. She went, and came back ten minutes later with a message. 'It was the ghastly little man on the desk. He chatted me up, and he gave me this. Masses of Japanese in this hotel, have you noticed? But the room next door was free, so I've got that, isn't it excellent?'

I was looking at the message.

3.6.92 am
Ring Martin Kely

it said, with a number. It gave me a prickling feeling at the back of my neck. If Kelly came through, his whole fantasy of whatever evil he'd found at Rissington Abbey could be laid out before me, and I could stop looking for corruption in the break buns.

'He was very apologetic.'

I was reaching for the telephone. 'Who was?'

'The Trainee person.'

'Why?'

'The message. It was overlooked, he said. Mislaid.'

I looked again at the date, and time. Yesterday morning. 'Shit,' I said, and dialled the number. It rang and rang. I let it ring thirty times. Unless he lived in Buckingham Palace, he'd have had more than time to get to the phone. Maybe he was out. I grabbed the phone book, flicked through it, dialled the *Banbury Courier*. A man's voice answered. 'Martin Kelly, please.'

'Sorry,' said the voice, gravelly and phlegmatic, a Drunken Has-Been. 'He's not in today.'

He'd told me Tuesday was his afternoon off. Today was Thursday. Why hadn't he been in? 'Is he off work?'

'Dunno. He's not in, that's all. 'Bye.'

'*Wait!* I've a home number for him. Could you check it for me?' I gave him the number, and waited. The Trainee could have garbled that, surely, he cocked up everything else.

'Confirm that number,' said the voice.

'Did he call in sick?'

'No idea.'

'His address,' I said. 'Give me his address, and I'll get off the phone.'

' 12 Waterford Avenue,' he said. 'It's in one of the little streets behind the church at the top of the town. Now some of us have work to do. 'Bye,' and this time he rang off.

'What's the matter?' said Claudia. 'You look – shocked.'

'Not really,' I said. 'We'll eat in here, tonight, OK?'

'Not in the hotel restaurant,' she said, looking equally shocked.

'No. In the room. I want you to go and buy us food. Healthy food,' I said. 'Free of additives, low in cholesterol, expensive. And picnic cutlery, and plates. Can you do that?'

'Where will you go?'

'I'm going to pay a call on Martin Kelly.'

'Then I'm coming too. I'll get the food after.'

'No. I want to go by myself. It'll be quicker.'

'I've paid you for training. I can't be trained if you protect me. What are you afraid of? Do you think something's happened to the priest?'

'You can come on one condition. That you promise to do exactly what I say, when I say it.'

'I've already promised that. And I've done it. Haven't you noticed?'

She had. And she had. And I had. So I let her come.

Waterford Avenue was a quiet little cul-de-sac, semi-light industrial. Number twelve was tucked away at the end, between a van-hire yard, now closed, and a Baptist chapel which looked as if it had been closed since Cromwell. The few remaining houses, down the other end of the street, were in multiple occupation, judging from the peeling paintwork and the plethora of rickety bells, but Kelly's was in spanking condition.

We'd parked down the road, and walked. Now we stood outside the neat little house with its fresh curtains and weed-free path, and I looked at the milk-bottle on its side on the front step, and the dried pool of curdled milk that had seeped into the rosebed. I rang the bell. It whirred in the silent house. We waited, and I rang it again.

Then I stepped onto the tiny square of lawn under the front window and looked in. Nothing. A tidy parlour, with a crucifix on the wall.

'It's got a back garden,' said Claudia. 'If we go down the side of the chapel, we can climb over the wall into the garden, and break in.'

'We won't break in,' I said. 'We'll find the back door is open.'

'How do you know?' she said, following me down the narrow damp alley beside the church and giving me a leg-up over the wall, then scrambling up behind me. We both jumped down onto the back lawn.

'I know the door will be open because breaking in is illegal,' I said. Nothing and no one, as far as I could see, overlooked the garden and the back door. The catch was a simple Yale. 'Giss a credit card,' I said. She passed me a platinum American Express card. 'Don't you have a less useful one? I'll wreck it.' While she sorted through her collection, I checked, through the window, that there was nothing upsetting in the kitchen.

'Harvey Nichols?' she said.

'Thank you. That'll do nicely.'

Whoever'd used the door last hadn't left the catch on. I well and truly mangled the card – Claudia'd have to omit Harvey Nichols from her shopping plans for a day or two – but the lock clicked back, I pushed the door with my elbow, and we were in.

The kitchen was clean, and tidy except for an empty bottle of whisky and one glass on the small Formica table, and a grate overflowing with ashes and scraps of burnt paper.

'Stay here,' I said. 'Don't touch anything.' Then I went upstairs, towards the smell and the buzz of flies, to discover the body.

I'd hoped it would be an overdose, but it was a hanging. It was darkish on the stairs: as I reached the top I could see his body up to his armpits. The upper part was hidden by the ceiling. When I got closer, holding my breath, I could look up through a trapdoor in the ceiling to his face, the noose and a rope thrown over a beam in the attic above. I only looked at his face once, to check it was him, though I realized as I quickly looked away that I'd confirmed it already by the bitten nails on his swinging hands.

I leant against the wall and waited till the giddiness went. At least his neck was broken. He'd been lucky: he could have just throttled. It hadn't been a long enough drop to guarantee a quick death. By his feet was a torn sheet of paper. Printed on it: GOD FORGIVE ME.

I looked beyond him, into the front bedroom. Neat, bare, another crucifix on the wall, with a palm cross tucked behind it. The back bedroom and the bathroom door was shut.

I went down again. Claudia was standing exactly where I'd left her. 'Come on,' I said. 'Don't touch anything as we go.'

'You told me that already,' she said mildly. 'Is he dead? What's the smell?'

'Double incontinence,' I said closing the door behind us, using my T-shirt to hold the handle. 'He's dead. Hanged. With what could be a suicide note by his feet, or could just be a page from one of his notebooks.'

'Why? What did it say?'

'God forgive me.'

'He wrote that all the time, didn't he? I've got that from his notes about six times already. Do you think he was mad?'

'Depressed. Guilty.'

Back in the street again, I headed for the car, and Claudia followed. 'What are we going to do?'

'That's up to you.'

'Up to me?'

'Yes. We've found a dead body. We should report it.'

'What would you do if I wasn't here?'

'Nothing.'

'Then that's what we'll do.'

'We're breaking the law.'

'*Tant pis*. We must have a reason. I expect you'll tell me in due course.'

I didn't want to tell the police because I didn't want them tying Kelly in with Rissington Abbey. Not yet. I didn't want that particular ant's nest overturned for a day or two, until I'd had a chance to work it out for myself. I should be able to: he'd given me the notebooks, probably for that very purpose. I didn't know if it was suicide or if someone had fixed it to look like that. If he hadn't killed himself, I wanted to find out who had. I hadn't known Kelly at all, but I felt for him. He'd been trying to work something out, and if he'd been killed before he'd resolved it, someone had cheated him.

We went back to the hotel. When Claudia had gone shopping, we settled down to a picnic. I didn't notice what I ate. She put the food on a plate for me, poured me what she said was fresh-squeezed orange juice, and waited.

Eventually I explained why I didn't want to tell the police. She nodded. 'What do we do this evening?' she said.

'Get sorted. First, I want you to finish going through Kelly's notes, and we'll look at what you've got.'

'Thanks,' she said.

'What for?'

'For letting me keep on with his notes. When you gave it to me, it was a rubbish job, to keep me busy. Now, it's important.'

'No big deal,' I said. 'If you're given a job to do, you should do it. There are enough people in television already who make every small thing a three-legged hurdle race.'

'Alan wouldn't have left it to me.'

'Alan doesn't like anyone to pee without getting it cleared by a conference. Now bugger off to your room and don't come back till you've finished.'

Chapter Eighteen

When Claudia'd gone to her room, I watched the news. The Rio summit: Major ruled out a referendum on Maastricht: nothing else, much. I turned it off. I wished I hadn't taken Claudia along to Kelly's. She seemed very subdued by it, even though she hadn't seen the body. She didn't seem worried by the police, though, and I thought the chances of the police ever tying us in with Kelly were slight. I also thought they'd take his suicide at face value.

I turned off the lights, lay on the bed and watched the sun set. I'd never seen a hanged man before, though I'd seen photographs. I hoped I'd never see another one.

He'd meant it about the evil at Rissington Abbey. One way or another, I was sure, it had killed him. I'd come to Banbury: he'd given me his notes: he'd called me, the hotel had cocked it up, I hadn't called back, and he'd died. I looked at the sun flooding the horizon with pink and let my mind float on the day, on what I'd seen and heard, what I knew. Something would come, if I didn't force it.

After a while it was dark and I sat up, put the light on, and wrote down what my thoughts had come to. They looked sparse enough.

What's the connection between Brown and Kelly?
What's the Major's hurry to get the documentary made?
Who's keeping a watch on me?
Why did Alistair Brown ask me to dinner?
Where's Mrs Ellis, and why?

I felt melancholy. Work was the answer, and it would help to keep Claudia going, so she didn't fall into a melancholy too. She'd been tiptoeing round me with her food and orange juice and gentle voice.

116

She needed to learn that feelings had to be put aside, if she was to be a professional.

Then she came back.

She had very neat, sloping, foreign child's writing. Easy to read. And most of what she'd found was easy to eliminate, because she hadn't recognized references to British news items over the past two years. 'When did you move to London?' I asked.

'Three months ago,' she said.

It figured. My pencil raced down her five A4 sheets, crossing out. When I'd finished, I looked at what we'd got. Apart from the ever-recurring 'God forgive me', it all came in the pages relating to the Rissington Abbey sports day.

dark armour
buttocks on the diving-board spotlight
0325 63812 RP 86 28833311
Bernard Corrigan
031 22331

Very little, entirely obscure. Kelly had certainly meant me to work for it, if there was anything to work for.

'I can't make anything of it,' said Claudia, 'but that's what I've got. I've been thinking. Suicide's a terrible sin. The sin of final despair. And look, if he keeps writing "God forgive me", he obviously hasn't renounced the faith, has he?'

It was what I thought too, though I said, 'He could just have been depressed. Unbalanced. If he was drunk, too. He could have been a recovering alcoholic, and starting to drink again might have pushed him over the edge.'

'*Buttocks on the diving-board spotlight*? That doesn't even make sense. You don't have spotlights on diving-boards.'

'That came from his notes on last year's Rissington Abbey sports day, didn't it? Could be any of the divers.'

'Perhaps Olivier?'

'Perhaps.'

'But why did Kelly write that?'

'Maybe he fancied the anonymous buttocks.'

'Is he queer?'

'Say gay.'

'Why?'

'It's more politically correct.'

'My mother says "queer".'

'Your mother isn't hoping to work in the media. Trust me. You should, you're paying me enough. He may be talking about himself.'

She looked at me oddly. 'Are you feeling better?'

'What do you mean?'

'Just then. You were talking to me as if – as if a man hadn't died.'

'I'm not feeling better. I wasn't feeling particularly worse,' I lied. 'In this business you can't afford to give in to your feelings all the time. We're doing the same job, and we must do it just as well.'

'But if we make no sense of it, where do we start?' she said.

'Always start with the facts. Here, it's the telephone numbers. Too late to ring either of them now, and we won't get an answer if they're business numbers anyhow. We could place them. Find where the first dialling code is. The other's Edinburgh.'

She rang the operator. 'Darlington,' she said. 'What do we do now?'

'Leave it,' I said, 'until we can call tomorrow morning.'

'How important do you think this stuff is?'

I'd been thinking about that. 'To him, very,' I said. 'He seemed to make a decision before he gave it to me.'

'Why do you think he rang you?'

'I wish I knew.'

It was melancholy. I kept remembering his bitten nails, his fierce and willed smile. 'Tell me what you think you learnt today,' I said.

'I talked to Peter Newman. He was in my French class and the history class. D'you want to hear?'

'Please.'

She fiddled with the tape. 'This is before the history master came in, between lessons.'

'Hang on. I thought Alistair Brown taught history. He was with me.'

'They split the teaching of A-level history between two teachers who each do a different part of the syllabus. Schools often do.'

'Does Rissington split other subjects as well?'

'I didn't ask. Does it matter?'

'I don't know.'

'This is the bit,' she said, and put the recorder on the table.

CLAUDIA: I saw in the paper about Olivier Desmoulins. Wasn't it sad? I've always been a terrific fan of his father, I lived in France, you know, and Michel Mouche is very big in France.

BOY: I could tell. Your French is great.

CLAUDIA: Olivier was at school here, wasn't he? Did you know him?

BOY: Sure.

CLAUDIA: What was he like?

BOY: He was an OK guy. Bloody good diver.

CLAUDIA: How sad, it was that killed him, wasn't it?

BOY [Knowing laugh]: The vodka, more like.

CLAUDIA: I often wonder about premonitions and things like that, seeing into the future, I believe in the paranormal, do you?

BOY [Hesitation. But he fancied her enough to lie]: Yeah. Right. We can't know everything, can we?

CLAUDIA: What's your sign? I'm Aquarius.

BOY: Leo.

CLAUDIA: Wow. Leo. That's the leader's sign.

BOY: [Flattered laugh]

CLAUDIA: And I wonder if we know when we're going to die, like animals do, elephants go to a graveyard and stuff, don't they?

BOY: I've heard that. Yeah.

CLAUDIA: Did Olivier know? The day before he was going to die? Did he have a premonition?

BOY: He didn't say if he did.

CLAUDIA: Was he happy?

BOY: Yeah, he was. Kind of – pleased about something, but he didn't say what.

CLAUDIA: Had something happened?

BOY: Like what?

CLAUDIA: Maybe he'd had some good news from home, or something, like a letter?

BOY: He never opened his letters from his mother.

CLAUDIA: What do you mean?

BOY: She wrote to him a lot, and he just looked through the envelope, you know, held it up to the light to see if there was a cheque in it, and if there wasn't he just chucked them on his desk.

CLAUDIA: Was there a letter from his mother, that day?

BOY: Dunno.

Claudia stopped the tape. 'Then the teacher came in,' she said.

I was impressed. 'Well done,' I said. 'That was smooth. What else did you get?'

'Lots of background. Nothing else about Olivier.'

'What was the teaching like?'

'OK. That's the thing, Alex, it just seems like an OK school to me, all round. Bit peculiar with the military stuff, but no odder than Eton with those penguin suits. And I like the Major, he's a sweetie. What did you get?'

I looked at my list. 'Brown was in a seminary. He originally wanted to be a priest. So the Matron said.'

'That's terrifically important!' fizzed Claudia.

'Why?'

She thought. 'I don't know, but it just is, it must be.'

Since her reaction was the same as mine, I didn't give her a hard time. I went on, 'And Brown asked me to dinner. I don't know why. To get me out of the way? To pump me? To brainwash me?'

'He could just like the look of you.'

'I don't think he's seen me at all. I don't think he sees beyond his glasses. He's a closed system.'

'Why didn't you go?'

'Because we had work to do. A whole dinner would be a waste of time. If there is something he wants, he'll try another way to get it.'

'So you think he's up to something? He must be!'

'Don't know.'

We kicked it around for another hour. By then it was ten o'clock and I felt tired and heavy. I wanted a bath, and bed. I wanted Martin Kelly not to be dead. Two out of three ain't bad.

Claudia went to her room. I lay in the bath for a while, saying *dark armour* and *buttocks on the diving-board spotlight*, to see if the sound of the words helped. It didn't.

I was in bed and nearly asleep when there was a knock on the door. Claudia. 'I can't sleep,' she said. She was wearing a short nightshirt under a silk dressing-gown, and clutching a battered once-pink rabbit. 'I really find it difficult to sleep alone in hotels,' she said.

She took the other bed, and fell asleep very quickly. I heard her regular breathing for what seemed hours. I really find it difficult to sleep with pink rabbits in hotels.

Friday, June 5th

Chapter Nineteen

I woke at seven, to another sunny day. It was worrying. Claudia's bed was empty: there was a cooling cup of coffee on my bedside table. I drank it, gratefully, and put on track suit bottoms, an old white sweatshirt, and trainers. Running might help.

I banged on Claudia's door as I passed and told her where I was going. She responded with a warning squawk: 'Mind your knees! Run on grass!'

I started slowly, out of the hotel car park and along the grass verge towards Rissington Abbey. It was about two miles away, I reckoned. There and back would do me nicely.

When I got there, I stopped at the gates and looked down the drive. Nothing. I couldn't even see a fatigue party. I was hardly puffed, I'd been jogging so slowly, and I set off back at a faster pace. As I picked up speed, I noticed a car drawing level. It was going very slowly and I thought it might be someone from the Abbey I knew, but it wasn't, it was two Japanese from the hotel. I recognized them easily: I can manage Japanese, it's politicians I can't tell apart. I waved and they waved, but they respected my exercise and didn't offer me a lift. Or perhaps they wouldn't have anyway.

I did the two miles back to the hotel in sixteen minutes, which wasn't bad. By the time I was bathed and dressed (today's sweatshirt selection: dark blue, no logo) Claudia had finished what I imagined to be an arduous cleansing, toning, moisturizing routine and joined me for breakfast wearing yet another white shirt (lace-trimmed) and Gloria Vanderbilt jeans. The silver combs in her newly washed and conditioned hair remained the same.

I said nothing at breakfast: neither did she. She was speaking when she was spoken to, I realized. Sensible girl.

Back in my room it was just nine o'clock. 'Telephone time,' I said, and dialled the first of Kelly's numbers, the Darlington one. 'Department of Education and Science, Pensions Branch,' said the female voice that answered as if it had just sat down, vaguely resentful that anyone would ring before she'd had time to check her stars in the *Mail*.

'Good morning,' I said, then took a flyer. 'This number' – I read it to her – 'would it be your reference?'

'What do you mean?'

'Do teachers have numbers, with you? For their pensions?'

'Well, yes. Stands to reason.'

'And the number I just gave you. Is that a teacher's number?'

'It could be, but I can't give you any information about that.'

'It's a standard format, I suppose? What year would this number have been registered?'

'1986, of course.'

The first two digits. Six years ago. 'So, in the normal way, the teacher to whom this number refers would be in his or her late twenties?'

'I suppose,' said the voice. 'Depends when they trained. There are plenty of mature entrants to the profession.'

'Thank you,' I said, cutting the line and dialling the other number.

'Hello,' said an oldish, female, Scots voice. Unsurprising since I'd dialled Edinburgh.

'Good morning. Who am I speaking to?'

'This is St Anselm's.'

'A Catholic church?'

'The priest's house.'

'Could I speak to Father Corrigan?'

'He's away.'

'When will he be back?'

'Sunday morning, for early Mass.'

'What time should I ring, to speak to him?'

'After his breakfast.'

'Which would be?'

'Nine o'clock.'

'One more thing – is that Father Bernard Corrigan?'

'No, Father Patrick.'

'Sorry, it is Patrick, of course. I misread my writing. Thanks. I'll call back.'

'Is there a message?'

'No, thank you. No message.'

I told Claudia about both of them. 'Father Corrigan's probably a friend of his, a priest from his past. I've no idea who Bernard is.'

'So it might not be anything to do with Rissington?'

'We'll know on Sunday.'

'I hate waiting,' said Claudia.

So did I. 'Grin and bear it,' I said.

'We're no further forward, then?' said Claudia, disappointed.

'Yes, we are. I'm going to try another flyer.' I dialled again.

'Bartholemew O'Neill,' said Barty.

'Hi, Barty. I want you to ring the DES about your pension entitlement.'

'Hi, Alex. Who am I?'

'You're Alistair Brown, employed since 1986 at Rissington Abbey.' I gave him the school address, the teacher's reference number, and the DES telephone number.

'What do I want to know about myself?'

'If the reference number applies to you. Beyond that, any other details of your employment record.'

'OK. I'll be back to you in ten minutes or so.'

'So it's Alistair Brown,' said Claudia, as we waited.

'What is?'

'The evil. The person who's doing everything.'

'Doing what, exactly?'

She gestured vaguely. Her vagueness mirrored mine.

'That's the problem,' I said. 'It may be Brown that Kelly was after, but even if it was we don't know why. We don't know beans, really, until we talk to Father Corrigan, and even then he may not help.'

The ringing phone made me jump. 'Hi,' said Barty. 'John Alistair Brown here. Maybe I didn't like being plain John Brown, and I prettied it up. I wasn't working as a teacher from 1984 to 1986, after I left university. Other than that, my retirement holds no fears for me, and I can always buy-in the two missing years. What are you up to, Alex?'

'I'm not sure, yet.'

'Do take care.'

'And you.'

This time, at Rissington, our one-man reception committee was a Chinese boy. 'Good morning, Miss Tanner,' he said. 'I am Li Sung.

Please call me Sung. I've been asked to wait for you and act as your guide.'

He looked about sixteen, slender, suave, and very handsome despite a savagely short haircut. The uniform, khaki camouflage trousers and mud-green short-sleeved sweatshirt, emphasized his slenderness. His accent was old-fashioned Oxford English.

'Hello. My assistant, Claudia.'

'We met yesterday,' she said.

'Are you missing your break, waiting for us?'

He shrugged. 'That does not matter. One can only eat so many Rissington Abbey buns. I reached my limit years ago . . . Please, wait a moment . . .' Like the boy the day before, he nipped up the steps and into GHQ.

'I wish we knew who they all report to,' I said to Claudia.

'Now I am at your disposal,' said Li Sung, re-emerging. 'The Major thought you would be interested in the playing-fields. Follow me.' He set off, back along the drive. I began to move, then stopped. So did Claudia. When he'd gone about five yards, he turned. 'We're very proud of our playing-fields. Please, let me show you.'

'Another time,' I said. 'This morning, I want to speak to Mrs Brown.'

'She may not be well enough. Shall I check?'

'Please do.'

Back he went to GHQ. I followed him: so did Claudia. I felt like the experienced, ageing half of a synchronized-swimming team. He shut the door firmly in our faces and we turned away and went down the steps together. I raised one hand and waggled it.

'What are you doing?'

'Synchronized swimming. All we lack is pegs on our noses.'

'What? I don't understand.'

'Never mind . . . Here's Li Sung again.'

'Mrs Brown can see you,' he said, and we all moved off.

'Are you a private?' I asked.

'I'm an NCO. A prefect. As I am in the first year sixth I can only be a corporal. Perhaps, next year, I shall achieve higher things . . . The canteen, the CDT block, the squash courts.' He was taking us the long way round and we could hardly see the buildings: they were hidden behind towering old trees, some of them oaks, the only deciduous tree I can reliably identify. It didn't matter, because by now I could have conducted a tour of the place.

126

'I hear the school squash team is very successful,' I said. 'Are you in it?'

'I have that honour, yes . . .'

'We must cover it in our documentary,' I said.

'Ah. The documentary. Yes. The younger boys are very excited.' His tone was condescending.

'And you're not?'

'Well. There's many a slip between the cup and the lip, is there not?'

'Do you have any particular slip in mind?'

'No, not at all. My first English teacher, at home in Hong Kong, was very keen on proverbs. We had to learn lists of them . . . I try to use as many as I can . . . The playing-fields are—'

'The swimming-pool's up there, too, isn't it?' I said, peering through the trees. 'Built during the Second War, I believe.'

'Yes. It was intended as a temporary structure. I so admire the British capacity for making do . . . fifty years does seem a lot to ask of such a ramshackle construction.'

Behind his opaque black eyes, under his short blue-black hair, silently, Corporal Li Sung was laughing at me. Because he laughed at all adults? All Europeans? All women? Because he knew more than I did about something which affected me? Whatever his reason, I wasn't going to pretend I hadn't noticed.

'I expect it'll outlast Hong Kong,' I said cheerfully.

He was unfazed. 'You may be right. My father would agree. Unfortunately, we were unable to obtain American visas, so we have transferred some of our assets to this country, and bought a pleasant house near Oxford.'

'Why do you suppose the Major picked you to meet me?' I said.

He smiled. 'Because of my whole-hearted loyalty to the school, naturally. On our right, beyond the trees, is the First Eleven cricket pitch . . .'

He'd set a cracking pace, faster than a normal walk. Claudia and I were both handling it, but I slowed down and looked through the trees across the expanse of grass. It was flat, green, with two wickets. Exactly like a cricket pitch. It was, however, the one part of the school I hadn't yet seen: presumably Alistair Brown had told Sung that. Or told the Major that, and the Major had told Sung.

Below us on the drive, a crowded minibus passed, heading for the gate. 'We can make our own way from here,' I said. 'Mrs Brown's flat is on the end of the Duke of Wellington Annexe, isn't it? I know the way.'

'Surely . . .' he began, but I'd had enough.

'He travels fastest who travels alone,' I said. 'Perhaps your list of proverbs included that.'

'It did. Just before "look before you leap",' said Sung.

I wasn't going to win a proverb war. The English teachers at my comprehensive had thought them outdated, élitist, and middle class. For ideological reasons, they only ever spoke to us in words they thought we knew already.

I nodded to the boy and turned away, Claudia at my heels. My abruptness dared him to follow us. He didn't. He said: 'Go up the steps of the Annexe, then turn left and follow the terrace round the building. The flat has a separate entrance.'

It did. It had flowers in tubs on each side of the door, and hanging baskets, and a flagged patio. The door was opened by a woman in a wheelchair.

'Can I help?' she said, and I looked down at Mrs Brown, beloved mother and master organizer.

She was in her fifties, with shortish fluffy hair probably dyed from a packet which called itself Glowing Chestnut or Blazing Autumn. The strength of the colour didn't help her skin, which was pale, crumpled, and dry, but her teeth were good and she showed a lot of them in a determined smile.

I introduced Claudia and myself. She paused for a moment, watching me, still smiling, then spun the wheelchair backwards down the small vinyl-tiled hall with skilled turns of her wrists. 'Come in! Come in!' she said. 'Corporal Li said you'd be dropping in. I'm Mrs B. My Alistair's busy at the moment, training in his study.' She waved at a door as she passed. 'How exciting! Television! You work in television! You are so lucky. Have you met Terry Wogan? I'm a real fan. Come in, my dears.' Her voice was high and sweet, with the breathy softness of a Highland Scot. As she spoke, she smiled.

Training in his study? Intellectual exercises? Advanced time-tabling? Preparing the Standard Aptitude Tests in evil? She was still talking at us: now she was out of sight, because the hall had an L-bend. 'And Sir Jimmy Savile? Have you ever met him? That's a truly good man.' I followed her, answering her nonsense as sensibly as I could, wondering why there was such an overpowering smell of a smart Italian after-shave. The smell hung in the corridor, it didn't come from her. But if it was the Second-in-Command's, it must be an off-duty luxury: he didn't wear it normally.

She'd stopped her chair outside a door at the far end, waiting for us. 'The living-room's at the back of the annexe, with what we think is a charming view of the trees, and our private garden.'

'No boys?' I said.

She laughed. 'How right you are! It's a joy to get away from them now and then, I must admit, though I do love the boys! Heartwarming young rascals, they are!'

The living-room was very light and too warm. I felt a radiator as I passed: it was hot to the touch. Perhaps, being ill, she felt the cold. A large glass sliding door to the garden occupied most of one wall, and the sun poured through it on to the beige fitted carpet and the light blue, newish sofa and matching chairs. There were no little tables: the floor area was mostly clear, to give space for the wheelchair, I supposed. A fitted bookcase held romance paperbacks and an assortment of gardening and cookery books. The walls, painted light yellow, displayed watercolours of Highland scenes, including a particularly hapless cow. 'Sit down, both of you,' she said, still smiling. 'Can I offer you refreshment?'

'No, thank you,' I said. I was trying to work out what it was about the room that rubbed me the wrong way. The sofa was comfortable, everything was clean – what was wrong?

Nothing. That was it. Nothing was wrong, out of place, individual; it had no meaning and no character, like the emptiness of her smile. 'I hope you're feeling better today,' I said.

'Quite well enough for visitors,' she said, and waited.

While I asked her automatic questions (How long had she worked at Rissington? Eight years. How did she like it? Wonderful! wonderful! The Major's an inspiration, and Mrs Ellis such a gracious lady, and so kind!) I tried to imagine the life the Browns led. I couldn't, and the room didn't help. But maybe that was just a failure of my imagination.

Claudia asked to go to the lavatory. 'Second door on the right,' smiled Mrs Brown, and Claudia shut the door behind her.

By the time she came back, five minutes later, I was well into the particular needs of the sanatorium at Rissington. 'Because they're so active, we do get a higher than usual incidence of sports injuries –

broken bones, strained muscles, etc., but they're very healthy otherwise.'

I remembered Tim Robertson, in the san on the night of Olivier's death. 'And I suppose the normal run of colds and flu and things,' I said.

'Bless you, they wouldn't go to the san for colds. Influenza, perhaps, if it was serious.'

'And you're not in charge there any more?'

'Sadly no, not since my illness. I do help out, I'm always glad to help, when I'm well enough. And of course, I keep house for my Alistair, and I'm unofficial housemistress. When the boys need a motherly shoulder to cry on, I'm always here.'

She seemed to me as motherly as a combine harvester, as genuine as a two-pound note, and as warm as an Eskimo's ice-box, but I never like false smilers or gushing women, and I couldn't forget Martin Kelly's loneliness which somehow I connected with her. I'd probably suspect anyone, this morning.

'One thing that interests me,' I said. 'I didn't go to boarding-school myself—'

'Neither did I, dear, neither did I! I came from a very simple home.'

I bet it wasn't half as simple as mine, I thought, but I wasn't going to get into a 'we were too poor to afford a hole in the road' contest with her. 'So I don't know much about boarding-schools at all. But I'd think the boys might feel homesick, and so on. I suppose the chaplain would be a help? Do you have a chaplain here?'

She looked puzzled, as well she might, but said, 'Oh, yes, of course! Not a resident chaplain, but the school attends St Peter's near by and the vicar there conducts confirmation classes.'

'And for boys of other denominations? The Catholics, for instance?'

'The Catholics go to Mass in town.'

'By themselves?'

'Oh, no. Catholic members of staff accompany them. I'm a Catholic myself and it used to be my responsibility to take charge. Then, when my Alistair came as housemaster here, he took over.'

'Mr Brown originally trained as a priest?' I tried to sound uninterested.

'Yes, dear, he did. Later, he decided to do God's work in the teaching profession.'

Claudia was looking excited. I wished she wouldn't and I coughed, to warn her. She wiped her face blank, before Mrs Brown saw her, I thought.

The telephone rang, Mrs Brown answered it. 'Yes ... Yes ... Of course, straight away.' She turned to us. 'You're wanted down in GHQ.'

'Immediately?' I said.

'I'm afraid so, dear, yes. Wish we could chat all morning.'

She bundled us out of the flat, past the open door to Brown's study, now empty. Then she watched us on our way.

'What's all this about?' said Claudia, hurrying to keep up with me as I increased my pace.

'No idea,' I said. 'Originally, Li Sung was keeping us away from something or someone, I suppose.'

'What do we do now?'

'What we're told. Eventually, try and find out what they want to stop us from doing, and do it.'

'Why didn't you say something about Olivier?'

'She was sharp. I've already asked her son. I told the solicitor no one at Rissington would know what I was after, and I've got to make that good.'

'But you've told the fat boy. Tim Robertson.'

'And he can't afford to tell on me in case I tell on him.'

'Tell what?'

'Tell the school that he couldn't run the community service programme properly. That he lied about what Olivier was doing when he should have been working on Matilda Beckford's house.'

Claudia was still talking. 'How do you know? You said to cross-check everything, right, not take one person's word?'

'Not now,' I said. 'Tell me later.' I was waiting to see who came out to meet us. I was sure it would be Alistair Brown, or possibly a boy following his orders.

But it was the Major who came down the front steps and walked towards us.

Chapter Twenty

'Another lovely day,' I said, but the Major wasn't interested. He was looking at Claudia. His expression was wistful, almost sad. 'You're here, Miss Tanner,' he said. 'With your assistant.'

'Yes,' I said.

'My wife's come back,' he said to me flatly. 'She'd like to see you.' He took a handkerchief from his sleeve and patted away sweat from his face. Was he anxious? Ill? Perhaps he saw the documentary, his immortality, being dashed from his lips. Perhaps Mrs Ellis had come back to stop it. 'Better all round if your assistant waits in the hall, huh?'

'I'd like her with me,' I said. 'She's part of the team.'

Claudia grinned delightedly. He hesitated, then shrugged, as if prospects were already so bad that an assistant more or less would make no difference. He hurried us through the hall, up the *Gone with the Wind* stairs, down the corridor to his private quarters. We passed two boys on the way: they both stood back and saluted, then watched the receding seat of Claudia's jeans.

The Major opened the door for us and waved us through to the sitting-room where a woman stood waiting with her back to the window. 'My wife,' he said. 'Miss Tanner. And – um – Claudia.'

'Mrs Ellis,' I said, we shook hands, and I took stock of the original of the 'artistic' photographs, thirty years on. Kelly's newspaper article had placed her at fifty-three and that looked about right, I reckoned, though her face hadn't dropped. She was tall, much taller than her husband, and her hair was still black. Her eyes and complexion showed that she had once genuinely been very dark but the condition of her hair shrieked 'dyed'. There was masses of it which she wore on top of her head in carefully arranged disarray, stuck through with wooden hair ornaments like small African spears. Her large dark eyes swam in reddened whites, surrounded by faded bruising. She looked hungover

132

and not at all pleased to see us, but she'd dressed up enough to make an entrance down the stairs. She wore a deep red linen skirt, a short, fitted cream linen jacket, high-heeled red and blue leather sandals, and a liberal sprinkling of some expensive perfume. When I met her eyes her personality engulfed me in waves. It was rich and rather over-fruity, and so was her voice.

'How do you do, Miss Tanner,' she swooped, like a contralto loosening up in the dressing room before a recital. 'I'm not at all sure about this documentary.'

The Major was jittering from foot to foot and looking at his watch. 'Perhaps we should ask our guests to sit down, my dear? Huh? Ah – coffee?'

He waved us all to chairs, especially Claudia, who Mrs Ellis had ignored, and started distributing cups from the waiting tray. I was surprised. I'd thought him the sort of man who would have expected serving coffee to be a woman's privilege.

Impatiently, she sat down too and accepted a cup. Then she started niggling. The coffee was too weak. No, she didn't want him to make any more. No, she didn't want him to ring for the duty batman to make some. Oh, she'd drink it, and why didn't he stop fussing? I watched her irritated gestures. She often pushed at her hair, to lift it off her neck. She was big, deep-breasted, handsome, and self-absorbed.

Eventually she turned to me with the air of someone whose attention was worth getting. 'I hope you won't be too terribly disappointed if we send you packing,' she said.

'Not at all,' I said blandly.

The Major looked at his watch again. 'I really must go. I have an appointment.'

'Nobody's keeping you,' said Mrs Ellis scornfully. 'Why don't you run along?'

'I'll see you later, Miss Tanner—' The door closed behind him.

I turned to Mrs Ellis. 'I thought you were coming back next week,' I said mildly. 'Change of plan?'

'I came as soon as I heard about this ridiculous programme . . . Really, I can't imagine what he was thinking about, letting the media in. We run a school, not a circus.'

'My producer is most discreet, and you'd be consulted every step of the way.'

She chuckled. It was a low, expressive chuckle. She had an air of over-ripe sexuality that was flaring up for the last time before the pension-book and the cocoa and before her breasts met her waist in the run-up to Matilda Beckford's old age. 'You would say that, wouldn't you?' she said, 'But I'm not sure the parents will like it . . . and I don't think the Major realizes how dangerous the media can be. You could easily make him look a fool. He's not, he's an idealist.'

But you treat him like a fool, I thought, and wondered about her motives. 'You're not committed to anything yet,' I said. 'We'll need your permission to film, of course, and then before that, Alan may not decide to use your school. So if I were you I wouldn't worry about anything, yet. And we're nearly finished with the preliminary research.'

'What does *she* do?' Mrs Ellis lit a cigarette and waved it at Claudia. 'Can she talk?'

'I said "How do you do" when I came in,' said Claudia politely. 'I don't think you heard. I'm Alex's assistant, learning the job.'

'Learning the job. And what have you learnt so far?' One eyebrow raised, a quizzical, denigratory swoop of the self-conscious voice.

'It's very interesting. Your school is fascinating.'

'Is that so?' Mrs Ellis turned back to me. 'What do you have left to do?'

'I'd like to speak to some of the boys. And I'd like to hear from you, of course. You're almost as involved in running the school as your husband is, I expect.'

'Almost,' she said ironically, puffing the smoke in my direction. I wondered why she'd cut short her holiday. If she wanted to throw me out, she could just have rung up and told the Major the documentary wasn't on. She certainly had enough clout with him to do that. What didn't she want me to find out? Or did she just want to make sure that she had a big enough part in the eventual programme?

And who, or what, had she dressed up for?

She made me uneasy. There was a turbulence in the air about her: she overflowed with undirected resentment. I'm disappointed, her manner said. Make it up to me. I could suggest we filmed her in a white dress clinging to a basketball stand: other than that, nothing sprang to mind.

*

What she appeared to want, for the rest of the morning, was our company. She talked about her father, the founder, about her exciting youth (she'd been a beauty: many men had been after her: she'd chosen Geoffrey because her father, the pop-eyed Colonel, had wanted him as a successor). 'My father the colonel' cropped up so often I felt I was in the Katherine Mansfield short story. I turned on the tape, Claudia took notes, and we both pretended that Alan might use them. Her mother, Mrs Colonel, had died when she was three.

I looked at the photographs, starting about the time of her mother's death, and wondered. What had the relationship been? Had the little girl in the white dress been fixed by her father at some early stage, and was she suffocating behind the façade of the well-dressed middle-aged Mrs Ellis?

I found it hard to pay attention. Her voice annoyed me. I watched the tape go round in my recorder and promised myself that I'd listen to it later.

I switched back on when she started talking about money. According to her, the school was a profitable business. All their building – the craft block, the Sports Hall – had come out of profits. No building appeals. They had no problem with numbers. They filled a particular niche in the market and the applications weren't dropping. Not, of course, that you automatically believe business people talking about their own profitability, but she really didn't seem concerned about it. Neither did he, when he rejoined us an hour before lunch.

I asked her about the specific difficulties of the boys who paid the higher fees rate: how 'disturbed' they actually were. She refused to talk about that, though she was ready enough to join the Major in talking about old boys. They were equally interested in their successes, remembered the details of their failures. 'Brooks – such a sad boy – and we couldn't do much for him, could we? Ended up in court for forgery,' she said.

'Terrible. When he put up such a fine show at the endurance exercise on the Brecons in '82. Almost as good as Eggleston in '79.'

'Eggleston's doing splendidly in the Scots Guards . . .'

Her dissatisfaction might have been with herself or with the Major, but it wasn't with the boys, although she refused to discuss general educational points. The National Curriculum: 'Can't make head or tail of it. Everybody knows what they should learn anyway.' The Major plunged into another explanation of the Rissington syllabus changes: I

135

switched off. I was trying to decide what to pack for my weekend away with Barty. Should I borrow Polly's little black Lycra dress? She said I looked stunning in it. I thought my tits looked too big. My body's in good condition but I think there's too much of it. Besides, where was Barty taking me? Black Lycra'd be fine in Paris or Rome but if we were going to an unspoilt Greek island I'd look like the town tart. On the other hand wasn't black Lycra last year's news anyway? And I'd have to remember to ring Father Corrigan on Sunday. I hoped, wherever we were going, that there'd be a functioning phone . . .

Mrs Ellis was talking again. I tuned in. She didn't sit down consistently: she often got up and walked about as she spoke, or stood by the window, smoking. She was smoking by the window now. That was probably why she didn't bother to buy decent chairs, I thought shifting my tortured bum to the one spot on the chair I hadn't yet tried. She was telling us about her athletic prowess. Apparently she'd just missed the British Olympic gymnastic team in the late fifties, and later taken up swimming at a high level. She'd only do things she was good at, I reckoned.

Just before lunch, the Major popped out again, Claudia asked to go to the lavatory, presumably to check on any change in the status of the medicine-cabinet, and we were left alone. Mrs Ellis took up her place by the window, arms folded across her chest, one well-shod foot tapping. It seemed that she was impatient with our presence, yet she had kept us there. And was the documentary still on, or not?

Before I could ask, she said, 'Still interested in us, Miss Tanner?'

'Very,' I said.

'Well, perhaps I won't throw you out just yet. By the way, I'm sorry about your appointment with Tim Robertson.'

'My appointment . . .?'

'You were supposed to meet him this morning, I believe. After break.'

The bogus appointment he'd talked about in his room while we were fixing the real one, scribbling in my notebook. Her spy system worked well.

I was appalled. All my usual sharps were blunt. I'd completely forgotten. I'd been mooning over Barty, the day of my first meeting with Tim. What else had I missed? 'So I was,' I said. 'How silly of me. Perhaps I can see him in the lunch break.'

'I'm afraid not,' she said, smiling. 'He's well on his way to Wales by now. A last-minute place was available on this weekend's Brecon trip . . . My husband decided it would be just the thing for Tim. He isn't as fit as we'd like.'

She was watching for a reaction, which I didn't give. 'What a pity,' I said. 'Perhaps I could see him next week?'

'If you're still here, of course. Ah, here's your little assistant.' Claudia, back from the lavatory, smiled sweetly and sat down. She wasn't little. She must have been five foot eight. Mrs Ellis was probably jealous because Claudia had just as much hair as she had, in better condition. 'I haven't heard much from you, my dear,' said Mrs Ellis, patronizing. 'Have you any questions you'd like to ask?'

Claudia looked at me. I nodded. 'Well, yes, there is, Mrs Ellis,' she said in her elfin I-come-from-nowhere voice. 'What's going to happen when you and the Major retire?'

Mrs Ellis glanced at me. 'Haven't you discussed that with the Major?' I shook my head. She looked, fleetingly, relieved, and went on expansively: 'Of course we're giving it thought. Much thought. Nothing's decided yet. My father's vision mustn't die, but the Major's mortal, and the time will come when he must hand over to a younger man.'

'I see that,' said Claudia, 'but I don't see the financial side, quite. You've got a lot of capital tied up in the property, haven't you? Will you sell?'

'I don't see that it's any of your business,' said Mrs Ellis. 'As I understand it, your documentary is dealing with education—'

'But unfortunately,' said Claudia, 'education costs money, doesn't it? Like everything else. And part of the problem with evaluating educational systems is the cost. Like the problem with health services. If money was unlimited, then there'd be fewer difficult decisions to take.'

Good for Claudia. She was already strong on flannel. But we were never to know if Mrs Ellis had managed to work out that what Claudia'd said had nothing to do with the Major's retirement plans, because the phone rang.

Mrs Ellis answered it. 'Yes— Yes— Oh, I suppose so.' Ungraciously, she thrust the phone at me. 'I think the caller wants to speak to you.'

'Miss Turner? This is the Wanderotel. I have an urgent message for you.'

It was the Accelerated Trainee.

Chapter Twenty-One

I didn't know who might be listening in on the Rissington Abbey phone line, or what Mrs Ellis could overhear – she was standing very close to me. So I told the Trainee I'd come back to the hotel for the message, and rang off. It was a good excuse to avoid lunch in the canteen, anyway.

Mrs Ellis saw us down the stairs, across the hall and right into the car, as if to make sure we spoke to no one on the way out. She seemed irritated by our departure, and her four-square, arms-folded stare was following us up the drive every time I looked in the rear-view mirror.

'Who do you think the message is from?' said Claudia. 'Maybe the police have—'

'It won't be the police. Probably not ever, and certainly not yet. And don't waste time speculating on soon to be established facts,' I snapped priggishly. I was furious with myself. I'd cocked up. Forgetting the fake appointment with Tim was bad enough – on top of that, I'd lost him, perhaps just for the weekend, perhaps for ever. And I'd told him too much, all of which Mrs Ellis and her spy team might already know.

'Sorry,' said Claudia unapologetically.

I told her about Tim. 'Bad luck,' she said.

'Not bad luck. Bad judgement and bad management.'

'*Tant pis*,' said Claudia. 'Mrs Ellis had a good lift, didn't she? It'll be fine, once the bruising's gone.'

'What?'

'It was a face-lift, wasn't it?' Of course. But I didn't think it through, because Claudia was rattling on. 'I've got something for you. From the Browns' bathroom, look.' Another of her medicine-cabinet lists.

'I can't look, I'm driving,' I said. 'Tell me.'

'The usual aspirin etc. Hair dye, Mountain Ash. But – the really crucial thing – a diaphragm, and contraceptive cream.'

'So she had a late menopause and she's cautious,' I said. 'So what? She may be keeping them for sentimental reasons.'

'No, she isn't, not judging by the sell-by date on the cream. 1995 sometime, must have been bought quite recently.'

'So she's still sexually active. Good for her.'

'But who with?' said Claudia. '*Who with?*'

I saw what she meant. In a boarding-school: in a wheelchair: living with her son. 'It'd be difficult, having a lover,' I said, 'but not impossible. If he lived near by, with a place of his own.'

'All the same . . .' said Claudia.

' "My Alistair", you reckon?'

'That'd be evil, wouldn't it?'

'That'd be extraordinary,' I said.

'I bet Father Kelly would have called it evil. Plus, I went into Alistair's study by mistake on purpose. He was there.'

'What was he doing?'

'Working out. With weights. He has incredible muscles, a great body, if you like that kind of thing.'

I turned in to the hotel car park. 'Well done, Claudia. We'll talk about it in a minute, but we've got to pick up the message. Smile at the creep, but not too warmly, because I want him to concentrate.'

The Trainee was pleased with his skill in tracking us down at Rissington Abbey, and he wanted Claudia to know how he had done it. 'I had no idea where you were, of course, but then I remembered I'd taken a message with a local number, and I tried it, on the off-chance, and—'

I took my key and the message form.

5.6.92 am
Ring Mr Plumber MOST ERGENT

I dragged Claudia away from a still-talking Trainee.

'You were right about being nice to him,' she said. 'I bet he wouldn't have bothered trying to find us if I hadn't . . .'

Back in my room, I dialled Plummer, expecting to talk to his secretary. He must have given me his private number, because he answered. I'd never had a call answered by a solicitor before. I'd never even been put straight through to talk to one. They're always with a client.

So I knew before he spoke that it was indeed 'most ergent'. His creamy smooth voice could only be *almost* ruffled, but it was that. 'Miss Tanner? My client has expressed his urgent wish that you meet him, in France, tomorrow.'

'You'd better tell me who he is.'

'Baron Charles de Sauvigny Desmoulins.'

So it was the French grandfather. At least I'd been right about something. 'Saturday?' I said. 'What's so urgent? What's wrong with Monday?'

'I think it better if he explains that himself,' said Plummer with a distancing distaste. 'He is, of course, prepared to pay the appropriate weekend rate. And if you let him know the time your plane arrives at Toulouse, he'll send a car for you.'

I wouldn't do that. I'd hire a car of my own. Never depend on other people's transport; you can't get out.

I didn't actually have any choice. My time was bought and paid for. I got the address and telephone number from Plummer.

Next, I sent Claudia next door for packets of sugar that I didn't need, and rang to cancel Barty. He sounded disappointed. I expect, so did I. 'Where were we going?' I asked.

'Venice,' he said.

'Damn.' I've worked in Venice, and Florence too, and I loved them both. Polly's black Lycra dress would have been fine.

'Next weekend, maybe?' he said.

'I hope so. Let's talk on Monday.'

'I want to see you tonight. Can I come round for a drink?'

'I've got things to sort. I don't know when I'll be finished, and I may be leaving early on Saturday.'

'Nine o'clock. I'll be at home. Ring me if you're not through.'

There was no reason I could give for refusing, especially not the real one, that while he was on my mind I couldn't concentrate. I could always put him off . . .

Claudia was delighted. We were going to France. France she knew about. She didn't doubt for a moment that we were both going, and thinking about it, of course it made sense. She'd pay her own expenses and she could speak the language fluently. I expected the Baron to speak English, but there might be other solely French-speaking people hanging about that I'd want to communicate with. I'd almost lost sight of the central Olivier question in dealing with the peculiar shenanigans at Rissington Abbey.

Actually, the original problem remained unresolved. Why did Olivier's grandfather want to know his state of mind? If I could deal with that, and Kelly's turned out to be a straightforward depressive suicide, then I needn't even think about Rissington Abbey, perhaps. Or perhaps it would suddenly click into focus.

Claudia went ahead of me back to London by way of the *Banbury Courier*. I wanted a copy of the article Kelly'd written on last year's sports day. I warned her to pretend to be surprised if Cycling Shorts was full of the news of Kelly's tragic suicide. 'Of course,' she said.

I also gave her the Baron's address and telephone number, and the job of finding a morning plane, booking the flight, reserving a hire car, and ringing the Baron's house to tell them what time we'd be likely to arrive, making allowances for delays in the plane, etc. 'Can you handle that?' I said finally, when I'd explained.

'No problem. Give me your driver's licence number.'

'You'll need my credit card number as well.'

'No. I'll do it on mine.'

'OK, but make sure you're not out of pocket. Keep a record of your telephone calls, too. You can stay at my flat tonight, we'll need to get our act together. Get there about seven.'

When she'd left and I had the room back, I enjoyed the silence. I took my boots off and padded around packing and thinking about Kelly, especially our first meeting, and my first sight of him at the bar, lonely, with his cigarettes, Diet Coke, and crossword.

When I was packed and ready to go, I rang the station to check on the next fast train to London, the hire car place to tell them I was returning the Nissan, and then Polly to find out when she was leaving for the country.

She sounded plaintive. 'I'm not sure, Alex... About five, perhaps...'

'Five's hopeless for the traffic. Earlier or later. Make it later and we'll have time for a chat before you go. I'll be back about half-past four.'

'OK. When shall I leave?'

'Eight. Ring your parents and tell them not to wait dinner.'

'Eight's too late.'

'Seven?'

'The traffic won't be much better then.'

'I'd like to see you before you go.'

'OK, if you must.'

It was most unlike Polly to be so limp, and so sarky. The sooner I could see her, the better, I thought as I dialled Rissington Abbey and asked to speak to Mrs Ellis.

'Oh,' she said, sounding piqued. 'So you won't be coming back to us this afternoon?'

'No. Something urgent's come up in London . . . I was hoping to see you on Monday, if that's all right . . .'

'I'm not at all sure it will be,' she said. 'Perhaps you can telephone on Monday and see.'

A power freak, Mrs Ellis. 'If that's what you'd prefer,' I said obligingly, and put the phone down swearing under my breath.

Then I rang Barty again. 'Tell me the Baron's cancelled,' he said. 'Make my day.'

'No, sorry. You do crossword puzzles, don't you? OK. *Dark armour.*'

'Nine letters?'

'No idea.'

'A quick crossword, I presume?'

'Why?'

'It's hardly a clue at all.'

'What is it hardly a clue to?'

'*Blackmail.*'

Blackmail. Of whom? By whom? Kelly'd written the word on a page with his notes of last year's Sports Day at Rissington, just before *buttocks on the diving-board spotlight.* Say it was Olivier's buttocks: we knew he was diving. He'd been Olivier's priest. Maybe he knew Olivier was being blackmailed. Or blackmailing. More likely blackmailing, because young people weren't good victims for blackmail. They didn't have enough money, and they didn't have enough to lose.

That might be a reason for killing him. But there was no reason to suppose he was killed. And even if he had been, presumably his secrets had died with him. If he'd kept any evidence it had long gone: cleared away by whoever had gone through his room before Tim got there the morning after Olivier's death.

Tim. Observant, clever Tim, who'd shared a room with Olivier for nearly two terms. He'd know, probably. Wherever he was in the Brecons now, I wished I could talk to him.

Would he have confided in anyone? Surely not. Knowledge was power. He'd keep anything he knew close to his chest.

And then I remembered something. Matilda Beckford's kitchen: Matilda Beckford's eyes: Tim's barren study.

Her number was in the phone book.

'Mrs Beckford?'

'Yes?'

Her telephone manner was rusty. She held the receiver too far from her mouth and her voice trickled faintly across the wire.

'This is Alex Tanner here. Remember, I saw you last Tuesday, about the television programme on Rissington Abbey?'

'Oh, yes.'

'I've been talking to Tim. Isn't he nice?'

'Yes?'

'He's had to go away for the weekend unexpectedly. To the Brecon Beacons.'

'Oh, dear,' she said with more animation, 'poor Tim, he does hate the outdoors.'

'And he was worried about something. He asked me to check with you.'

'Yes?'

'The things he left with you for safekeeping.'

Silence. Had I bluffed her?

'Yes?'

I had bluffed her. Good. 'Everything's OK with them? They're still with you?' I asked at random, because I'd already found out what I wanted to know.

'Oh, dear, oh, my dear – is something wrong?'

'How do you mean?'

'Well, I gave them to the nice Chinese boy. Did I do wrong?'

'No, of course not, I soothed automatically. She sounded distraught.

'He brought the note, you see, the note from Tim, and so I gave them to him.'

'When was this?'

'About an hour ago. I never thought—'

'Tim probably changed his mind since he spoke to me and asked his friend to fetch them. That'll be it.'

She blethered some more, I soothed some more.

Then I rang off. I'd got something. But what?

I'd think about it later. Time I went to London.

Chapter Twenty-Two

Polly looked terrible. Her flat was hot, musty, and Poison-filled: the windows were shut against the world, and she wouldn't let me open them. Her sofa was a tangle of duvet and pillows. She sat in the centre of it, in a track suit that was much too big for her, which she hadn't changed as far as I knew for the past two days. Her hair was grubby, and for the first time since we'd met, I had the feeling that I didn't want to breathe in too deeply in her vicinity.

It was Friday, late afternoon. She hadn't been out since Barty had brought her back on Wednesday morning. I didn't think she'd washed. She'd drunk a bottle of gin in two days and her eyes looked as if they were colour co-ordinated for Christmas.

'We're going out,' I said.

'Let's have a drink first.'

'No. If you want a drink, we're going out to have one. And not a strong one, either, because you're driving. A healthful orange juice with a tiny trace of gin in it.'

'I haven't had a drink all day. We finished the gin last night.'

That was a better sign than it sounded. She was evidently confining herself to gin, because the house was full of other spirits left over from the party.

'You finished the gin. I was drinking coffee.'

'You always do,' she said cantankerously. 'Caffeine's very bad for you.'

'Get washed and changed and we'll go out.'

'I'm not going out. I can't put any make-up on.'

'Why not?'

'I can't bear to look at my face.'

'If you want a drink, we're going out. You needn't wear make-up. Just get clean.'

She complained all the way upstairs and into my bath. She complained when I washed her hair and when I took a flannel and soaped her, nearly all over. 'Flannels are unhygienic,' she said. She reminded me of Claudia. Why was I fated to deal with people who made massive fusses over tiny things? People who were probably much less healthy than me? I hadn't had a day's illness in my life, literally. The only time I was in hospital, as I told you earlier, was when someone else broke my leg. People's obsessions are strange. I don't argue with them. I just kept soaping her so she had to move, to wash the soap off, because I was using a supermarket own-brand and she only used special high-fat extra olive-oiled ultra-expensive soap which would keep her beautiful longer. That was a problem I didn't have.

Eventually she stood up and I dried her and pointed at the clean clothes I'd laid out on my bed.

'What if someone sees me?' she asked querulously. 'Those are my house-cleaning jeans. And that T-shirt's dreadful. It looks like one of yours.'

Nothing wrong with the T-shirt. It was old and thin, but clean, bright white, and easy to wear. Soft, baggy, cool enough for the sweltering weather, that's why I'd chosen it. 'If you don't want to wear those, choose your own,' I said briskly.

'I can't be bothered . . . But what if someone sees me?'

'If you're not done up they won't recognize you,' I said.

'I don't care anyhow . . . Just so long as we don't go to Faxes.'

That suited me fine. The cafés, bistros, and wine bars around our neck of the woods are all more or less smart, but Faxes was far and away the smartest. It was always full of the well-groomed twentysome-things that swarmed round Ladbroke Grove, looking as if they knew they were already something special, just watch this space for fame. Plus, usually, at least three or four of the genuinely famous or near-famous.

When we got there, Faxes had tables out on the pavement, in honour of the heatwave: so did Forty-Three, the smaller, less crowded place just opposite, also on Westbourne Park Road. I wanted to sit out but Polly insisted she didn't want the sun on her face, not without blocker. So we went into Forty-Three and I followed her to a far table near the window but screened from the rest of the room by two huge cheese plants.

The waiters at Forty-Three are always, for some reason (A gay

146

owner? An Australian?) tall, muscular, and blond, looking as if they've just stepped off the Bondi Beach Shuttle. Our waiter introduced himself as David. He was well up to the usual standard and I tried not to stare at his jean-hugged crotch as I ordered Polly a double freshly squeezed orange juice and two ham and cheese croissants, her favourite, and myself some coffee.

She looked round uneasily at first, then relaxed a bit when she saw no one she knew. They couldn't have seen us through the cheese plants, as it was. 'Now you can tell me what's really the matter,' I said.

'Clive's left me,' she said blankly.

'I know that. But you didn't want the relationship to go anywhere anyway. I'm worried about you, Polly. Trust me. You know I'll never tell another living soul.'

She started to cry without sobbing. Tears rolled down her cheeks and plopped on to the T-shirt. 'I can't say ... It'll sound so stupid ...'

'No it won't,' I lied.

'It's my life. My meaningless life. I'll be thirty next birthday, and what have I done? I don't have a proper man, I don't have any children. Both my sisters have children, people to call them Mummy, people who they matter to ... I haven't done anything. OK, I've been famous, but that makes it worse. I've been something, it's past, it'll be all downhill from here, my looks'll go, and who'll I be?'

'You've got more money than you ever need. You'll be a chartered accountant, so you'll have a career. And you're one of the nicest human beings I've ever met.'

'I'm not nice at all. And even if I was, that's not enough ... And the money's nothing. You keep on about it, Alex, it matters to you. It doesn't matter to me.'

'It'd sure as hell matter if you didn't have any.'

'I need something to live for. I've got to have something to live for, something to look forward to when I get up in the morning, something to buy clothes for and put make-up on for – oh, shit, it's Clive.'

'Forget Clive,' I said impatiently.

'No, I mean it's Clive, over there at Faxes – it's Clive, with Cassie.' My eyes followed her pointing finger. There, at one of the pavement tables opposite, was Clive. And, smugly under her writhing red hair, Cassie. Loyalty to Polly didn't prevent me from noticing that Cassie looked deliciously cool in a yellow linen shirt and a tiny pale green linen skirt.

'Let's go,' I said.

'I'm not walking out there past that woman. Not looking like this. I don't want him to see me looking like this. He'll guess I'm upset. I don't want him to know I'm upset, or her, I don't want them to know—'

Her voice was sliding upwards towards hysteria. 'If you start screaming, they will know,' I said flatly. 'Get a grip, Polly. If we just walk straight out, past them, he won't even notice. You don't look like yourself. You just look ordinary, like me. He won't give you a second look.' I didn't point out also that he was so busy looking into Cassie's eyes and showing off that the chances were he'd notice nothing but Cassie anyway, even if Madonna strutted past in a bustier.

David brought Polly's hot croissants and, as he put them down, he winked at me. That was the first time, ever, that when I was out with Polly a man noticed me, not her. She'd noticed, too. She looked at the croissants and pushed them away. 'Hey' – I caught David's attention as he turned away – 'is there a back way out of here? There's someone outside we don't want to meet.'

He shrugged his shoulders and spread his hands. 'Sorry. Just the one entrance.'

Polly was lamenting. 'I didn't even bring my bag – I've got no make-up – Alex, you told me not to bring my bag – You made me wear these awful awful jeans and this rag of a T-shirt—'

'I told you not to bring your bag because you didn't need money. I didn't know you'd have to do a quick change into Polly Coyne, Top Model.'

'It's all your fault,' said Polly helplessly, and I lost patience.

'Come on,' I said, grabbed her by the upper arm and started dragging her through to the back of the wine bar.

'Where are we going?'

'To the lavatory, in case there's a window.'

I opened the lavatory door and pushed her ahead of me into the tiny space. There was an outer section, just large enough for condom and sanitary-towel machines, a basin, and a vanity top under the wall mirror. Beyond, a door led to the lavatory itself. I checked it for a window: there wasn't one.

'I'm not walking out past Clive.'

'We can wait until they go.'

'It'll be hours, I expect. Once he's got to a place, Clive doesn't like to leave.' She began to cry again, presumably at the tender memory of Superlimpet Clive.

It wasn't a moment for sympathy. With sympathy, she'd dissolve into wailing screams, I'd have to carry her out in a fireman's lift, and even Clive would glance away from Cassie's eyes and break off his minute-by-minute account of his triumphs at nursery school to watch our progress. The whole street would see. Probably even the dope dealers would stop trading and the undercover policemen stop watching them. And if there were any journalists—

I up-ended my bag on the vanity top, emptied my jeans pockets on top of the pile, and said: 'That's it.'

'What?' sobbed Polly.

'That's what we've got. To tart you up, so we can go home.'

Polly's shaking fingers poked through my organizer, credit cards, money, boiled sweets ... 'I can't do anything with this.'

'Yes, you can. Think. It's your job. It's what you're good at. Start with the clothes. What can you do with the clothes?'

She looked down at herself, at the worn, baggy jeans and the loose T-shirt. 'Nothing,' she said helplessly.

'Your legs. You've got to be able to use the legs. They're twenty feet long, Polly, they're luscious and brown and shapely – How about rolling up your jeans?' Her huge, empty eyes were fixed on me, and I saw the second her brain clicked in.

'Don't be silly,' she said, picking up my army knife. 'Does this thing have scissors?'

'Sure,' I said. 'Where do I cut?'

She showed me. I started sawing through the tough material of the jeans legs seven inches above her knee. 'Is this going to be short enough?' I asked as I cut.

'Of course not,' she said impatiently, 'then we roll them up to my buttocks – hurry up, Alex, I need to get started on the T-shirt.' When the second leg fell away she unlaced her trainers, took them off, and kicked the spare denim into a corner. 'I need your socks,' she said. 'And your belt. Give me the scissors.' She pulled the T-shirt over her head and started hacking away at it. We were standing close together. There was no other choice in there. I could smell the soap I'd washed her with, and the room-smell of drains overlaid with air freshener which

149

seemed to suggest a much worse smell underneath. But I didn't mind, because she was beginning to come back. She was beginning to be alive again.

'String. Or ribbon,' she said. I have to tie up my hair.' Her hair hung, limp and ageing, straight to her shoulders.

'Strips of the T-shirt?'

'Could. They'll look raggy and they won't grip, and I need colour near my face. How can you not have any make-up in your bag?'

I sorted through my change and fed it into the machine. 'Condoms,' I said when the packet came clicking out. 'Different colours. They'll grip.'

'Great. Trim them . . . Use the pink.' I clipped away at two pink condoms while she tied the now much shorter T-shirt just under her breasts and splashed her chest with water. 'Good,' she said when the cotton clung. She put on my thick socks, then her trainers, and rolled the socks down so they were thick against her ankles, and made her lower leg seem even slimmer, her calves more curved.

She knotted up her hair with deft twists of her fingers. 'Now, the face.' She looked at her face in the mirror and I looked with her. She was chalky pale and her eyes, undefined, looked insignificant. 'Matches,' she said. 'Burn some matches.'

'What for?'

'Eye-liner. Don't burn them too far.' I struck, held, blew out match after match. As I finished each one she took it from me and worked on her eyes.

When she'd finished we both looked at her face again. Her eyes were huge, dark, defined, but her face and lips looked even paler, especially against the warm honey-brown of so much exposed body-skin. 'I've got lip salve,' I offered. She put it on and then started biting her lips. I watched the colour surge back. 'The cheeks are easy,' she said. 'Just before I go, I slap them. Nearly ready, Alex?'

I piled everything back into my bag – my things, her discarded bra and jeans-legs – while she threaded my belt through the waistband of her jeans and fastened it tight. 'Hang on a minute,' I said, and went in search of David the gorgeous waiter. I paid him for the food and drink we hadn't used, and then explained the situation, very briefly. 'Walk her to the end of the road, round the corner, out of sight, OK?'

'Sure,' he said eventually. He wasn't quick, but he was beautiful, and Clive wouldn't be measuring his IQ.

I opened the door to the lavatory again. 'Face-slapping time,' I said. 'Here's your prop,' waving a hand at David, tall, stupid, eye-catching.

'Holy shit,' he said as she took his arm. 'You used to be Polly Coyne.'

She still was. I grabbed the cheese and ham croissants – I'd paid for them, after all – and followed Polly and David at a safe distance. She strutted her stuff along the catwalk of Westbourne Park Road, every eye in the place following her, including Clive's. He half-stood up: Cassie put a hand on his arm, pulled him down again. Polly looked up into David's face, sharing an intimate joke. They might have been lovers for weeks.

Round the corner we thanked and dismissed David and set off for home. 'It's all your fault, Alex. You shouldn't have made me come out like this,' said Polly.

I'd been feeling modestly pleased with myself, for thinking of the condoms and David, and the whole tarting-up procedure. My beltless jeans kept sliding down around my hips and, without socks, my boots rubbed. I didn't say anything. 'Now you're being patient with me,' she said. 'I can't stand it.'

Chapter Twenty-Three

The one-sided row went on, more or less, until I waved Polly off only ten minutes before Claudia was due to arrive. I trailed disconsolately round the flat trying not to remember that if my client hadn't summoned me to France on a whim, I'd have been packing for a weekend with Barty.

I hadn't told Polly about the change of plan because she'd have used it as fuel for renewed attack on me, and because she might have cancelled her visit to her parents. Better, if she was going to fall apart, that she'd be with them.

Even if I had no grip at all on what was going on at Rissington Abbey, at least I was nearer to understanding what was wrong with her. If I hadn't liked her so much I'd have seen it sooner.

Ever since I moved in next to Polly and our friendship began, it was always *her* being kind to *me*. I'd got used to it. She was the perfect one, I was the gauche outsider from the wrong side of the tracks. I didn't mind that role. It was nearly true. So I played it, and Polly was Lady Bountiful. What I was beginning to see now was that she couldn't cope if she wasn't the one giving all the time. She couldn't take.

She didn't want to go back to her family because she didn't want to take from them, she didn't want their sympathy. She'd chosen Clive because she always wanted to be in control. Now that had broken down she couldn't cope with it. Perfect Polly had gone. Perfect Polly, wounded, was a vulnerable flailing bitch. I hoped our friendship would survive it. I didn't mind her being a bitch. Everyone has the right to be a bitch sometimes. I liked her, if anything, rather more. She'd been too good to be true, before.

But her outburst must have been humiliating for her. People find it difficult to forgive you for watching them behave badly. There was a lot of water under the bridge with Polly and me: I hoped there was enough to wash away the aftertaste of this.

I looked around for the Rissington Abbey promotional video I'd asked her to watch. She hadn't mentioned it. I expected she hadn't even bothered to run it. I'd better have a look at it, I thought. It would be something mindless to do, and at least Claudia would shut up through it. I didn't want her discussing the case, asking questions I couldn't answer, and disturbing my thought processes. And as far as I knew videos didn't contain additives so she couldn't preach at me either.

I took a superficial look through Polly's flat but I couldn't find it, and after all it didn't matter very much. I considered starting work on cleaning up her flat, but my heart wasn't in it. I'd have time on Sunday, and I'd do it then, when her abuse of me wasn't ringing quite so loudly in my ears.

Back in my own flat, I packed for Toulouse. Only a toothbrush, clean underwear, and two clean T-shirts in case we had to stay overnight.

Then Claudia arrived, with her stepfather Dieter.

Dieter was in his forties, small, dark, dapper, bespectacled, and self-important. His scornful glance didn't think much of my flat. Not expensive enough, probably: you wouldn't have got much change out of seven thousand pounds for his pinstripe suit, Bond Street shirt and tie, Rolex watch, and hand-made shoes. The after-shave probably cost a bomb as well. It filled the air around him, soaring effortlessly over Claudia's now-familiar young girl's perfume – Chloe, perhaps, or Lagerfeld.

He didn't think much of me either. Who was I? What was I doing with his stepdaughter? Where were we going, the next day, and who would we see? When would we be back?

I kept my temper, just. I didn't point out that I was doing Claudia a favour, however much she paid me. I didn't point out that at least, unlike Alan (who he approved of) I wasn't trying to get into Claudia's pants, or that I knew several people who had poncy flats and regular jobs with big corporations and were still incompetent, or crooked, or both. I raked up impressive acquaintances for references, wrote down their names and phone numbers, gave him a cup of coffee, and nodded appreciatively while he told me how important he was and therefore how important Claudia was.

I didn't gather exactly what he did, though it seemed to be connected with banking. I switched off when he started in on the ERM and the weakness of the pound, and the lack of moral fibre and plain economic common sense of the British. I didn't even chant *Two world wars and one world cup, doodah, doodah*, though I was tempted.

After he went I smiled at an embarrassed Claudia. 'I am sorry,' she began. 'He's trying to look after me, at the moment. It's a difficult time for him.'

'Why?'

'My mother's new lover is an Englishman. Richer, and taller, and more attractive than Dieter. Besides—'

She hesitated. I hadn't known her hesitate before. 'Besides?' I prompted.

'He desires me. It is difficult, with stepfathers.'

'How many have you had?'

'Just two.'

'Do they both desire you?'

'Oh, yes.'

'And do you desire them?'

'Oh, no. I am a virgin.'

The logic escaped me. Myself, I'd been a very randy virgin, and so had my mates at school. Also – 'What were you doing with that kid at my party then?'

She blushed. 'Oh, just – messing around. I wanted Alan to think I was unfaithful to him, so he would not mind me leaving—'

'That poor red-headed kid. You held out on him all evening?'

'But of course. I am a virgin.'

I left it. Of all the unanswered questions I had on my plate at the moment, Claudia's sexuality had Priority Z. 'Tell me what arrangements you've made for tomorrow,' I said.

The arrangements seemed OK. We were on the British Airways 8.25 a.m. flight to Toulouse, due to see the Baron at 2 p.m., and we had reservations in the Wanderotel, Toulouse, in case we had to stay over. She'd brought maps. She wanted to show them to me and explain the route, but I wouldn't listen.

'And I've got the photocopy of Kelly's sports day article,' she said. 'The article isn't important but I'm sure the photograph means something. I just don't know what.'

It was a featured piece and the pic was portrait shape, four inches by eight. At the top of the frame, a figure poised on the diving-board. Olivier. Watching him, faces tilted upwards, a group of people.

Some were familiar: the Major, Mrs Ellis, Alistair Brown. One was famous: Peter Hayes the runner, the sports day visiting celebrity. The others looked like parents.

Olivier was in silhouette. 'There's our buttocks on the diving-board,' I said. 'Probably.' It might also be our potential blackmail victims, I thought, but I wasn't going to explain my *dark armour* theory to her now.

'So what does it mean?'

'Don't know, yet. Are you hungry?'

'No. I've eaten.'

I went to the kitchen, fetched the croissants, and ate them. I was sitting on the sofa: she sat crosslegged on the floor, opposite me, and watched me alertly. 'Shall we discuss the case?' she said.

I wanted to do anything but that. My mind works much better when I let things silt down into it. 'Can you use a word processor?' I asked.

'Of course.'

'Type up your ideas for me. Questions that need answering, leads we need to follow. It'll help you focus your ideas, and we'll talk about it tomorrow.' It was make-work, but it wouldn't hurt. I introduced her to my old Amstrad, left her getting acquainted, and lay on the sofa with my eyes closed until the printer's chatter told me Claudia had finished. 'This machine is very out-of-date,' she said dismissively.

'That machine was very cheap,' I said. 'And it works.'

'I have a portable Toshiba that runs MS-DOS. IBM compatible.'

'Bully for you. We'll use it when we need to talk to IBM. By the way, Barty's coming around soon, for a drink. You met at my party—'

'The man who threw me out?'

'The very one.'

'Do you want to be alone? I can sleep at home, tonight.'

'Stay. Much easier. We'll have to leave at some ungodly hour tomorrow—'

'Latest check-in time, seven fifty-five. I ordered a taxi for six-thirty, from here—'

'There you are then. We'll leave things as they are.'

'If you're sure.'

'Certain.'

'Anything else I can do?' she said briskly.

'Record a new answering-machine message. We'll leave the number of the French hotel in case Alan panics or Polly wants to ring.'

'OK,' she said, and set about it efficiently. The message she recorded began 'Alex Tanner and her assistant aren't available right now . . .' When she finished, she explained apologetically, 'I just thought it always sounds good, to have an assistant. The bigger your staff, the better you're doing. Oh, I forgot. I brought a video to show you.' She produced it from her overnight bag. 'Michel Mouche and Freedom Pertwee, and Olivier, about ten years ago.'

'Olivier? Was he a child singer, or something?'

'Not really, though he sings on this. How well do you know French television?'

'Hardly at all.'

'It's very in-bred and nepotistic. There aren't that many Francophone entertainers.'

'Francophone?'

'French-speaking. That's very important in France, where everybody knows that French is the best language and only fools can't speak it. So when they have a singer or whatever, he or she appears on television all the time, and quite often brings along his relations. The last television award ceremony I watched in France mostly consisted of three families giving each other awards.'

'How come you've got this video?'

'I was a fan of Mouche's when I was little – still am, come to that – and this was a birthday present when I was much younger. I moved all my stuff over to the flat in London when Mummy bought it for me – I wanted a place of my own, if Mummy and Dieter are going to be breaking up, I wanted somewhere of my own to keep out of it – I don't like the breakups – and I brought everything of mine over. I don't have enough cupboards, I never throw things away' – I reminded myself not to ask Claudia any open-ended questions if I wanted to keep her chatter-genie in the bottle. She was just finishing – 'so I have the video. I thought maybe you would like to see your client when he was just a boy.'

'And when he was still alive,' I said. 'Not that he's my client.'

'But he's your subject, the person all this is about.'

She put in her video and ran it back. 'We'll only see it in black and white, though it was made in colour. The TV system is different. And it's in French, of course, but most of it is singing anyway. I'll translate if you want – I thought you'd just like to see them.'

I settled myself on the floor with my back to the sofa, my favourite position for telly watching. Claudia came and sat beside me with the remote-control.

The first few minutes were typical light entertainment. The host had a wig, a frenetic line in chat, and a false-toothed, omnipresent smile. The set was cramped and dated. 'When did you say this was?'

'1982. Ten years ago.'

The set looked more old-fashioned than that. Six chorus-girls, wearing less than they would have ten years ago in England, waved their legs about more or less in time to accordion music. 'Claudia, do they still use that corny music?'

'Of course. It's very popular. Typically French.'

The girls danced off. A pop group came on, and sang. 'The sound quality's terrible,' I said.

'Different system. Pal, or Secam, can't remember which. Like the colour, it doesn't travel well. Here's Michel now. Isn't he gorgeous?'

He was in his forties, a big man, dark-haired, pale-eyed, shambling, three days unshaven, wearing jeans, a sweater, and what looked like old tennis shoes on bare feet. He began to talk. He was uncoordinated and his face was heavy and sloppy. 'He looks drunk,' I said.

'He probably is – he sounds drunk, as well.' I couldn't tell: all French speech was the same to me. 'He's talking about Freedom. He's telling an obscene story, about the first time they – made love.'

The host was looking equal parts enthralled and shocked, and he didn't try to interrupt. 'Translate, Claudia.'

'And she gripped me with her legs, and I possessed her all the way to her delicious teeth,' said Claudia obediently, 'and—'

The doorbell rang, Claudia stopped the video, I went downstairs to open the door to Barty. I was still laughing and I began to explain as he followed me back to the flat. 'Barty, you've met Claudia,' I said. 'She's my new assistant.' He looked surprised – perhaps at me having an assistant, perhaps at it being Claudia – but either way, it wouldn't hurt for him to know that I could surprise him. They greeted each other warmly, as if the party eviction had created a bond between them.

'Come and watch the rest of the video,' I said. 'We'll go out for a drink later.'

Claudia had paused the video on a frame of Mouche's face, decadent and drunk with the faint pause wobble making it seem as if he was

157

shaking, which most of the time he probably was. 'It's that fraud Mouche,' said Barty. 'The devil with blue eyes.'

'What?' I was lost.

'That is what they call him, in France. Because he is so beautiful,' said Claudia.

'Not any more he isn't,' I said. 'And I bet he looks even worse, now.'

'Why are we watching him?' said Barty.

'He's the father of the boy, Olivier, whose death I'm investigating,' I said.

'You didn't tell me that.'

'You didn't ask. You've come in at a critical moment. He's just possessed her up to her perfect teeth,' I said.

'Fair enough. Is squeaky-voiced Freedom the owner of the teeth in question?'

'Yes.' Barty began to settle himself on the floor between us, and Claudia protested. 'You can't sit on the floor! Not in a suit! And it is a *very* good suit, isn't it?'

'A Mother Teresa of suits,' said Barty. 'Good enough to put up with a little harsh treatment, I think.'

'Why are you wearing it?' I said. Barty dressed formally very seldom: usually only for court appearances, when someone tried to prevent one of his whistle-blowing documentaries being shown.

'What do you mean, a Mother Teresa of suits?' said Claudia. 'I don't understand.'

'She's literal-minded,' I explained. 'Don't worry about it, Claudia. Get on with the video, for God's sake.'

She pressed 'play' and we were off. Mouche was still talking, the host was aghast and smiling. Most of the studio audience looked stunned: the rest seemed comatose. 'Translate!' I demanded.

Claudia and Barty spoke at the same time.

CLAUDIA: I filled her with my angel-milk and she became a slave to love

BARTY: I came inside her and she liked it

CLAUDIA: And of this mating of the gods, beautiful Olivier was created

BARTY: That was when Olivier was conceived

158

'Stop the tape!' I said. 'Hang on. I can't cope with this simultrans. One or the other of you do it, I don't mind which.'

Barty bowed to Claudia, across me. 'Yours is more elegant.'

She bowed back. 'Yours is more English.'

I grabbed the remote control, ran the tape back, and told Claudia to get on with it. The host was talking. 'Will the beautiful Freedom like the secrets of her heart to be shared with three million viewers?' translated Claudia.

'He'll be lucky, three million viewers,' said Barty.

'Freedom is my love slave,' said Mouche, through Claudia. It was like a seance, with Claudia's reedy voice floating over his drunken politically incorrect growl. Then the camera shifted to fix on a tall slender girl in a clinging left-over-seventies jersey dress, who was slinking on to the set leading a beautiful dark-eyed six-year-old boy by the hand. Olivier, before the vodka and the diving-board hit him. He was dressed in a sort of page-boy outfit. Dark, though I couldn't tell in black and white what shade of dark, velvet and a wide white lace collar, and shiny shoes with buckles. He must have felt a prat, I thought sympathetically, as Mouche lumbered to his feet and picked the boy up in a bear-hug, then started covering his face in kisses, ending up in a kiss on the mouth.

'Lucky Olivier, to be so loved,' said Claudia. Barty and I were both cringing. No wonder Olivier had turned to blackmail. If he had.

Mouche was talking, still holding the boy, looking down into his face. 'Olivier is my life, my soul, my being,' said Mouche/Claudia. 'He is my future, my immortality.'

I felt uncomfortable at the display of drunken emotionalism. 'Bye-bye future,' I said.

'Now father and son will sing,' said host/Claudia. An amateurish pianist started an intro and then father and son went into an excruciating version of a song I didn't recognize but Claudia said was Mouche's. The boy kept missing his words and looking round for help, as if he wanted to escape. Freedom stood by smiling vaguely and tapping her bare, bony feet out of time to the music.

'She looks out of it, as well,' I said. She had rather thin, long hair. You couldn't tell the colour, but it wasn't dark. 'What's the song about?'

'It's about Freedom. About how she's called Freedom because her eyes are the colour of the sky.'

The song finished and father, mother, and son embraced. I paused the video and went to the kitchen to get drinks. Claudia wanted mineral water, Barty and I white wine. Barty called to me, 'I picked up something for you in the States. Two Sue Graftons and a Sara Paretsky. Remind me to bring them in from the car.'

'Thanks,' I said, coming back with the tray.

'Oh, please, get them now,' said Claudia. 'I'd like to see them.' She was standing by the French window, looking out. Barty and I shouted a warning at the same time:

'Stop!'

'Wait!'

She looked puzzled. 'It's the balcony,' I said. 'It isn't safe. It isn't a balcony, it's a shelf for window-boxes.'

She moved further into the room, shrugging. 'I'd love to see your presents,' she said.

Now Barty looked puzzled, but he stood up obligingly.

'Don't bother, Barty,' I said. 'She doesn't know they're books.'

'*Books*?' said Claudia, cheated. 'Oh, no, please . . . don't bother.'

Barty still looked puzzled. 'She thought you'd bought me designer clothes,' I said.

'I thought those names were new designers, that I'd never heard of,' said Claudia blushing. I distributed the drinks and waved at the television to cover her embarrassment: I hate looking a fool, myself, and I'm so half-educated that I often did until I learned to shut up if I wasn't sure. The video was still paused on Mouche, Freedom, and Olivier. I said the first thing that came into my head. 'Family group. Does anything strike you?'

Barty chipped in immediately. 'I've never liked Mouche. Drunken fraud. The woman's a nonentity, and I don't trust people who change their names.'

'Especially because their eyes are the colour of the sky,' I said at random.

Then it hit us both at once. Barty choked on his wine: I gasped: we stared at little Olivier staring at us.

'What is it?' said Claudia. 'I don't understand.'

'Genetics,' said Barty.

'Mendel and the peas,' I said. 'Two blue-eyed people can't produce a brown-eyed child. Not even in a mating of the gods.'

160

Chapter Twenty-Four

It didn't take Barty and me long to calm down and work out that the Great Olivier Discovery didn't get my enquiry much further forward. Apart from everything else, it was so obvious that it must have been commented on before. Surely Michel Mouche couldn't not have known. Perhaps his harping on, and on television yet, about his paternity of Olivier was a gigantic bluff, or at the least an attempt to cover his insecurity over the issue.

Either way, I didn't see how it fitted in with the information I had, or explained any of my unanswered questions.

Claudia was so excited that she insisted on telling Barty the whole story from the beginning, about Olivier and Rissington Abbey. When she started on Martin Kelly I shook my head, and she ground to a halt. Barty was getting restive. By this time it was nearly eleven o'clock and I expected him to go home, but he obviously wanted to talk to me alone.

'Let's go out for a drink,' he said.

I didn't want to be inside and I didn't want a drink. I wanted to be outside. I wanted to have an element of freedom, a possible escape when Barty broke whatever unpleasant news Barty was going to break. He knew I had an early plane to catch: I kept yawning: it wasn't like him to push it unless he really needed to get it over with. Anything personal with that degree of urgency about it couldn't be good news, I reckoned.

Claudia almost scooped me out, eventually. She, like Polly, seemed to take an interest in my love-life. I don't know why I attract that kind of interference. I don't invite it.

It was almost cool, in Hyde Park. We were walking south-west from Marble Arch, towards the Serpentine. I like the Park at night but seldom go there alone. Polly's persuaded me it's foolhardy. We were walking in as close to silence as you ever get in Central London.

After ten minutes we reached the Serpentine and started to skirt it. The café was just closing: eleven o'clock, it would be. All the boats were in. The few people left were drifting back to their cars, the ducks had gone wherever they go at night, leaving slimy droppings on the paths to remind us of their existence.

'Permission to speak?' said Barty.

'What?'

'Can I talk?'

'Sure. My ears have recovered from Claudia's assault.'

'She's a nice kid. With a crush on you.'

'Not specifically me. She's got a crush on Life and the Media, and how she's going to eat it up and spit it out.'

'Perhaps,' said Barty. 'Anyway, she's very excited about the Great Olivier Discovery.'

'Yeah. It doesn't make much difference, as far as I can see, whose child he was. It's very common, as well. I saw a statistic somewhere – research, in the West country I think – twenty per cent of babies born in one hospital couldn't have been their official father's child.'

'Why've you taken on an assistant, Alex? I thought you couldn't afford it.'

'I can't afford not to. She's paying me, to train her. Don't worry, it's just a whim of hers, and we're only doing a week, and I know, what kind of training can I give her?'

'She's lucky.'

I stopped by a bench. 'Why don't we sit down, and then you can say whatever you *were* going to say? I've got to catch an early plane.' I sat down, but he didn't. He stood with his hands in his pockets, frowning.

'I wanted to talk to you. About Miranda, among other things.'

Miranda's his ex-wife.

'Yeah,' I said. 'How is she?'

'Better. She's going back to her own place tomorrow.'

That hit me. Hard. I was ready to hear that they were going to give it another go, as soon as he mentioned her name. I was armoured for that and what I actually heard slipped under my defences. 'Good,' I said. 'Do sit down. You're towering over me.' It wasn't like him to be tense.

'I wanted you to know that.'

'Now I do, what do you want me to say?'

He sighed impatiently. 'I want to have a conversation with you. You know, a conversation, where two people explain things to each other and reach an understanding.'

'I thought we did.'

'No. You didn't. You can't. You're not stupid. You must know that when we talk you behave like Ronald Colman dancing up and down the castle steps in the duel in *The Prisoner of Zenda*.'

'That was before my time. I only saw the remake, on a Sunday afternoon. With Richard Todd.'

'Stewart Granger,' he corrected automatically. I didn't pursue it. I knew he'd be right, about Stewart Granger. Of course he was right about me.

Silence. I looked to my right, towards the stone that commemorated the help we'd given to some Scandinavian country during the war. Must be odd to remember a time when Britain was in a position to help the Scandinavians. I nearly asked Barty if he remembered which country it was and what we'd done for them, then realized he'd think it was another piece of rapier-waving. Which it might have been.

'I don't know any history,' I said. 'Not really. Not the kind you used to get taught as a matter of course, about what happened in England, and why the war finished us. We did Colonialism and Post-Colonialism in Africa.'

He sat down beside me. 'That's history too,' he said.

'Not mine. And there weren't any facts in it. Lots of empathy. I got top marks for my project. Diary of a Yoruba Tribeswoman.'

'Did you win a gold star?'

'You must be joking. Competition? Dirty word. We had no stars, not to stick on our work, not to look up to.'

'Do you resent it?'

'Not really. The teachers meant well. They just weren't very bright, or the theory was wrong, or something. They spent all their time trying to help us emotionally, which they couldn't, and they didn't teach us anything, which they maybe could. Which is why I can empathize with anything except an educated white middle-class male.'

'That's too neat to be true,' he said gently.

'It's too true to be ignored.'

More silence. We both pretended to watch a man in a macintosh walk past. A macintosh? In this weather?

'Flasher?' I said.

'Probably . . . Alex, you've got an early plane.'

'I just said that . . . Why are you in a suit? Were you in court today?'

'That was the other thing I wanted to talk to you about. The project I've been working on. Why I didn't involve you. Why I didn't hire you.'

'Don't tell me, you've found a better researcher.'

'There aren't any better . . . Some as good, though.'

'Name them.'

'If you're so smart, guess what I've been working on.'

'Worst possible scenario?'

'Yes.'

'Dangerous, or just likely to lead to weeks in court followed by months in prison?'

'Both.'

I'd thought we were half-joking. Now, I saw he wasn't, and kept asking. 'In America? East Coast?'

'And Chicago, and LA.'

'This side of the Atlantic, as well?'

'Yes.'

I thought I knew, but I couldn't believe that anybody I liked could be so stupid. Not even Don Quixote O'Neill, padded by inherited money, floating on aristocratic insouciance. 'Earth to Barty. Come in, please,' I said blankly. 'Tell me we're not talking about the American funding of the IRA.'

'We are.'

'Oh, shit,' I said. 'At least tell me you're employed by a big, big, well-insured production company, who'll pay your legal fees.'

'No.'

'Your own project?'

'Yes.'

I was speechless. No wonder he hadn't told me anything about it. Partly to protect me, maybe: more because I'd have given him such a hard time. Rule one, never mix with the IRA. They're unstable, ruthless, bigoted . . . Rule two, if you must, make sure you're backed by big money. If you get anywhere with the IRA, the British security services want to know about it. They want names and dates and places and they take your material and they prevent it being shown so you can't even cover the seed money you spent researching it, and they take you to court if you don't do what they want and the legal fees can be horrendous. That doesn't so much worry the British government, who are

164

backing the other side. But for a single small operator, they can wipe you out. Barty wasn't even really rich, I didn't think. He was rich by my standards, but not seriously rich. Not funding legal fees without thinking twice rich. And if he was in prison it wouldn't exactly help his business.

'You've been working on the one project all this year?'

'Yes.'

'And you've been funding yourself?'

'Yes.'

I thought about it. It explained a lot. Not everything: he hadn't been in touch with me for other reasons as well. 'And you didn't get in touch with me, also, because of your ex-wife?'

'I hadn't heard from Miranda for a year when she turned up, sobbing, two days before your party. I was giving you time to think. About me. Did you think about me?'

'Of course.'

'What did you think?'

'I didn't know.'

'Did you miss me?'

'Yes,' I said. 'Of course.'

He stood up. 'Right. Time you went home.'

I kept sitting. 'Is that it?' I said, rather blankly. I didn't know what I'd expected to happen, but it was more than this sudden dismissal.

'That's it. Are we on for next weekend?'

'Barring accidents,' I said flippantly. 'Venice again?'

'If that's what you'd like.'

'I'd like it very much. And you mustn't waste the tickets. Where are we staying?'

'The Danieli.'

'On your own money? You can't chalk it up to someone's expenses?'

'*You* probably could. I don't have your creative approach to accounting. I always meant to ask you, where did you learn, or was it native wit?'

'Mostly native wit. Helped along by an early boyfriend, a BBC cameraman.'

'That explains it . . . Come on, Alex, home. You're tired.'

I was. Most unusually, I was, probably because now he hadn't told me anything really awful I allowed myself to feel it. I'd tensed up to cope with whatever he was going to hit me with. And it hadn't been so bad. I didn't really think any harm would come to him from the IRA, perhaps because you don't believe those things unless they actually happen. It was an idea, not a reality, like the bombs you knew they planted round London but they didn't stop you living there and you didn't actually give them more than a momentary tut-tut unless they blew up in your face. There was too much else to do, and think about, just living.

My real fear had been that he would tell me something personal. That he was going back to his wife. That he'd met an enchanting American. That he was going into a monastery. That he'd decided not to hire me again. Anything final, irrevocable, that would mean I'd lose him. Not that I wanted him . . .

We walked back through the rustling trees. There was a breeze, a cooler breeze. 'I think the weather's breaking,' I said. 'About time. And I'm glad you told me what you've been up to, the last few months.'

'Why?'

He thought I was going to say something intimate. For a moment, so did I. But I wasn't ready yet to make concessions. I had to think, about what I wanted from him, about what we were going to do and be together. So I didn't. 'At least I can empathize with you now,' I said. 'You being mentally challenged, and all.'

Saturday, June 6th

Chapter Twenty-Five

Toulouse has a manky little airport, new and clean and smug, but at first sight, I quite liked the town. It reminded me of Birmingham, which isn't London but is a long way from country. Apart from that, it was hot and dusty and Southern, with the combination of big-city grubbiness and potential for violence which I find exhilarating.

So far, I'd only seen it from the ring road. We'd been met at the barrier by a chauffeur in full uniform carrying a placard:

Mlle TANNER, Alex

I'd sent Claudia with my driving licence to pick up the hire car, and now the smart black Citroën and its smart French driver was piloting us and the hired Peugeot through heavy traffic on the way out of Toulouse.

We went on to a motorway, and took a ticket: off the motorway, and paid the toll with Claudia's francs. I hadn't asked her to get any, but she had. Her common sense wasn't bad. Then we were on winding country roads, full of fruit trees, heavy with blossom. We couldn't go fast on the minor roads. I wound my window down, felt the sun on my arms, and listened to the first of Beethoven's late quartets. Claudia was being dutifully silent.

I was trying to enjoy myself and leave Rissington Abbey behind in England. I hadn't slept much the night before. I'd been thinking too much. Partly about Barty, partly about Martin Kelly. I'd found only more questions, no answers, on both subjects.

We were in deep country: the villages were tiny. We were just through one which seemed only to be inhabited by a very old woman, manning the petrol station, and a recumbent old dog enjoying the sun, when the Citroën slowed down and turned between large stone gates and up a hill towards a big, square stone house. 'More like a château than a shack,' Plummer had said. In fact it was a château, according to the sign: the Château Touffailles.

We parked at the top of the hill on a gravel space beside the Citroën and I saw that the house wasn't a completed square, it had one side missing, the side that faced the parking area. The chauffeur led us through a formal garden with a fountain in the centre towards the front door. He pulled the bell and introduced us to the maid who answered it.

The maid and Claudia talked French, then Claudia turned to me. 'M'sieu le Baron would like to speak to you alone. I'm to wait down here.'

Fine by me. We went inside: the house was built in several levels on the side of the hill so the staircase which led off the stone hall went downwards, not upwards. The maid took Claudia down the stairs, out of my sight, and tucked her away somewhere. Then she came back for me and we went to the right, along a stone-flagged tapestry-hung corridor to a corner room.

'Mlle Tanner,' said the maid, and I went in.

'How do you do,' said the Baron, and went into light chat about my journey. He was an aristocratic Frenchman of whom Central Casting would have been proud. About five-ten, dark, with grey wings of thick hair, dark eyes, a lean elegant face, and an elegant body draped somewhere near Savile Row in expensive English light tweed cloth. He was also nearing seventy so I didn't fancy him but I reckoned he'd pull ninety per cent of females over forty-five. He spoke really beautiful English, much better than mine, and his accent was distinctly more upper, which as he'd been to Eton seemed reasonable. He even managed 'th', which seems to be Beecher's Brook for Francophones.

He gave me one of the best cups of coffee I've ever had, poured from a silver set which would have cost a bomb back in the eighteenth century. The room was a study, with bare stone walls lined with bookcases containing books in French, English, and German. I was envious. Imagine if you could read in three languages. Many, many, many more books. Still, I've got enough to do with English. I've always comforted myself with that. And I can read a bit of Ancient Greek. Greek is wonderful. It's like Shakespeare and the Bible, you keep meeting bits you know. I'd looked forward to meeting the word for 'sea' because I thought I knew it from the *Persian Expedition* — 'thalassa, thalassa'. Except when I met it, it was 'thalatta' because of the dialect, which just goes to show that the closer you get to knowing the more you find out you don't know.

So I sat looking round the study, at the thick dark carpet, Persian I thought, the ornate gilded desk, the velvet chairs, the open wood fire with logs cut and hauled by his servants ready for the winter, and the narrow stone windows with spectacular views over the valley. The windows were as wide open as they'd go and the soft air billowed into the smallish room and filled it. The Baron looked tired, as if he'd not slept. The lines around his eyes were crumpled and yellow and his tension showed in the absent-minded manner of his courtesy, and after he'd asked (twice) if I'd visited France before, I thought I'd better help him out.

'Would you like an interim report?'

'Please,' he said, looking relieved.

'I've spent the last few days at Rissington Abbey. The Headmaster thinks I'm doing preliminary interviewing for a documentary on education. So far, there is no suggestion that Olivier was anything but happy on his last day. My sources are his roommate, Tim Robertson, his friend Peter Newman, and his housemaster and teacher, Alistair Brown.'

'Well done,' he said.

Silence. He looked unhappy and uncomfortable. I'd have to prise him loose.

'M'sieu le Baron,' I said (that's what Claudia'd told me to call him. I was pleased with the stab I made at the sounds, half-clearing my throat on the 'r') 'you must get on with it, otherwise this'll take hours. I don't believe that it's you who wants to know the information I was hired to find. I don't believe that you'd fly me out here just for a progress report. I don't believe that Olivier is the child of your son and Miss Pertwee.'

'Ah,' he said. 'And what conclusions have you drawn from these – suppositions?'

'None, so far. That's what I'm waiting for you to tell me.'

He looked sad, for a moment. Not so much sad, I thought looking more closely, as crushed, as if someone had taken his heart and squeezed. There's no mistaking real pain, and this was it. 'Were you very fond of Olivier?' I asked gently.

'No,' he said, and we were silent again.

There is something about grief which settles you. It doesn't exactly make you feel guilty for being happy. It's more a sort of awe. Pity and terror, I suppose.

'I think you're going to have to talk about it,' I said. 'I can't guess. I know it's painful.'

'Yes,' he said. 'I think you do. Miss Tanner, you're not quite what I expected. Plummer said you were young, and inexperienced. It was on that understanding that I employed you.'

'I am youngish. And inexperienced, as a private investigator. Why did you want someone incompetent?'

'Not exactly incompetent.'

'Not quite competent, then.'

'What do you expect me to say?' he asked with a graceful shrug and a thoroughly French spread of his hands in mock-surrender.

'I expect you not to waste my time,' I said. 'This is a Saturday. I had to cancel arrangements to be here. So far, I can't see any urgency in our meeting.'

'There is, I assure you.'

'So tell me,' I said, exasperated. 'Spit it out.'

'The urgency is not mine,' he said, getting up and going to look out of the window, presumably because he couldn't face me. 'It is Freedom's. To do with the stars. The aspects change tonight. Jupiter leaves the third house, or some such nonsense.'

'OK. What happens when Jupiter leaves the third house?'

'Come here, please,' he said, and waved me to the window beside him. 'My wife,' he said, and pointed. Just below us, in a garden at the side of the château, was a woman sitting in a wheelchair with a rug over her knees. What I could see of her was very thin, and yellow with illness (cancer?) probably younger than the Baron but looking older, looking one breath from dying, really. 'She loves the garden. Even now, she sits outside when she can, in the full sun. She feels the cold, you see.'

'Is she very ill?' I said gently.

'I'm afraid so, yes.'

That was the source of his pain, not Olivier. 'Look, Baron,' I said, 'you've hired me, and I always stay hired. When push comes to shove, I do what my employers tell me. Following that principle I've produced some of the worst documentaries in the history of television. Better one bad general than two good generals.'

'Napoleon,' he said, but he pronounced it French and it took me a second to recognize the name. 'And so?'

'And so you're the bad general. Tell me what you want me to do. Tell me what I need to know to do it well, and I'll never repeat it.'

'And your assistant?'

'The same goes for her.'

'I don't know if you know much about Freedom?'

'Tell me.'

'She's – she's not very serious.'

'An airhead,' I said.

'I do not know the expression. But she is – like a child. In the seventies, she was very pretty, very young, very spontaneous, with bare feet and a laughing face, always searching for happiness and truth.'

'And you slept with her.'

He shrugged. 'Not often. But she came to stay, with my son, and she believed in free love.'

'Was Olivier your child?'

He shrugged again. 'It's possible. I have dark eyes. So have many Frenchmen. But Freedom decided that I was. And now, in her search for truth, she has a spiritual guide. A Tibetan. She lives with him and other seekers for truth in a commune not far from here, funded by her. Her guide has told her she must set herself right with everyone she has injured in her life, if she is to reach a higher plane of awareness. She wrote to Olivier to tell him that my son Michel is not his father, and that I am.'

'Selfish cow,' I said.

He made a French noise, with pursed lips, like *pffff*. 'Olivier was a very pragmatic boy. I did not expect it to disturb him unduly. But when he died, she feared he had read the letter and committed suicide. I knew this could not be the case.'

'Why?'

'Because if Olivier knew, he would have written or telephoned to me.'

'Were you close?'

'Not at all. You misunderstand. He would have asked me to increase his allowance.'

'I have reason to believe that Olivier didn't read his letters from his mother. He didn't even open them, unless they contained a cheque,' I said.

'Unfortunately the unopened letter was not among the belongings returned to his mother. So she was disturbed, and she wanted to know what his last day was like, whether he had killed himself. She asked me to find out.'

'So you hired me.'

'I wanted a woman, and someone – not insensitive.'

'You wanted someone who wouldn't find anything.'

'Perhaps.'

'And you'd have shut Freedom up with my report. Why did I have to come over, then?'

'It is the aspect of the stars, I told you. Freedom's guide told her that she must deal with this matter before Jupiter moves, tonight.'

'Why couldn't we have spoken on the phone?'

'Her guide must meet you, to feel your cosmic vibrations, to see if you're telling the truth.'

'What happens if he doesn't believe me, or she isn't satisfied?'

'Then she will speak to my wife.'

Chapter Twenty-Six

Half an hour later Claudia and I were back in the car, following the chauffeured, empty Citroën. This time Claudia was driving while I explained. 'So we're going to a commune in the Gers,' she said. 'I've never been to a commune.'

'Neither have I.'

'The poor, poor Baron.'

'Poor Baron my foot. He shouldn't have banged his daughter-in-law if he didn't want trouble, especially not a hippy twit like Freedom. Besides, his wife probably knows anyway, she's been married to him for long enough, and if she's dying she'll have more important things to think about than a legover eighteen years ago.'

'Why does he annoy you?'

I nearly denied it. Then I realized what a bad example I'd be setting. Most cock ups, in my experience, are compounded by people covering because they don't like looking foolish. She'd hired me to train her. So I'd train her. 'Because I feel humiliated,' I said. 'I was pleased when Plummer gave me the job. Now I've found out I was chosen to fail. I don't like that.'

'I'm sorry,' she said.

'Not your fault. Anyway, some good's come out of it. He's agreed to keep paying me until I'm satisfied that Kelly's death was suicide and nobody at Rissington was involved. It was the least he could do.'

We drove for forty minutes, through some dead villages and a medium-sized town with a city-sized traffic problem, not helped by the French habit, which I rather admired, of parking their cars wherever it suited them. Then the country roads got smaller and smaller, and finally the Citroën stopped. The chauffeur got out and Claudia went to meet him.

'The commune is here. Down this lane,' she said, getting back in the car and waving goodbye to the chauffeur.

The lane was narrow, overgrown, and deeply rutted. It would be a nightmare in winter. It wasn't a barrel of laughs in summer, and I was glad it wasn't my car's suspension it was punishing. It was also steep: we were going down the side of a small valley. About three hundred yards along the view opened out and I could see a cluster of buildings below us. A farmhouse, outhouses, a barn, all built in the local greyish-white stone, in a reasonable state of repair. There was a small area of grass shaded by a large tree in the quadrangle formed by the buildings, with a group of children dressed in flame-red flimsy cotton, playing. Both boys and girls wore loose trousers gathered at the ankle and knee-length tunics.

Beyond the buildings, on ground sloping down to the valley floor, there was an orchard. About twenty men and women, also in flame-red cotton, were working among the trees. It reminded me of Rissington: only the costumes were different, and the hairstyles. Long hair and beards for the men, long hair for the women, but otherwise it was a fatigue party. There were no other buildings or farms, as far as I could see, in the valley. There's a lot of empty country in France.

Claudia stopped the car and we went towards the farmhouse; I didn't expect Freedom or her spiritual guide to be working. The front door was open. 'Hallo,' I shouted. 'Anyone at home?' I waited. Claudia looked at me for direction. 'Someone'll come,' I said. 'You'll see.'

Freedom came, barefoot under her red shift. The colour was too strong for her: it washed out her pale skin and hair. She hadn't changed her hairstyle since 1969; it was still straight, and parted in the middle with a fringe. She looked bony and stupid and vain, or perhaps I was prejudiced, maybe she just looked bony. She had huge feet.

We were sitting in the main room of the farmhouse, on cushions on the wooden floor. There was no furniture. Books were piled around the walls: there was a star-map over the rough plaster of one wall, an astrological chart on another; the other two walls were hung with brightly coloured Eastern materials, some with small circular mirrors as part of the pattern. The room smelt of damp, pot, incense, and yesterday's curry, and reminded me of the Portobello Road.

I didn't say so: I was on my best behaviour. I wanted to get the business done for the Baron and get out of there. My other encounters

176

with fringe Eastern guru-crooks didn't give me any grounds for optimism on that score. They can usually bore for the cosmos, and if you try to hurry them they lapse into spiritual silences.

This one, according to the Baron a Tibetan, was small and dark and entirely bald, though judging by his five o'clock shadow only some of the baldness was natural, in a white shift and trousers. He sat crosslegged on a bigger, more impressive, probably more comfortable cushion than ours. He spoke only French. He spoke, Freedom translated.

'You are welcome to our ashram.'

'Thank you.'

'You must say "Guru",' prompted Freedom.

'Guru,' I said.

She translated. He spoke. 'In the matter of the child of light Olivier,' she said. 'My daughter Freedom must know whether his spirit soared un — un—'

'Unfettered,' suggested Claudia.

Freedom didn't look grateful for the help. 'Unfettered by earthly cares.'

'It soared unfettered,' I said. 'He was happy, the day before he died. Guru.'

'Do you have proof of this?'

'His friend Peter Newman says so. His friend Tim Robertson, who shared his room, says so. Guru.'

'You need not say "Guru" each time, like that,' said Freedom. 'It is a term of respect.'

She was sharper that I'd thought. I resolved to weave my respect into the garbage I was talking like a seamless garment.

He was speaking again. 'What is your star-sign? When were you born?'

'April, Guru,' I said. 'I'm an Aries.'

Claudia said nothing. She didn't even twitch, though she knew it'd been my birthday party on Monday.

'A fire-child,' said the guru/Freedom. 'You have brought truth to us. Saturn is in Aries. You were guided by a spirit greater than ours.'

And the shit is in the fan, I thought. Not just a crook. A completely unintuitive crook. I'll get away with it.

'In the matter of the letter,' said the guru/Freedom. 'My daughter Freedom wrote a letter to her son just before he died. We wish to know whether he received this letter.'

177

'He never opened it, Guru,' I said. 'The letter arrived after he died. It was destroyed by the boy who shared his room.'

Freedom started to cry. I hadn't thought she was capable of so much emotion. I didn't warm to her, exactly. I just despised the guru more. She didn't translate for him: she said directly to me 'Honestly? Is that really true?' For the first time she sounded English, like Mary Anne Pertwee from Sydenham.

'Honestly,' I said. 'My word of honour.'

She leant towards me, took my hand and kissed it. 'Thank you,' she said.

Half an hour of spiritual uplift later, she showed us out. I found walking difficult, at first: the damp cushions and the cross-legged posture had hammered my bad leg. I exaggerated my difficulty to slow us down on the way to the car. I wanted to talk to her. 'Where's Olivier buried?' I said.

She waved at the grass under the central tree. 'All around us,' she said. 'We scattered his ashes here. In a simple ceremony. We all chanted and then I sang two of my songs. And the Guru blessed his ashes so he can breathe pure air.'

The pure air of fraud, I thought. 'Freedom,' I said, 'tell me about Olivier. When he left Eton——'

'I was glad,' she interrupted. 'I didn't want him to go there. But it was part of the divorce settlement. Michel insisted. Well, his father insisted, because his father paid. And his father pays my allowance. Not that I need it, because my records sell well, but I'm glad, because I can spend it on helping the Guru with his work.'

'Why doesn't Michel pay?'

'He's an artist. He can't handle money.'

'When Olivier left Eton, what kind of trouble was he in?'

'It was only because he was so clever.'

'So clever?'

'Yes, so clever with his hands, just like my father. With wires and microphones and things.'

'Electronics?'

'Yes.'

'He fixed up electronic equipment? And then he used it to listen to other people's conversations?'

'He was a seeker after truth, like me. He wanted to know. He wanted

178

to understand. In his own way, he was looking for a higher plane of awareness. He was a very religious boy. He had a spiritual guide too, at Rissington. A priest. When he first went to school there, he was lonely, and the priest was his friend. Olivier wrote to me every week, then.'

'The priest? Martin Kelly?'

'Yes.'

'I'm afraid he's dead.'

We'd reached the car, and stopped. 'But he was young,' said Freedom. 'Olivier told me he was young, and handsome. Looks mattered very much to Olivier. And youth. He always said I was more like a sister than a mother. I was very young when he was born. Young, and unwise.'

And no wiser now, I thought. On the other hand Martin Kelly was no longer young and handsome.

'He stopped writing to me,' she said. 'Last year, he hardly wrote at all. And he didn't come here for Christmas. When he died, I hadn't seen him since August. Seven months. Seven months . . .'

'That's sad,' said Claudia, as we drove away. 'Imagine not seeing him for so long, and then he dies. Your only son.'

'Imagine getting on a plane and going to see your only son,' I said, 'instead of getting stoned on pot and lapping up the drivelling of a third-rate crook.'

'Mmm,' she said, unconvinced. 'Maybe it's even sadder, for her, because she feels guilty. And you lied about the letter.'

'So sue me.'

'But you lied on your word of honour.'

'I think what I told her was probably the truth. It might have been. But anyway it's better all round if she believes me.'

'You shouldn't do evil that good may come of it. The end can never justify the means.'

'Who says?'

'It's basic ethics. I was taught it by the Jesuits.'

'Some people don't want or deserve the truth. That's basic ethics too.'

'Who taught you that?'

'Twenty-nine years and five days. Now drive like hell to Toulouse. I want a bath.'

Chapter Twenty-Seven

The Toulouse Wanderotel was in a main road right opposite the railway station, in a row of middle-range hotels. When we checked in, at eight o'clock, the bossy old woman at the desk gave us directions to the hotel car park, two keys, and a map. Because of the one-way system we had to drive for half a mile before reaching it, the last third of which was in the red-light district. The car park itself was down a side-street which contained two strip shows, a pornographic video shop, three patrolling prostitutes, and a patrolling poodle, though the poodle may just have been a dog out for an evening stroll. Claudia was chastened. 'Do you think it's safe?' she said.

'Sure. We've only got to walk fifty yards to the main road,' I said, more confidently than I felt. I wasn't worried about the street but about the car park, which was very big and dark, under an apartment building. It had a system of electronic gates and separate lock-up garages which suggested a high risk of theft, and if I'd been a violent petty thief who didn't mind a bit of mugging on the side I'd have zeroed in on Claudia. I promised myself to fetch the car alone the next day, then backed us in, with some difficulty as our garage was tiny.

We made it to the hotel without any trouble and went up to our rooms on the fourth floor. Mine was small, crammed with cheap, chipped modern furniture and a lumpy double bed, with a battered green carpet whose ugly patterns were only partly obscured by dirt. It was also very stuffy, and devoid of coffee-making equipment. I wrestled one of the French windows open and admitted a high level of traffic noise and polluted air. The balcony was only just large enough to stand on, with a view across to the backs of other hotels and down to a kitchen well and dustbins. There was, I was glad to see, a fire escape. Judging by the state of the wiring, some of which was hanging free of the decaying plaster, we might need it.

Claudia's room, next door, was worse. But we did have a bathroom each and we both had baths. The air was so oppressively hot that the tepid water didn't matter. I changed my T-shirt, pants, and socks; Claudia changed everything except the silver combs. Then we went out for dinner, to a big restaurant on one of the main roads leading down to the station, chosen by Claudia.

The food was very good but extremely rich. Our main course was a local duck dish which seemed to me ninety per cent fat. When I pointed out this to Claudia, she was scathing. 'That's not cholesterol,' she said. 'That's proper cooking. Goose fat and butter. You can't make *confit de canard* without it.' I'd have to remember to tell Cassie.

When we got back to the hotel the manageress spoke to Claudia and gave her a piece of paper. Because I couldn't understand, I stood by and admired the manageress's courageous approach to the passing years. A chestnut wig, the same piercing colour as Mrs Brown's hair. Dyed black eyebrows. False eyelashes. A department store full of make-up, a low-cut tight black dress, shiny stockings, and spike-heeled black shoes. Perhaps she'd originally worked the side-streets, and when her feet hurt too much she'd invested her earnings in a share of the hotel. A wise career-move, judging by the hotel prices.

'Come on,' said Claudia, 'hurry. We need to get up to your room. Polly rang and she's going to ring again any minute.'

Polly sounded better. Her voice had life in it that wasn't spite. 'Hi, Alex, how are you? I'm so sorry – really, I don't know what came over me – I'm really sorry, I didn't mean any of it.'

Of course she had, but she meant the apology too. 'Forget it,' I said. 'Couldn't matter less. I know I'm a pain sometimes.'

'So'm I. You've been fantastic, I've been awful. I didn't mean it, really. But I'm not just ringing for that. I watched the video today – the Rissington Abbey promotional thing. Have you seen it?'

'No. What have you got?' I said, lurched back into the case, which I'd been managing to ignore through dinner.

'It's probably nothing. I may just have made it up because I was looking too closely and because I was suspicious, you know how it is. I may be completely wrong.'

The skin on the back of my neck was prickling. 'Let's have it anyway,' I said.

'It's the deputy head.'

'What's wrong with him?'

'Everything. He doesn't need those glasses, for a start. You wear glasses for long or short sight, right? Well, when he's talking to the camera he wears them and blinks as if he can't see, which he probably can't, they're so thick and distorting. Then there's a long shot of him reading the Bible in Assembly, and he hasn't got them on then. And when he's on the assault course – he's the course record-holder – he isn't wearing them either.'

'Contact lenses?' I said.

'Could be. But it's not just that. He doesn't need to stoop, surely. He's incredibly fit and strong, and he could be very good-looking. It looks put on, to me. Like an actor trying to look like a schoolteacher. And his Scottish accent comes and goes. I told you it mayn't be anything, but it's just a feeling I have.'

I thanked her, we chatted a bit, I rang off. I wasn't entirely convinced by her arguments. She'd wanted to find something for me: she'd looked: she'd found it. That didn't mean it was there. But it was interesting she'd picked on Brown.

Brown. Not just a name, a colour. I knocked on Claudia's wall: she came in. 'Bring me the list you made from the Browns' medicine-cabinet, would you?'

She brought it.

Paracetamol
Milk of Magnesia
Several drug-names I didn't recognise – presumably for the MS
Diaphragm & contraceptive cream
Hair dye – Mountain Ash

There was more, but I stopped there. I was sitting on the bed, with Claudia beside me. 'What colour do you think Mountain Ash is?' I said.

'Have you found something?' She seemed to crackle with excitement.

'Not sure. What colour?'

'Well, it could be a pale ashy blonde.'

'Or?'

'I suppose, a light ashy brown.'

'But not bright chestnut?'

'Of course not.' She stared at me. 'I don't understand—' and then she clicked. 'Not Mrs Brown. It couldn't be Mrs Brown's! Which means – it's Alistair's? But what . . .'

182

'He could have gone prematurely grey, I suppose, but I doubt it.'

'So do you think it's a disguise?'

'God knows. Polly thinks his short-sightedness and stooping are a disguise. She watched the school video for me . . . Claudia, how old do you reckon he is?'

'Mid-thirties?'

'That's what I thought when I met him. He's supposed to be thirty.'

'It's possible, I suppose. An old-looking thirty. He's very lined about the eyes.'

'Could be all that blinking.'

'But why would anyone disguise themselves in a school? It doesn't make sense. Do you think he's a criminal on the run?'

'Two reasons for disguise,' I said, thinking aloud. 'One, not to be yourself. Two, to be someone else.'

'Really to make yourself look like someone else is impossible,' said Claudia dismissively. 'People's faces are all very different.'

'Unless they're identical twins. But if they were identical they'd have the same height and hair colour naturally . . . Don't know. Maybe Father Corrigan will cast some light on it tomorrow.'

Claudia sat expectantly. 'What do we do now?' she said.

'Go to sleep. It's nearly eleven.'

'Oh,' she wailed, disappointed. 'But it's only ten in England.'

'We're in France and I'm tired.' I wasn't, really, but I didn't want to talk any longer.

'Can I sleep in here?' she said. 'I know it's only a double bed but I'm a very quiet sleeper and I'll keep right over to my side, and I really, really don't like sleeping alone in hotels.'

'OK.'

'I'll be right back. I've got to fetch my handbag, and Lappay.'

'Lappay?'

'My pink rabbit. When I was small, my first stepfather – the French one – he was very sweet to me and he began teaching me the language, and the French for rabbit is "lapin", so he taught me that and I couldn't say it so I just said "Lappay" and I've called him that ever since . . .'

'Belt up, Claudia.'

'OK.'

Sunday, June 7th

Chapter Twenty-Eight

I went to sleep at two and woke at seven, six English time. It was light but only just: the sky was heavily overcast, though it was still warm, and not much light filtered down the well and through the dirty windows anyway. I could hear traffic, and kitchen noises from below, and close by, a television was blaring. Claudia was still asleep, clutching the rabbit. Her hair, freed from the combs, covered all her square hard pillow and most of mine. As I watched her, she woke, stretched and smiled at me. 'I had such a happy dream,' she said. 'Madame la Baronne went to Lourdes and she was healed. Wasn't that lovely?'

'Lovely,' I said. 'Did a tape rewind also take Olivier back up to the diving-board? Did it take Martin Kelly back down from his rope?'

'What?'

'Never mind. Get up, there's some things I want you to do.'

'Great,' she said. 'Have you had an idea?'

I sent her off to get washed and dressed, book us a return flight at noon or later, pack, and bring her overnight bag into my room.

When she came back with the news that we were on a two-thirty flight, I was ready to go for coffee, but first I said: 'Give me Kelly's notebook, the one with the sports day notes, plus your summary page.' She fished them out, and I compared them. One line – the line I'd remembered somewhere in my hours of wakefulness – was different.

Claudia had written: *buttocks on the diving-board spotlight*

Kelly had written: *buttocks on the diving-board Spotlight*

'What is it?' said Claudia. 'Oh, what is it, have I made a mistake?'

'A small mistake. Look.'

She looked. 'I left off the capital letter. Is it important?'

'It could be, but you weren't to know that. My fault, I should have seen it anyway. Buzz down to the desk and ask Madame Wig if the hotel has a fax machine, and if it has, get the number.'

She did. It had. She gave me the number, and I dialled Barty.

He'd been asleep. He was at his worst in the early morning. It took him a while to work out who he was, let alone who I was, and that I was talking to him on the telephone. Finally he said, 'Hell, Alex, it's six-thirty.'

'Not in la France. Do you still have those 1980s *Spotlight*s?'

'Yes.'

'What's *Spotlight*?' hissed Claudia.

'It's a casting directory. Ssshhh.'

'You've rung me up at six-thirty to tell me that?' complained Barty.

'I was talking to Claudia. Barty, look someone up for me. Start 1980 and work forward. Could be one of several names: try surname Bernard, maybe Alistair Bernard. Or surname Alistair, maybe Bernard Alistair. Or surname Brown, with any of the other names first. Born about 1958, height five eleven to six foot, blue eyes, maybe blond hair. Probably under Young Actor but could be Leading, not likely to be Character but try anyway. Bone structure like Kevin Costner, high-bridged nose, high forehead. Muscular, athletic. Might offer stunting or a martial art.'

'What are you casting?'

'*Evil at Rissington Abbey*,' I said. 'Maybe. If you find him, fax the picture to me. Mark the fax with my name, Room 402.' I gave him the fax number.

'You will be careful?' he said.

'As careful as you'd be,' I said, rather meanly, and put the phone down on his protests.

Then I explained to Claudia.

'Alistair Brown's really an actor? Is he really Alistair Brown?'

'His name doesn't matter. He certainly isn't Mrs Brown's son, the thirty-year-old who got a degree from Edinburgh and then wrestled with his soul in the seminary. Whose passport probably says, height, five foot ten, colour of hair, brown.'

'But why? Why should he do it? What could he gain?'

'He could marry Mrs Ellis. The Major's got a heart condition.'

'Would he want her?'

'She owns the school, remember?'

'Why would he want to own a school?'

'If you close the school, what have you got?'

Claudia blinked. 'Property,' she said, with reverence. 'Land. In an area with good road and rail links, ripe for development. That's what Dieter said when he read the school prospectus, and I thought he was being narrow and mercenary, like a banker. But why would Mrs Brown do it?'

'For a share in the profit. It was probably her idea. She was there first.'

'And the contraceptives – perhaps he's her lover!' said Claudia, almost choking with excitement.

'And perhaps she's having a fling with the Craft, Design, and Technology teacher,' I said. 'Don't let's go mad. Time for breakfast.'

It was a wonderful breakfast. We went to a café along the road, and I had two basinfuls of coffee second only to the Baron's, and croissants that would have melted on the plate if I'd given them time. I felt relieved. I was sure that at least some of my questions were answered. There were plenty of details left to sort out, but the link with Kelly seemed clear enough. I didn't know much about priests and trainee priests, but I thought theirs must be a smallish world, rather like mine, in which you bump into most people, sometime. If Kelly had known the real John Alistair Brown, perhaps while Brown was at the seminary, then he'd have spotted the Rissington Second-in-Command as a ringer.

How Kelly knew he was an actor, I didn't know. It didn't much matter.

Claudia paid the bill and got up to go. 'Hang on a minute,' I said. 'What have you forgotten?'

'I've got my bag.'

'Much more important than that. The bill. Keep the bill and log the expense.'

'Alex, it's only coffee and croissants.'

'Who is training who?'

'Sorry.'

'And get a bigger organizer, I told you.'

'Sorry. I haven't had time.'

'And never say you haven't had time. That's the ultimate confession of failure. If you want an explanation, say you bought an organizer yesterday but the producer lost it.'

'Why?'

'Always blame the producer, except to his face. It's a union requirement.'

Madame Wig beckoned us over to the desk, where the fax machine was whirring. I watched the face inch out, younger, sharper, predatory without the glasses, the head tilted back and looking upwards, the neck strong on broad shoulders. A very handsome man. Worth having a face-lift for. His hair was longer, in the photograph. Long and straight and heavy and fair. He was, to the last detail, the sort of man I find attractive. So why, after the first few minutes, hadn't I?

I took the fax and we went back to my room. 'It's him,' said Claudia, and looked at me reverently. 'Don't look at me like that,' I said. 'It was easy. Kelly gave it to us, and Polly, Barty and you did the work. Why the hell the priest couldn't just tell me—'

I looked at the fax. Apart from the photograph, the entry said:

ALISTAIR BERNARD. Height, six foot. Eyes, blue. Photograph taken 1982. c/o *Spotlight*.

Underneath, Barty had written:

He's in 1983–86. 83's the earliest I've got. Young Actor. Half-page ad, thinks a lot of himself. I've seen him doing one-liners in cop series, nothing for years. He was terrible. Good hunting.

I gave it to Claudia to mull over. 'What does it mean, c/o *Spotlight*?'
'That he didn't have an agent.'
'So what do we do now?'
'Sight-see. I've never been to Toulouse, and we've got the whole morning.'
' "*Sight-see*"? But Alex—' She stopped, when I sneezed. Then I sneezed again. 'You've got a cold!' she said accusingly. 'Lack of Vitamin C!'
'Hay-fever,' I said. 'I didn't bring enough anti-histamine. I didn't know we'd be going into deep country.'
'There weren't any in your medicine cabinet.'
'That's because I keep my drugs in the kitchen.'

She was taken aback. 'That's cheating,' she said, then rallied. 'Aren't you going to ring Father Corrigan?'

'Not till we get back to England and I've had time to sort out what I think I know, and see if he confirms it. I'll get more that way.'

I needed Claudia-free time to work. Maybe I'd even wait until after I'd spoken to Tim Robertson. Meanwhile we were in Toulouse, on expenses.

Chapter Twenty-Nine

I dropped Claudia off at her flat near Queen's Gate at half-past four and took the taxi on home. I couldn't wait to be alone. I had plenty to think about and I looked forward to a whole late afternoon, evening, night all to myself in the flat. Polly wasn't due back till sometime next week.

It was overcast in London too. And hot, and clammy. First stop, take my clothes off and stuff them into the washing machine. Next stop, a bath. I paid off the taxi and went in to the house, kicking several Kentucky Fried Chicken boxes off the steps on the way. Four houses away, further along the road, there was a party. Probably Saturday night's, still going. Bob Marley thundered from huge speakers balanced on the first-floor window-ledge.

When I shut the front door behind me, the noise lessened, but only a little. I picked up the Saturday mail, and sorted it. Bills for me: proper mail for Polly. I took it in to her flat. Her place was still the festering mess she'd left, but now we were back on friendly terms I felt more like sorting it out. Besides, the hay-fever had affected my sense of smell and the faint waves of Poison that reached me were almost pleasant. I got a black rubbish bag and collected her duvet-cover, pillowcases, and towels. Then I took another and emptied her linen-basket into it.

Trailing the two bags and my overnight bag, heavy with all the material – mine, and Claudia's – on the case, I went upstairs.

I was home.

I dropped everything on the floor, closed the door behind me, sneezed twice, and took off my boots. The flat was stuffy; I opened the living-room windows, including the French window.

I didn't feel up to Beethoven, but I didn't want Marley. I put on a Mozart violin concerto (Perhaps *the* Mozart violin concerto – are there more than one?) on the CD, loud enough to screen the heavy background thumps, and turned on the hot water. I'd have to wait abut half an hour for my bath. Time to make coffee and sort the washing.

When the coffee was ground and filtering, I took the black bag with Polly's linen-basket washing up to the bathroom to add mine to it. On the way up the stairs, I passed the bookshelves I'd made for my American private eye paperback collection. Sitting on top was Barty's present, the two Sue Graftons and the Sara Paretsky. I hadn't read any of them. I'd read one in my bath, I thought. I could afford an hour or so before I got to work. But which one? I prefer Grafton, so normally I'd have read Paretsky first. On the other hand you shouldn't read two books by the same author one after another because the mannerisms get on your nerves.

I opened the tiny bathroom window, and it got stuffier. Could London actually be sucking oxygen out of the atmosphere, like a reverse rain forest? I sneezed again, and blew my nose, and then I smelt it.

Not Poison. Not London. After-shave. A familiar after-shave.

I closed my eyes, and remembered. A beige carpet: a woman in a wheelchair. The Browns' flat.

Alistair Brown. Bernard Alistair. He'd been here.

Maybe he still was.

I was bent over my linen-basket, scooping out the dirty clothes. I didn't stop, and I didn't turn round. It was superstition. If I didn't turn round, I wouldn't see him. If I didn't see him he couldn't be there.

I'd been into every room of my flat except the tiny spare bedroom beyond the living-room. And my bedroom, next door. I'd smelt the after-shave up here. I listened, but all I could hear was Mozart.

I took two deep breaths, and turned round.

He was standing in the doorway, between me and the stairs. He didn't look like the Second-in-Command. He looked like his casting photograph, ten years on. No glasses: hair hanging over his face: a white T-shirt straining to cover his chest, with short sleeves over muscular arms, tight faded jeans, trainers, and short black leather gloves. He looked like a body-builder or a bouncer or a walk-on villain in a cop series. No wonder I hadn't found him attractive. He was gay, or so narcissistic that he was asexual.

But that didn't matter, now. I didn't like the look of the gloves.

I jumped. I gave a little scream, which wasn't entirely affected. I dropped the black bag I was holding. 'What the hell are you doing in my flat?' I said. 'How did you get in here?'

'Up the back drainpipe, in through the bedroom window. You really should close the metal gate on that window. This is a rough area, isn't it?'

'I like it,' I said. If one of my local burglars had turned up at that moment, I'd have given him the video and a box to carry it away in.

Silence. I'd better fill it: I didn't want him to get to the point. I didn't think I'd like it. 'Mr Brown, you're wearing eye-liner,' I said. 'That's unusual.'

'Not very. Plenty of guys do, if it makes them look good.' The Scottish accent had gone. In its place was an actor's voice, with undertones of nasal London.

'How did you get time off school?' I said. The Major'd told me how important the housemasters were at weekends, how a boarding-school stood or fell by its weekend provision, that the housemasters had light time-tables and a day and a half off during the week for that very reason.

'Don't play games,' he said. 'I want the letter.'

I didn't have to pretend ignorance. 'What letter?'

'Martin's. The letter he sent you on Wednesday.'

'I never received it. When did Martin Kelly tell you he'd written to me?'

'Wednesday evening. Just before he died.'

'Did you kill him?'

'I didn't need to. He was crazy. He'd been in the bin, did you know that? You couldn't trust a word he said. Plus he didn't have the guts to come out of the closet. Plus he had a drink problem. A serious drink problem. No self-control. No self-discipline. Did you see his nails?'

'Why did you go to see him on Wednesday?'

'You said you'd read the piece in the *Banbury Courier*. You might have spoken to him. He'd promised to keep quiet about me, for John's sake, but I wanted to check.'

'Did you watch him die?'

'Yeah. Had to be sure, didn't I? Like I asked you to dinner, to find out what you knew, if you'd got the letter. I wanted to be sure.'

We looked at each other. His eyes were empty but flickering and quick, like a computer game, full of bright, smug, childlike violence. I was glad Claudia wasn't there, and sorry for Martin Kelly, who had surely, even if indirectly, died at this man's manicured hands. I was also very angry. 'How long had you known him?' I said.

'I only *met* him last summer. I knew *of* him for years, ever since he met John. John talked about him all the time. Martin this, Martin that. Typical cousin John. He never could keep his mouth shut. He talked about me all the time, too. And showed off my photograph. God, he was stupid.'

'What happened to John?' I said.

'Chopped to dogmeat by some boy he met in the souk, in Marrakech. A fine man of God, our John.'

'Did you have an affair with him?' I said.

'*Me*?' he was shocked, and outraged. 'I'm straight. Martin and John were the lovebirds. True love. Romeo and Romeo. Antony and Antony.' He groped for other names.

'Tristan and Tristan,' I suggested. 'Kevin Costner and Kevin Costner—'

'Shut up,' he said. 'I want the letter.'

Actually, just then, he didn't. He wanted me to be frightened of him, and I was, but only partly. I hadn't got any grip on his personality at Rissington, but I had now. He was familiar to me. I'd eaten bacon butties from the location catering truck, many a time, standing beside actors like him. They thought they could act because they were good-looking and they waited to be the new James Bond. He was very strong but he wasn't very bright: I should be able to outmanoeuvre him. I'd have to be careful, and organized, and quick. And it would have to be soon.

'Can we go downstairs?' I said. 'The coffee should be ready, and I want to put Polly's bedlinen in the washing machine. I told you, I haven't got any letter.' I moved towards him. He didn't step aside to let me pass, and I had to stop, my head level with his over-developed chest, my breath choking on his after-shave.

Finally he moved down the stairs. 'Why not?' he said. 'It won't help, you know.'

I followed him. He was at the front door, double-locking it. He struggled to put the keys in the back pocket of his jeans. 'Your jeans are too tight,' I said. 'Have you put on weight?'

'No.'

'They were a bad buy, then.'

'What?'

'Or a bad fashion choice.'

'Will you shut the fuck up about my jeans?' he said, and pushed me on to the sofa. He was not only strong, he was quick.

'Why are you here?' I said.

'I told you, to get the letter.'

'Why? If I know what's in it, what good will the letter do you?'

He didn't answer, and I could only half guess. If he planned to get rid of me – but then he'd have to dispose of Claudia too – no, it was stupid. But then he was fairly stupid: actors often are. So are television researchers who don't follow up broad hints from sources, however crazy. I'd sat on Kelly's notes until he died. I hoped I'd live to regret it.

'Do you want some coffee?' I said.

'No. Turn off that sodding music.'

'You don't like Mozart?'

He stepped over to the music centre and pulled the wires from the wall. No more Mozart. Just the thump of Bob Marley from the party along the road.

'It's got to be an accident, you see,' he said. 'Desmoulins was an accident. Martin was suicide. You'll be an accident, then the girl can be a sexual crime.'

'What sort of accident will I be?'

'The balcony, I think. Dangerously low, those railings.'

The balcony. My balcony, that I owned and understood, and he only knew by sight.

'Nobody'll believe it,' I said. 'I never go out on the balcony. I'm afraid of heights. I've got vertigo. All my friends know that.'

'All the better,' he said. 'If you stumbled on to the balcony by mistake, you'd panic, and fall.'

'No,' I said, sobbing, burying my head in my hands till I could squeeze out enough tears. 'No, no, not that. Please – please let me get some coffee.' I made a dash for the kitchen and managed to grab the coffee jug before he grabbed me. The tepid liquid splashed over me, soaking my clothes. He'd leapt back to avoid it, balanced and agile. Only a few drops reached him.

'Clear up the mess,' he said. 'Now.' I mopped at the floor with a J-cloth while he watched me critically and pointed out splashes I'd missed. When I'd finished, he said, 'Change your clothes.'

'Why?'

'Just change them. And wash the coffee off.'

I suppose he didn't want me to have an unusually stained corpse. Neither did I.

'Can I go to the bedroom?' I said eagerly, sending him thought-waves, 'drainpipe, drainpipe' till the veins in my head stood out. He received them, or he'd worked it out for himself.

'Change in the bathroom. You've got clothes in there, I saw them.'

'They're dirty,' I complained.

'Get on with it.' He looked at his watch. 'I want to be back for dinner in the Mess.'

I went, looking reluctant, up the stairs to the bathroom, with him right behind me. I went into the bathroom. He stood on the stairs outside and didn't object when I pulled the door half-shut.

I couldn't get out through the bathroom window and I wasn't going to try. Even if I could have squeezed through, there was at least a forty-foot drop to Polly's garden beneath, and no drainpipe or trellis to climb down.

I had other plans. I shucked off my clothes, showered away the coffee, dried myself, and slavered handfuls of sun-tan oil on my legs and arms. I rubbed my hands with a towel until they were dry, and concentrated. I told my body what it had to do. I went through every step, twice. Then I put on Polly's costume: the cut-off jeans, the sawn-off T-shirt. I took the broad, heavy leather belt out of my jeans and threaded it through the loops, then fastened it, three holes looser than usual. That should be enough. Any more, and he might have noticed.

The door banged open and hit me. 'That's it,' he said. 'Time's up.'

He pushed me down the stairs ahead of him. In the living-room, I said: 'This is a joke, right? Tell me this is a bad joke.' I was managing to cry again.

'On the balcony,' he said.

It was ten feet from where I was standing, across the room, to the balcony. He was fast, but I'd leave him standing, because he wouldn't expect it. I relaxed, then I tensed and ran. To the French window, and through it, to the ledge outside. Two careful steps along the narrow window-ledge, facing the wall. I looped my belt over the previous tenant's blessed anchor-spike, held the spike with both hands, and waited.

He hesitated at the window. I could see him. He didn't want to be seen from the road. But he couldn't reach me from there, so he stepped on to the balcony, and it went from beneath him.

As he felt himself falling, he grabbed for me. One hand reached my calf, and held. I could feel the bones in his fingers through the gloves, and my flesh. Then his frantic grip slid smoothly down my oiled calf to my ankle: my foot: and then air.

I looked down. He'd fallen straight into the basement well and broken his neck.

Monday, June 8th

Chapter Thirty

I woke at six, and it was raining. It must have been raining for hours: when I left the house half an hour later the gutters were swollen and the pavements greasy and slick.

The train to Banbury was crowded, damp, and hot; all the seats were taken. I stood up in the buffet, tried to spill only twenty-five per cent of my coffee down my steaming leather jacket, and watched the rivulets of rain slide sideways down the windows. The Major was expecting me at nine. Between breakfast and break. He'd wanted me to come when the school would be at work: he'd insisted.

I'd called him, last evening, right after I called the police, and long before they came. I thought he should know he had to replace his Second-in-Command. He hadn't sounded shocked, or even surprised, when I told him. He just said: 'You are safe, Miss Tanner? Not hurt?'

'Not hurt,' I said. 'In any way. You'd better break the news to Mrs Brown. I'll tell the police I've told you.'

After that, I'd spent hours with the police, first in the flat, when they'd taken the keys from Brown's pocket and let themselves in, then at the Notting Hill station. I could have called Plummer and told him to find me a lawyer more conversant than he was with bodies in basements, but I didn't need to. What I told them was the truth, though no more of it than they needed.

They were cautious at first, then sympathetic. That was worse because they lumbered me with a WPC fresh from a Victim Support training course who plied me with offers of tea I couldn't refuse and gave me every opening to discuss my trauma. I did my best for her: she did her best for me. By the time my statement was typed and signed, we'd both been a little desperate.

*

The car-hire firm at Banbury station gave me another middle-range Nissan. It was the only one they had left. One of the stereo speakers was out of service, but that was enough. Beethoven's Ninth could cope.

Banbury was grey in the rain, and when I bumped and splashed my way over the ramps in the Rissington drive it was dark enough for some lights to be on in GHQ. They looked forlorn, not welcoming.

There was nobody on the steps, either, and the front door was shut. I didn't try it: I rang the bell.

The Major answered. He must have been waiting. He was wearing grey trousers, a blue shirt, a tweed jacket, and a regimental tie. The civilian clothes made him look even smaller, and even neater. The badge on the tie was gold, on a dark blue background. It looked like crossed monkey-wrenches, but that couldn't have been right.

'Miss Tanner,' he said. 'The weather's broken.'

'Yes,' I said. Not only the weather, I thought. His head was still upright on his neck, but it looked as if he was keeping it there by an effort of will: as if it had been snapped as finally, as unnaturally, as Alistair's. I'd been glad about Alistair. I wasn't glad about him.

'Best if we go up to the private quarters, I think,' he said, and I followed him, though I didn't need to. I could have found it in my sleep.

There were no lights on in the flat, and it was quiet, apart from the crack and spit of distant shots from the firing-range. I had to pick my way through cardboard boxes on the floor of the living-room.

When he switched on a standard lamp, I saw that the walls were bare. No photographs. They were in the cardboard boxes. 'Did you take them down from the cloakroom as well?' I said.

'Yes. I'm afraid I never liked them . . . I didn't tell my wife, naturally. Are you sure Alistair didn't hurt you?'

'No.' I said. 'Not in the least. But I was lucky.'

'Believe me . . .' he began, checked, coughed and kick-started himself again. 'Miss Tanner, I had no idea. No idea at all, that you would be in any danger. If I had . . .' he drifted off into silence.

'Shall we sit down?' I said.

'If you like.'

I sat on the sofa, he sat on a chair. I waited for him to speak. He waited for me. Eventually, I said, 'Did you kill Olivier?'

'No.' It wasn't a denial, just a statement of fact.

'Did you let him die?'

'Yes. I found him diving, purely by chance. I'd given my wife her late-night cocoa. I looked out of the window, and saw the lights from the swimming-pool. Of course I had to investigate. He was practising a difficult dive.'

'And you could have stopped him?'

'Of course. It was a failure of my duty of care, I know that. But I had other things to consider. Huh?'

'Other things, such as . . .'

He stopped me with a raised hand, like a traffic policeman, or a well-prepared child in class. 'Miss Tanner, forgive me. I'm very tired. Perhaps you could tell me what you think you know.'

'Alistair Brown wasn't Mrs Brown's son. He was an actor called Alistair Bernard, perhaps a relation—'

'Her nephew.'

'Mrs Brown brought him in to make up to Mrs Ellis, with a view to persuading her, perhaps eventually by marrying her, to give him a share of the profit from closing the school and selling the land for industrial development. He used John Brown's degree and references. John Brown had been killed by a homosexual pick-up in Morocco. He had also had an affair, probably while he was at the seminary, with a priest called Martin Kelly, who left the priesthood after a breakdown and worked as a reporter on the *Banbury Courier*, and who had seen photographs of Brown's handsome actor cousin Alistair. He recognized Bernard, probably from a photograph taken at last year's sports day, when Bernard wasn't wearing his glasses and was in a similar pose to the one he adopted in another photograph familiar to Kelly. He knew he wasn't John Brown as he claimed to be. Bernard was successful in his pursuit of your wife. Olivier, either through Kelly, who fancied him, or Bernard, who might have fancied him too, or through bugging and spying generally, discovered some or all of this and blackmailed—'

'Yes, yes,' said the Major. 'Quite. Tell me one thing. Did you mean to kill him?'

'Yes.'

'Well done,' he said with an echo of his former heartiness, a touch of bracing Leadership, and as I watched him I realized how much I liked him. He was a gallant little man. And a subtler man-manager than I'd reckoned.

' "Choose your junior officers wisely and then let them get on with it," ' I said. 'You said that to me, the first time we met. I didn't know what you had in mind. Did you actually think I'd find out about Alistair?'

'Knew you'd stir it up,' he said. 'Asquith said you were sharp. And stubborn. Actually, forgive me, the word he used was "bloody-minded".'

Whereas Asquith was just bloody, I thought.

'He advised me against letting you in to the school,' the Major went on. 'He said your boss – Protheroe, is it? – was a toadying nonentity, but he warned me to steer clear of you.'

'Why did you ignore his advice?'

He sighed. 'I don't know. I couldn't let it go on. I couldn't let Brown have Rissington.'

'Your life's work,' I said.

He smiled. 'Did I say that? It's nearly true. Like most of the things I told you.'

'What wasn't true about it?'

'Anthea,' he said heavily. 'Anthea . . . She was my life's work, too.'

'Why didn't you just clear it up yourself? Face your wife. Chuck Alistair out. Keep the school going.'

'I couldn't hurt her. I couldn't bear to hurt her. She wasn't – an ordinary person, you know. She was very beautiful, but of course you know that. And her upbringing was unusual.'

Past tenses. But I wouldn't pursue that just yet.

'It was you who kept an eye on me, wasn't it?' I said. 'It was you who didn't let me take a step without a chaperon. Why?'

'Couldn't let you near the boys. Huh? The parents trust me. I'd have been mad to let you loose in the school . . . Too many grubby little adolescent secrets.'

Involuntarily, I looked into one of the boxes. Fifteen-year-old Mrs Ellis dreamed back.

'Was it child abuse?' I said. 'What was her relationship with the Colonel?'

'Very close. He was Artistic. I didn't ask for details . . . I didn't want to know. But she could never be as happy as I wanted her to be,' he said. 'She could never be happy at all. I just couldn't manage it.'

'I don't expect anybody could.'

'It was like that disease. The bleeding disease.'

'Haemophilia?'

'Everything that touched her made her bleed. Inside. And when she started to bleed, she didn't stop. D'you see what I mean?'

I saw what he meant. He'd spent twenty years pouring himself down the bottomless pit of her needs. Now he was drained, and she was still flushed and full, like a vampire after a good night out. All ready with her face-lift, and her full range of Elizabeth Arden, and the Colonel's dowry, to launch herself into life with Alistair Bernard.

'How did Mrs Brown take the news of Alistair?' I said.

'Quietly. She didn't say much. I didn't expect her to. She was a proud woman: she always kept herself to herself. Wonderful organizer.'

'She didn't manage to organize Alistair into control of the school,' I said.

'Not quite. Nearly.'

'Nearly doesn't butter the toast,' I said. 'Have you told Mrs Ellis about Alistair?'

'No need. It would have upset her.'

'You'll have to tell her sometime.'

'No.'

We looked at each other and I felt his grief. It was as heavy as the Baron's.

'She's dead?'

'Yes. She never knew . . . I always made a nightcap for her. Cocoa. She was very fond of gin . . . Milk's good, they say. A coating for the stomach. Protects the digestion.'

'What did you put in it?'

'Last night? Amytal. She died peacefully, early this morning. That's when I took the pictures down. I had to do something. Hate idleness. Always have. Which brings me to you, Miss Tanner. I have a favour to ask you.'

'Ask.'

'It's Rissington, d'you see. A question of inheritance. Under my will, a trust is set up. To keep the place going. She left everything to me. So it's important that there's no confusion over time of death.'

'How could there be? Forensic medicine's very accurate.'

'I thought so, until the case of the Birmingham Five.'

'Six,' I said. 'There were six of them. So you want me to discover the body?'

'Please.'

'Now?'

'I think so. Through the hall: the first door on the right.'

I went in to the bedroom. She was laid out on the bed, washed, in what must have been a fresh nightdress. Her hair streamed over the pillow. She looked old.

I checked her carotid pulse. There wasn't one. Her skin was cold and my fingers shrank from it. I would have shrunk from her living skin.

Then I went back to the living-room. 'Isn't she beautiful?' he said.

'Yes,' I said. No point in telling the truth. Not now. Not ever, to someone who has invested all their dreams and all their insecurities in a dud stock. Polly and Clive. Geoffrey and Anthea. Freedom and Olivier. And possibly, Martin and Olivier, John and Alistair.

'She was everything I ever wanted,' he said. He opened a drawer and took out an old army pistol, a piece of set-dressing for a Second War drama. 'Miss Tanner,' he said, 'this is a gun.'

'Yes, Major,' I said, undisturbed. He wasn't going to use it on me.

'On no account must any of the boys be allowed in here. You understand? Please do what you can in the way of damage-limitation. For the school. And I must ask you not to make any attempt to pursue Tim Robertson.'

'Did you know I met him in the town?'

'Yes. He told me.'

But Tim hadn't mentioned that I was a private detective in pursuit of Olivier, or surely the Major would have said so. It was a relief. I'd been slow enough on the uptake all through without having to reproach myself with making a massive miscalculation as well. 'Did you send Li Sung to fetch Tim's stuff from Matilda Beckford?'

He answered slowly, as if I was pulling him back to a present he'd already put behind him. 'Matilda Beckford?'

'The old woman in the sheltered housing.'

'Oh, yes. Robertson told me he kept some material there that he didn't want you to get hold of. Miss Tanner—'

I wasn't letting him go, yet. 'Major, how did you find out about Alistair?'

'I knew about the affair, of course. Desmoulins told me about the impersonation. Not an attempt at blackmail. Simply to make trouble. He was a very disturbed boy. Now, if you would wait outside?'

'Why me?' I said.

'I can trust you. We have something in common.'

'What?'

He tried to smile. It didn't come off. 'Risen from the ranks,' he said. 'I told you I'd risen from the ranks.'

'And?'

'The Army's run by the NCOs.'

'NCOs?'

'Non-commissioned officers. The effective ones, who carry out the orders or carry the can. "Sergeant, take that hill." Like you and me. But you know that already.'

He pointed to the door, and I went out.

I didn't go far, and I didn't have to wait long. The shot came in the middle of a fusillade from the firing range, and blended with it, though it was much louder.

I'd spent my time at Rissington Abbey, though I hadn't been aware of it, as the Major's pawn: bringing out into the daylight secrets that were no secrets to him. Following his sealed orders.

This time the orders were explicit. Usually I resent doing what I'm told, even by employers who are buying my obedience. But I'd accept it, just this once, from the Major. He'd invested his life unwisely, I thought, in a vain, shallow, and crazy woman, and a school full of boys who'd have forgotten him by the second day of the holidays. But that was his decision.

So I opened the door and discovered the body.

Tuesday, June 9th

Chapter Thirty-One

I slept in, the next morning. Soundly, and dreamlessly. At ten-thirty, bathed, dressed (sweatshirt selection: black, short-sleeved, no logo), I went downstairs, put the coffee on, and faced the hysterical flashing of my answering machine. Two calls from Polly. Two from Barty. Eight from Claudia. Three from Alan Protheroe. By the last, hysterical call, he'd heard from Claudia, who'd rung Rissington and found out the Major and Mrs Ellis were dead. He sounded as if he was trying to give birth to an aircraft carrier.

I'd ring them later. I was fed up to my back teeth with explanations. The Banbury police had been even more sympathetic than the Met, but they'd also been more interested. The Major and Mrs Ellis were important local people: Rissington was an important local employer. I'd told them some truth, some fiction. I'd left out Olivier, Kelly, the Baron and Plummer, the Alistair – Mrs Ellis affair, and the Alistair impersonation. I'd given them Mrs Ellis the unstable suicide, Major Ellis the inconsolable husband, and Alistair Brown the incomprehensible. They'd found Brown the hardest to swallow. I'd looked puzzled until my facial muscles seized up, then I'd settled for shocked. It was easier.

I went down to fetch the mail. One letter, for me, postmark Banbury. The envelope was in Kelly's writing. Wrongly addressed: I live in Ladbroke Crescent. Kelly had written Ladbroke Terrace, which is much posher: whoever it'd been delivered to had bothered to mark it 'not known at this address' and re-post it, instead of using it to protect the furniture from coffee mugs, which is what I do.

It wasn't signed. It said:

I thought Providence had brought you to me. I was wrong. I
am unworthy
I sent you into danger

self-deception is the dark armour of the soul
please forgive me

I sat at the kitchen table and looked at his scrawly writing. I'd been wrong about *dark armour* and it was too late to wish I'd paid attention to him earlier. The Rissington Five were beyond help.

Poor Kelly. Like Tim Robertson, like all neurotics, what went wrong wasn't because he didn't know what to do, it was because he couldn't make himself do it. Easier to know than to act.

But I wasn't going to make the same mistake twice and ignore an expert on her own subject, so I rang Polly. She was nearly better. She was burbling. 'Where've you *been*, Alex? What've you been doing? I'm coming back to London tomorrow—'

'Good,' I interrupted. 'I need you. I'm going shopping, and I need help.'

'Shopping? You? What for?'

'Clothes. For a weekend at the Danieli.'

She jabbered clothes for ten minutes. I ignored most of it, but by the time I put the phone down I'd gathered it was going to be expensive. I'd have to do a really creative invoice for Plummer. But first, I had a phone call to make.

I dialled, then listened to the single Continental ring. Freedom answered. I reminded her who I was. 'Oh! Alex! Of course I remember! the fire-child, who set my spirit free!'

'That's what I'm ringing about,' I said. 'I'm not an Aries. I'm a Gemini. Your guru didn't know it, and he's a crook.'

'What do you mean?' she said. 'Did you lie to him?'

'Yes I did, but that's not the point. If he's so spiritual he should have known. He's a fraud. He's taking you for a ride.'

'I don't understand,' she said. She sounded more London by the second. 'Did you lie to me?'

'No. I only lie to crooks,' I lied. 'You said you were a seeker after truth. Well, I've just given you some. You should get shot of that guru.'

'Really,' she said. She spoke thoughtfully, and dragged out the flattened vowel – 'reeely'. It was pure Sydenham, and I preferred it to the semi-French accent she usually affected. 'You reeely think so?'

'Yes,' I said. 'I reeely do.'

It wasn't a sound I'd used for years. I thought it was ugly, and I'd got shot of it when I started work at the BBC. But now it came easily to my tongue.

'I wonder—' she said. 'Alex—'

'Yes?'

'Would you consider being my spiritual adviser? We can seek the true path, together.'

Spiritual adviser. Not likely. Once an airhead, always an airhead.

'So Martin Kelly killed himself?' said Claudia. 'I'm glad. At least Alistair didn't murder him.'

I wanted to avoid a lengthy post-mortem, so I wasn't about to suggest that from Kelly's point of view, suicide might have been worse.

She was cross-legged on the floor, I was lying with my boots up on the sofa, thinking about nothing.

'So whose fault was it?' she said.

'Everyone's, partly. In a small way, the Wanderotel management's, for sending a trainee to do a man's job. If I'd got Kelly's telephone message on Wednesday morning he might just have told me about Alistair.'

'I don't think that's fair,' she said. 'About the trainee. You have to learn somehow, and it was a very small mistake, and I don't even think it was his, he told me one of the girls had forgotten . . .' She was speaking on behalf of trainees everywhere, I thought as I watched her eager defence of a boy she didn't like. She was still talking: '. . . and that's how you learn things, by doing them, you're thrown in at the deep end, like me in this case, and you do your best, but you're bound to make mistakes, like me and *Spotlight* because I didn't know . . .'

'OK, OK. Belt up.'

'So whose fault was it really?'

'Mrs Brown was a ruthless scheming cow. Alistair was amoral and utterly selfish. Olivier was spoilt rotten: a cruel, manipulative adolescent. And Kelly and the Major wouldn't do their own dirty work. They were afraid to look.'

'What at?'

'At themselves. At what they'd made of their lives. At what might happen. So they made us do it.'

'They made *you* do it,' she said. 'Don't you mind?'

'No. I enjoy it. It's important to look.'

213

'Why?'

'It's always a temptation not to face the truth. I have to keep reminding myself of that. Once you've looked, then you've set yourself free to look away.'

'Oh,' said Claudia. 'That's really – significant. It's serious. It's almost French.'

I was grinning.

'What is it? Alex, what is it? Are you teasing me? Didn't you mean what you said?'

'I was just thinking. Freedom Pertwee. If I became her spiritual adviser—'

'You wouldn't!'

'No, I wouldn't. But if I did, I could charge astronomical fees.'

Other Virago Crime Fiction of interest

TROUBLED WATERS
Pat Sweet

Money had never meant much to Cat O'Connell. At forty-five, freed of maternal duties, she changed jobs – from being a lucrative city lawyer in central Glasgow to a private investigator with an ever increasing overdraft. She needs work badly. So when an American oil company, Yukon Discovery, asks for a confidential investigation into a series of suspicious looking 'accidents' on the rigs, Cat is forced to consider it. Meanwhile the body of her old friend and lover Donald Grant, employee of Yukon, is found in Aberdeen harbour. Accident or murder? Cat won't rest until she finds out.

Skilfully mixing tension and excitement with wonderful characters and a sharp wit, Pat Sweet launches the indomitable Cat O'Connell into the world of perilous streets and chilling encounters.

ROLLERCOASTER
Barbara Crossley

A body on a bonfire draws Anna Knight into a nest of intrigue in the switchback world of seaside fun-parks. Anna, reporter on the *Northport News*, investigates the murder of Llew Madden, boss of the resort's leading amusement park, who was locked in a competition to the death with a ruthless new rival. Why was a grieving mother sending him hate-mail? And an embittered man seeking revenge? And why can't Anna Knight sort out her love-life as she switches from the ebullient fun-park manager Matt to the handsome and dangerous Guy, Llew Madden's brother? With quirky humour, Anna rollercoasters her way through clues and countdowns to find Llew's murderer in the ashes of guilt and corruption.

Virago also publishes *Candyfloss Coast*.

I'LL BE LEAVING YOU ALWAYS
Sandra Scoppettone

'Ms Scoppettone has created an original and daring detective'
– *New York Times*

Lauren Laurano doesn't fit the mould of the typical detective. Pretty, funny, clothes-conscious and gay, she lives with her psychotherapist lover, Kip, in Greenwich Village. When Lauren's oldest friend Megan is found brutally murdered behind the counter of her Greenwich Village jewellery store, she is hired by one of Megan's former husbands to investigate. Lauren begins to dig and discovers nothing is the way it seems. She has to accept difficult truths about her friend, whom she thought she knew intimately, and about herself, as she pursues a trail of bewildering and unsavoury clues to discover the murderer's identity in a shattering and tense denouement.

Virago also publishes *Everything You Have Is Mine*.